STRAIGHT

AND

LEVEL

Books by Penelope Haines

The Lost One
Helen Had a Sister
(previously published as Princess of Sparta)
Blood Never Lies

The Claire Hardcastle Series:
Death on D'Urville
Straight and Level
Stall Turns

STRAIGHT
AND
LEVEL

A Claire Hardcastle

Mystery

PENELOPE HAINES

For information contact;

www.penelopehaines.com

Published by Ithaca Publications, Wellington, New Zealand

Straight and Level/ Penelope Haines. -- 1st ed.

ISBN 978-0-473-39820-0

For Michaela Haines,

my granddaughter

"The most effective way to do it, is to do it."

Amelia Earhart

CHAPTER ONE

"NO," I SAID.

Roger, my boss, typically chose to ignore my protest. "Like it or lump it, but you're coming to this meeting, Hardcastle. It's a good sales opportunity for us and I'm not doing it on my own."

"But ..."

Roger stopped me with a look. I knew it was childish, but I had no interest in wasting a couple of hours at a cocktail party. I wouldn't even get to be dressed up and glamorous; I'd be in uniform. Although I was proud enough to wear it for work, I wasn't so keen when every other woman there would be fashionably dressed and I'd be in a white shirt, tie, epaulettes, navy trousers and sensible shoes.

The Kapiti Coast Chamber of Commerce was hosting the function at the reception rooms of the Southward Car Museum, and the car park was full when Roger and I arrived. Business owners from throughout the Kapiti Coast were attending and it was, as Roger had said, a good sales opportunity for Paraparaumu Aviation. I knew I was being trotted out as a show pony – not just because I was very visible in my uniform, but because I'd also featured in the local press a few months before after an incident at the airport. Roger wanted to get as much mileage as possible out of the publicity.

I loved my job, and was fond of my boss, but I was a pilot, not a salesperson. I followed in Roger's wake as we walked up the steps. I didn't kick a single one, which I thought showed considerable restraint, given how sulky I felt. He paused in the doorway. "You go left," he said. "I'll work the right," and he urged me on my way with a slight push.

I had learned to work a room from my ex, who had fancied himself a rising star in New Zealand's accounting firmament. David canvassed people at the parties to which we were invited with the mindset of a campaign manager launching a political candidate. I'd forgotten how artificial I found such enforced socialising and glared at Roger as he abandoned me.

A waiter offered a tray of drinks. My hand hesitated over the glass of bubbly and moved on towards the orange juice. I sighed. I'd have loved to have some Dutch courage to help me out, but Lisa, my best friend, had bullied me and Jen, my other best friend, into signing up for Dry July.

"It will be great for both our health and our figures," Lisa, whippet thin with not an extra gram of fat on her person, had enthused.

Jen and I had rolled our eyes at her, neither of us considering health or beauty sufficient reason to embark on sobriety.

"And it's for charity," she'd added desperately. "Think of the good that we can do."

After that, Jen and I caved. It seemed churlish to insist on our right to a glass of wine in the evenings when we could alleviate poverty, find a cure for cancer and end up looking like Kate Moss into the bargain.

We were a fortnight through the month, and so far, I'd stuck to my pledge, although tonight I regretted it bitterly. I sipped my OJ and made my way towards the nearest group of people. As I approached they parted and admitted me.

Studies have shown pilots are the most respected and trusted people on the planet. We outrank doctors, lawyers, priests, dentists and, by a large margin, politicians. Thanks to my uniform,

I was clearly identifiable as a member of that most desirable of professions and tonight this worked in my favour. Every group I approached opened up to let me in. I smiled, answered obvious and repetitive questions about my job and dutifully tried to sell the possibilities of aviation to them.

I may have had no aspirations as a salesperson, but I've got a wonderful job and, like most pilots, could talk about flying for hours. There's an old joke: *How do you tell who's the pilot in the crowd? . . . They'll tell you!* which pretty much summed it up. Consequently, for Paraparaumu Aviation's sake, I did my best to please and charm.

"Yes, of course you can fly; it's accessible to anyone. I'd love to take you up and share my world with you. You should give it a go."

"Yes, a voucher for a Tiger Moth flight would make a wonderful present for your dad. I'm sure he'd love it," and so on.

I kept an eye on Roger as I worked my way through the crowd. With any luck, we'd bump into each other soon and I'd force an end to our evening.

I was three-quarters of the way around the room and had joined a fresh group of people. Names I didn't bother trying to remember were exchanged. I was excruciatingly bored and frantic to go home. I kept casting pleading looks in Roger's direction.

Then I encountered *him*. He wasn't particularly tall, short, fat or thin. He was neither handsome nor significantly plain. There was a slightly quirky cast to his features which could, in another man, have been unattractive, but here had been enlivened by the very obvious intelligent humour in his eyes. His hair was a startling snowy white, at odds with his vigorous physical presence. Although his skin showed a normal degree of middle-age sag, both his face and physique were attractive. He wore the years well. I put him in his late-forties, well-groomed and well suited. In every facet he was a model of a typically successful businessman.

It was his unshielded vitality which stopped me. I suddenly

focused as I automatically extended my hand.

"Jim Mason," he introduced himself.

"Claire Hardcastle," I replied as he shook my hand.

I wondered what he did for a living. The others in our group had faded into a nondescript blur. One was the owner of a local supermarket – was it Pak'nSave, or Countdown? I had no idea which. The other couple owned a lighting business. Again, I hadn't made the effort to remember their names, or their businesses. All of them were mere extras to Jim Mason's leading-man performance.

"I read about you in the local paper," he said.

"They have to fill the pages with something." I didn't want to discuss the events that had led to my brief notoriety.

He looked amused. "Then we have something in common. I, too, dislike being discussed in the media. But if I recall, you emerged as the heroine of the piece?"

"They say you can't always believe what you read in the news."

The supermarket guy had entered the conversation, jockeying for some attention. The slur in his voice suggested he wasn't participating in Dry July. I wasn't sure if his statement was meant to be taken on its own merits or whether he intended some slight to me. Whatever the case, it earned him a frown from Jim.

"I'm sure the article stated nothing less than the obvious when it acclaimed Ms Hardcastle," he said, shortly.

The lighting guy and his wife immediately nodded their heads in agreement.

That's Mr Supermarket put in his place, I thought, as I watched him flush and back off. I was impressed Jim's opinion was so highly regarded and wondered again who he was.

Jack would know, I thought. I missed my sometime lover, not least because, as a detective senior sergeant in the police force, he tended to know all the local personalities and would undoubtedly have been able to tell me who or what Jim Mason was.

Unfortunately, Jack was currently unavailable, being on secondment for a month in the Solomon Islands, providing specialist training in criminal investigations to the Royal Solomon Islands Police Force. He'd been gone a fortnight, and I was missing him like crazy.

Others joined the group, and conversation flowed back and forth. Most of the people there knew each other. Even as I smiled and answered the usual questions about being a female pilot, I was aware Jim's attention was focused on me.

It wasn't easy to ignore. He had a powerful presence and enormous charisma. A ladies' man, I decided. It was hard to mistake that twinkle in the eye, or the overwhelming sense of sexual awareness that surrounded him.

Mr and Mrs Lighting said their goodbyes.

"Lovely to meet you," said Jim. He held the wife's hand a nanosecond too long. "I've no doubt we'll meet again. Kapiti is such a small place." He oozed pheromones over the poor woman.

The woman simpered girlishly as she drew her hand away. I could see she was captured by Jim's attention. "I hope so," she gushed, before her husband led her away from danger.

Mr Mason was definitely a player. He was too old for me to worry about being a notch on his belt, but he certainly intrigued me.

"Hardcastle?"

I turned to find Roger had come up behind me.

"How are you going?"

"Good," I said. "May I introduce you? Have you met Jim Mason?"

"No," said Roger.

The men shook hands. It would be interesting to see what Roger, no mean ladies' man himself, would make of Jim. So far he appeared impervious to the man's charisma.

"Ready to go?" he asked, after he'd run through the niceties.

I nodded.

We said our farewells and made our way to the door. We passed from the foyer through the first set of doors into the vestibule.

At the outer doors I stopped and looked out. "Oh, crap." Since we'd been inside, the weather had turned. It was now bitterly cold and rain was teeming down.

Roger was all right. He at least had a jacket, but I had no coat with me. He took in the situation. "Stay here, Hardcastle," he commanded. "I'll go and get the car."

"Thanks," I said, grateful for some old-fashioned gallantry for once.

Roger ran across the driveway. For a man well into his sixties he was surprisingly athletic, particularly considering he'd broken an ankle not more than three months ago. I watched as he disappeared across the large car park. We'd arrived later than most of the attendees, so his vehicle was miles away on the far side.

I retreated into the warmth of the foyer. A classic old sports car was displayed on a podium. Cars, ancient or modern, meant little to me, but I admired its high gloss and the complicated arrangement of pipes attached to its engine.

Across the room a young man also waited. He was young and slight. Rain had glued his curly blond hair to his forehead, framing the chiselled cheekbones of his narrow face. He was so thin the lines of his long neck and a prominent Adam's apple were clearly visible above his T-shirt. Damp jeans clung to his skinny legs, and his jacket looked worn. Hanging around his neck was a beautifully carved bone pendant.

I nodded at him. "Two refugees from the storm," I murmured.

He had a particularly sweet smile as he acknowledged my greeting and looked me over.

"Are you a pilot?" he asked. "Were you at the meeting upstairs?"

I nodded. "My boss thought it would be a great idea if I showed up in uniform. I think he hoped it would sell aviation to the business community."

He grinned, his eyes laughing at me. "The things we do …"

I nodded wryly. "The things we do, indeed."

His smile was warm and friendly.

"What about you?" I asked. "Were you upstairs?"

"No," he said. "I'm just a journalist working on a story about one of the guests here. There's a protest planned in connection with his company and I want to get a few comments at the end of the shindig."

"That's a beautiful pendant," I said, nodding at the carving which hung around his neck.

He looked down and touched it.

"It's antique," he said. "It was presented to me a couple of months ago in recognition of work I'd done preserving local ecosystems. I was very honoured to receive it; It's a valuable taonga. They even carved my initials into the back of it so no one can nick it from me." He gave a slight, deprecating laugh.

"It's lovely," I said, admiring its sinuous curves.

The outer doors opened again, and a number of people entered the vestibule together. As a collection, they didn't match the dress code or social spectrum of those at the reception upstairs. This was a varied group: elderly; mixed race; some clearly Maori, others Caucasian and other ethnicities; both genders; and several young people whom I assumed, given their slight scruffiness, were students. Many carried placards. These would be the anticipated protesters, I realised.

My companion gave me a faint smile of farewell as he walked through the doors to join them.

I waited a few more moments, watching for the lights of Roger's car.

"Fuck," I heard, and turned to see Jim Mason standing behind me. He saw me looking and smiled. "Sheltering from the rain?"

I nodded.

"Are you going to be all right? I'd offer you room under my umbrella, but I think I'm about to run the gauntlet." He lifted his chin to indicate the group in the lobby.

"Yes, thanks. Roger's gone to get the car. He won't be long. Perhaps I should ask you if you're going to be OK. Is that reception committee for you?"

I was now thoroughly curious.

He snorted. "I'd guess so," he said. "Bloody idiots. It's all stuff and nonsense."

He shrugged then turned his twinkly eyes on me. "Well, if you're all right, good night then. I hope to meet you again," he said, giving me a final megawatt smile before stepping out through the doors into the lobby.

He was immediately surrounded. The doors effectively cut off all sound, so I couldn't hear any comments, but I read the placards: Keep Your Hands Off Our Land; No to Development; Profiteering Bastard.

So Mr Mason was a property developer? I had no fixed position on this profession, but he'd obviously annoyed at least some of the locals.

I watched him say something to the hecklers, and after a moment the protesters backed away, letting him through, apparently content to wave their placards and leave it at that. Jim appeared relaxed and good-humoured. I thought he had it all well under control. Whatever he'd said had defused the situation.

He'd just reached the outer doors of the vestibule and was about to pass through, when one of the protesters abruptly broke ranks, stepped forward and blocked him.

It was like watching a silent movie. I was frustrated I couldn't hear what was said, but the young man was clearly passionate about his cause. He tried to grab Jim by his coat sleeves and, when Jim stepped back, followed him, jabbing his forefinger into Jim's chest as he made his points.

I suddenly realised it was the man I'd spoken to in the lobby.

In an instant Jim's demeanour changed. He stepped forward and said something short and sharp to his accoster. Even from behind the glass I could see the menace expressed in his body language. It caused the journalist to back off, obviously intimidated.

"Fuck." The voice from behind startled me, and I had a deja-vu moment.

I turned, and found two other men also watching the action in the lobby.

"He'll be fine" the one reassured the other. "He can look after himself."

"That fucking faggot of a journo needs to be dealt to. He's bloody trouble, sticking his nose in where it's not wanted." The speaker was young, tall, slender, and wearing a leather jacket. I wasn't sure whether his aggression was due to an objection to the journalist's sexuality or his profession. Either way I disliked his attitude.

The other man, was older and smaller, dressed in a non-descript jacket and trousers. "Don't be stupid," he replied.

He'd registered I was watching, and gave me a slight placatory smile as he shut his companion up.

I swung back to watch Jim who was studying the group aligned against him. I assume he said something scornful. The expression on his face was withering and his opponents looked thoroughly cowed.

Just before he turned to stride through the doors, Jim looked up and realised I was still standing on the far side of the glass.

I saw the slight shock on his face before he recovered, gave me another twinkly smile and walked out into the night.

The lights of a car swung around the drive and drew up in front of the doors. I recognised it and went into the vestibule, making my way through the group of protesters which had now gathered supportively around their spokesperson. In the fluorescent light of the lobby his face looked white and shocked.

CHAPTER TWO

"DO YOU KNOW WHAT HE DOES?" I asked Roger.

My boss looked confused. "What *who* does?"

I had one of those moments when I realised the gender gap is unbridgeable. I could guarantee every woman in that room knew there was only one significant '*he*' at the function that evening.

Roger's denseness was genuine. I took pity on him.

"Jim Mason," I said. "I've never heard of him before. Do you know what he does?"

"Oh, him. There was a piece about him in the local paper a few weeks back. Don't you ever follow the news, Hardcastle?"

"I do follow the news," I said. I was indignant. "Just not necessarily what's in the *Observer*."

I checked out *Stuff*, the online news site, on a regular basis. I just didn't have a lot of time for old-fashioned newspapers cluttering up my space. I didn't like to mention that the main use I had for the *Observer*, delivered free each week to my letter-box, was to use the pages as twills to start my log burner.

Roger shook his head in obvious despair. "I'll never understand your generation. Anyway, to quote the article, Jim Mason is a property developer. He made a packet and has moved from Auckland to Kapiti; said the property market in Auckland has become over-heated and he's looking for new opportunities. In particular, the land Tranzit acquired to build the new motorway, or rather, what happens to the unused surplus when the motorway is completed. He's eyeing it up and claims he wants to be part of developing the modern Kapiti resulting from the new infrastructure."

For the last few years, the New Zealand Transport Agency, better known as Tranzit, had been a major purchaser of land along the line of the motorway development. Back when I'd been at college the first families in our area had been forced to move to make way for the new road. Now the corridor extended as far north as Levin.

"There were protesters in the lobby," I said. "They didn't seem very pleased with him, and one of them was quite passionate."

Roger shrugged. "Goes with the territory, I suppose."

I ran over the scene in my mind. "The thing is, Jim Mason seemed to be quite relaxed and charming until the young journalist guy tackled him, then he really turned on him. It was nasty, even though I couldn't hear what they were saying."

"Mason gave me the impression he's a tough man. I guess he's handled plenty of scenes like that before. He's probably a bit of a villain as well. Most of his ilk are."

"A smiling damned villain," I murmured, remembering Year Thirteen English literature lessons and *Hamlet*.

"He's got twinkly eyes," I added. "A real ladies' man."

I was startled when Roger snorted. "I imagine that's been very useful in getting where he is today."

*   *   *

The next morning, I was leaning on the counter which separated the waiting room area from the pilot's offices, trying to read Greig's writing. He had booked me out for a lesson at ten o'clock, but I couldn't work out his scrawl.

"You're late," I observed when he arrived.

"Sorry, I know. There was a police cordon down Arawhata

Road, and it took me ages to get through. Apparently a dead body was found there this morning."

"Really?" I was curious. We don't often get dead bodies in our streets.

"Probably some drunken bastard who went to sleep in the middle of the road and got run over," said Greig.

I shrugged. "What does this say?" I asked, pointing to the roster.

Greig peered over my shoulder at the entry on the flying sheet.

"Pete Funnell," he said. "He told me he wanted to learn to fly, and asked for you as instructor. He said he knew you."

I looked at the writing again. I suppose there was a universe in which the letters spelt out Pete Funnell, but if so, the rest of humanity hadn't stumbled on it yet.

"You *do* know him, don't you?" asked Greig.

I could see the calculation in his eyes. If I didn't know him, and Greig had taken the booking, then by the company's internal rules, he would be Greig's client.

I grinned evilly. "Keep your sticky fingers off him. Yes, I know Pete. He's a friend and colleague of Jack's. We've met on several occasions. He just never said he wanted to learn to fly."

"Seems he does now."

Greig went to help Nick pull the aircraft out of the hangar, and I drew down the pilots' personal files to check everything was up to date. Maintaining them was part of my job, and I never understood how information got outdated so quickly. Qualifications, ratings, flying hours, last medical examination, it all had to be detailed. Technically, each pilot was responsible for their own file, but experience had taught Roger it was a chore we all avoided, so he'd given me the job of chasing everyone up.

I brought mine up to scratch. Roger's was so abysmally not current it was a wonder it showed anything more than a Private Pilot Licence dated 1955. As he is in fact our Chief Flying Instructor, and Chief Pilot he had a squillion other qualifications and ratings that needed to be current, maintained and signed off in his record. I dumped the file on his desk with a request for him to complete it, but I already knew who'd be updating it.

Nick, our newly qualified and *junior* 'C'Cat instructor, as Greig referred to him, had an immaculate file, complete in every detail. I made a mental note to applaud him – not that he'd had much time to complicate his record having qualified a bare six weeks ago.

Greig, who now styled himself the *senior* 'C'Cat, had a file almost as antique as Roger's. I scrawled a legible, but nasty, note requesting he bring it up to date. None of us liked the paperwork involved in aviation, but it had to be done, and we were due for an audit sometime in the next few months.

I greeted Pete as an old friend. I'd originally met him when he interviewed me about the death of a client. Subsequently I got to know him socially because my boyfriend worked with him and they were good mates.

He gave me a quick hug. "Hi Claire. You keeping well with Jack away?"

I nodded. "Yeah. He Skypes when he can, although reception's usually lousy." I shrugged. "He'll be back soon."

"Well, if you get lonely, you can always give me a call." Pete gave me a charming smirk and wiggled his eyebrows suggestively. I wondered whether he was joking. I wasn't always certain how to take his sense of humour.

I rolled my eyes at him. "I think I'll just wait for Jack to get home."

"I thought you'd say that, but you can't blame me for trying." Pete was unrepentant. "Not that I'd actually poach on Jack's territory," he assured me. "You're the best thing that's happened to him in a long time. We were beginning to think he'd never get over Samira."

I was instantly alert. "Samira?" I asked, my tone carefully casual.

Jack had never mentioned a Samira. In fact, we had never talked much about our lives or the partners we'd had before we'd met. My ex, David, hadn't been important enough to me to discuss, although I was certain I had mentioned him in passing. I would have remembered if Jack had talked about an old flame.

"Yes, his wife," said Pete.

I felt the blood drain from my face. Jack had certainly never told me about that.

"Wife?" I echoed, as my stomach went into freefall.

Pete suddenly realised he'd put his foot in it. "Shit. He hasn't told you, has he."

I shook my head. "Not that he's married, no."

Pete bit his lip. "Shit, shit, shit. Why did I open my stupid mouth? No, Jack's not married. At least, he is; I mean, he was." He stopped himself and took a deep breath.

"Samira died."

"Oh crap." I was appalled. The conversation kept getting worse. "What happened?"

"They met when they were both recruits at Police College. It was a great romance apparently. They fell in love and got married a couple of years later. I'd only just met Jack, but at the time I thought he had it all. Lovely wife, great relationship and a good career ahead of him. Poor bastard. They were just coming up for their first anniversary when she was killed."

"That's awful," I said. "How did she die?"

"Motor vehicle accident. The young woman who drove head-on into Samira's car, had no driver's licence, her car wasn't warranted or registered, and she was four times over the limit. Samira died at the scene. The other woman lived, with only minor injuries to show for it."

"Holy crap," I repeated. I wished Jack had told me. I was appalled by the pain he must have been carrying that he'd never mentioned.

"Crap, indeed," agreed Pete. "Jack suffered terribly of course. Not that he'd talk about it, but he changed overnight. He shut people out and became very intense and focused on his work. It's why he's done so well with his career but he's had no social life. It's been five years since that accident, and we'd almost forgotten just how funny he could be when he relaxed. Then he met you and you've transformed him."

I said nothing, just stared at Pete.

"Please don't tell Jack I told you," he begged. "Let him tell you in his own time. He'll kill me if he thinks I've interfered, although I didn't mean to. I genuinely thought you'd already know."

I shook my head. It was almost too much for me to take in.

I gritted my teeth and returned to territory I knew.

"I didn't know you wanted to learn to fly."

"It's always been on my bucket list and it struck me it could be a useful tool in police work. Now that I know a flying instructor personally, it seemed like the right time to actually do something about it." He shot me a sideways glance, as engaging as he had ever been.

"Fair enough," I said. We were both being scrupulously polite, but I had a job to do, and Pete was here to learn. I wrapped the mantle of my professionalism around me, ushered him into the briefing room and delivered the formal lecture for his first lesson, by the end of which some normality had returned.

"Can I take the camera with me so I can get some shots of the town?"

"Sure," I said. "We can do a bit of scenic flying as well."

I led him to the aircraft and settled him behind into the pilot's seat.

"A cockpit is an alien environment, and the controls don't act as intuitively as you might expect," I warned. "That's why this first lesson is called *Effects of Controls*. It introduces you to all the instruments, knobs and buttons. You can pull and push them until you're familiar with what they do and some of the side effects."

He nodded, serious for once.

I enjoyed teaching Pete. His understanding was quick, and he had a natural physical confidence and coordination which boded well for future lessons.

We were returning to the airport when Pete asked, "Can I take some shots now?"

"I have control," I said automatically, taking charge of the aircraft as Pete rummaged behind his seat, reaching for his camera bag. I glanced at it as he drew it out. It was a serious bit of kit. The lens he screwed on to it was almost as long as my arm.

He gave me an apologetic smile when I had to lean back in my seat to give him space to use it as he turned in my direction.

"Anywhere in particular you want to go?"

"Can we fly over the college, and then line up on Arawhata Road? There's a property I want some shots of."

I radioed the tower to let Sam know where we'd be operating. I wanted to make absolutely sure that no other aircraft wandered into our path while I was pre-occupied with the photos, although technically we were on the 'non-traffic' side of the airfield, and shouldn't be at risk from other aircraft.

I could see a line of police cars still parked along the road and remembered Greig's news that a body had been discovered in the vicinity that morning.

Pete indicated the house he wanted.

"The one with the green roof?" I asked.

He nodded. I banked the aircraft, and circled around a few times.

"Got it," he said eventually.

I straightened the aircraft up as he packed the camera away.

"Here you are, you can fly us back home," I said, handing control back to him. I made a radio call to let Sam know we were on our way in.

"Why the interest in the house?" I asked. "Is it in relation to the body they found, or are you looking at buying it?"

"Body?" asked Pete.

"Greig told me a body was found on Arawhata Road this morning. I wondered whether that was why you were taking photos."

"No," said Pete. "I know nothing about that. The place I was photographing is a gang house we've been keeping under surveillance. We've recently had intelligence from an informer that something big is going to happen, but no one knows any details. The obvious assumption is that it's drugs, and if so, we'd like to nip it in the bud before there's more shit out on the streets."

I realised I had inadvertently involved myself in a police operation, and wondered what Roger would have to say about that. He's careful about the jobs he allows our aircraft to be used for. Once I'd asked why he wouldn't release the chopper to go into the hills on a police orchestrated marijuana raid and he'd said there was too much risk for the company.

When we got back to the office I introduced Pete to Roger.

"Good lesson?" asked Roger.

"Yeah, great fun," enthused Pete. "I'm going to enjoy flying, although I can see it will be a challenge."

I explained our extra-curricular activities to Roger.

He looked at Pete thoughtfully.

"Our aircraft are clearly identifiable by their registration markings, and Paraparumu is a very small town," he explained. "Everyone knows where the airport is. I don't need some grudge-holding thug deciding to take revenge by chucking a Molotov cocktail at our hangar. If we're going to help the police, then it won't be on our home turf. Next time check with me first," he said.

"I apologise. I hadn't considered the risks," admitted Pete, "but I realised today just how useful a tool an aircraft can be for police work. I certainly hope you'll let us use it again as a resource."

"Under certain circumstances I'd consider it," said Roger. "Although I'm surprised you aren't using drones. I'd have thought it would be cheaper."

"We do," answered Pete, "but they're limited. If criminals see a plane in the sky, they probably don't give it a second thought. If they see a drone, they know they're being watched, which alerts them and we risk losing our suspect. Also," he gave us a disingenuous grin, "this is a way of getting the police force to contribute to the cost of my flying lessons."

Roger gave him a sharp look, but let the statement pass. "As it happens, today was probably the only day your flight's not going to matter. Anyone wondering why an aircraft was circling the area will assume it was press taking photos of police investigating the body they found, so we're probably safe."

I booked Pete in for his second lesson, and waved to him as he left.

"You'd better keep that one under control, Hardcastle," said Roger.

"Oh?" I said. "Apart from wanting to take those photos, he seemed very cooperative. I was impressed with him."

"I know his type," said Roger. "He's so used to taking control of the show, before you know it he'll be running you in circles. Make sure you stay on top of him."

I was amused, but agreed. "Fair enough. I'll keep him under my thumb."

Roger ran a tight ship, and wasn't going to allow a disaster on his watch. Time and time again he impressed on us all the importance of instructors being in control of their students. He argued that a good learning experience was separated from a serious incident by a very small margin.

*   *   *

Cloud rolled in during the afternoon, effectively ending flying for the day. We closed the hangar doors early, and shut the office at five o'clock, a rare occurrence.

I turned down an invitation to join Nick, Greig and Jayleen at the tavern. Dry July was wreaking havoc on my social life, but I couldn't be bothered going to a pub and drinking lemonade.

"I'm off home to my cup of hot chocolate," I told them as I waved goodbye.

Nelson, my Siamese cat, was pleased to see me home so early and made himself a major hazard, winding himself around my feet with every step I took. I lit the log fire, noting wryly that the newspaper I was using to start it came from old copies of the *Observer*.

Mindful of Roger's comments about being out of touch with current affairs, I switched the TV onto the news. I kept it on as background noise while I pottered around in the kitchen opening a tin of cat food and feeding Nelson.

My attention was caught when I heard the word 'Paraparaumu' and looked up to see a reporter standing in front of the Kapiti Road Police Station.

"Police have launched a homicide enquiry after a Paraparaumu man suffered multiple injuries," she said. "The body of the young man discovered this morning in the seaside town of Paraparaumu has been identified as 24-year-old, local journalist, Andrew Camborne. Police have launched an inquiry after Camborne's body was found on the pavement of Arawhata Road early this morning. Initial findings suggest the victim received multiple injuries, but the exact cause of death is currently inconclusive. Local police are conducting a forensic examination of the scene and are continuing to search for a possible weapon. Detectives have cordoned off a section of road between Tutanekai and Coleman streets and are carrying out a search of nearby properties in their continuing investigation as to how Camborne came to meet his death.

"A resident nearby, who did not wish to be named, said he heard a commotion in the street in the early hours of the morning, but did not investigate. Police are interested in hearing from anyone who may have seen the deceased, or anything unusual, in the vicinity of Arawhata Road late last night or early this morning. Please contact Detective Senior Sergeant Alistair Taylor at Paraparaumu Police Station if you have any information that may assist the police with their enquiries. Alternatively, information can be given anonymously via Crimestoppers on 0800 435 749".

A photo of a young man flicked up on the screen. Fine bones, curly blond hair and a shy smile that softened the ascetic lines of his face.

I took a sharp breath. I'd seen and spoken to him only last night.

CHAPTER THREE

I WONDERED WHETHER I SHOULD CALL THE police, then decided against it. There had been plenty of other witnesses who'd be in a better position than me to report the exchange between Andrew and Jim Mason. I hadn't even been able to hear what was said between them.

Only a few months earlier I had been part of a police investigation and I'd no desire to get caught up in another one. The only positive outcome of that adventure had been meeting Detective Jack Body.

It was late when I switched off the TV. I changed into my pyjamas, curled up on the bed with my tablet and Skyped him. It would be about nine o'clock with the two-hour time difference. I waited.

"Hi."

I know absence makes the heart grow fonder and all that, but before I'd become reliant on technology to contact him, I had never realised the beauty of Jack's voice. It was deep and mellow and ought to be bottled to drink on a cold winter's evening.

We got video connection, but the picture was broken and blurry. Still, it was at least a form of contact.

"Hi yourself," I replied. "How's it going?"

We chatted for a while about his assignment.

"I'm making progress," he said at last. "The guys here are a good bunch, but the biggest problems they face are culture and corruption. Everything gets expressed in such a round-about way. It's really frustrating. New Zealanders are so direct and assertive in their dealings. Here, no one wants to make a mistake and lose face, so they won't ask questions. And not just when they're talking to me. It's the same with their fieldwork. It's bloody hard to be a detective if you won't ask for information. Plus, although none of them have confessed to taking bribes themselves, they assure me everyone else does."

I chuckled. "I'm sure you'll get them sorted."

I'd spent most of the day dwelling on what Pete had told me. My emotions had swung between simple, uncomplicated grief for the pain Jack had known, to hurt and fury that he hadn't shared that history with me. We'd been together for three months. Surely by now he trusted me enough to have told me something so fundamental to his life?

In the end, common sense and caution won out.

Jack was a very self-possessed person. He was warm, loving and generous, but I knew him well enough to know he had enormous self-discipline and control. The natural dignity I admired in him was a product of his deep reserve, so there was always the possibility there were events he hadn't shared with me. A different man might have poured out the whole tragic story on our first date, in a sad attempt to win sympathy, but Jack wasn't like that. He did things in his own time.

It was unfortunate that Pete's indiscretion meant I had become privy to information I wasn't supposed to have, but I'd decided to put the conversation that morning behind me. If Jack ever wanted to tell me about his wife, then it was his right to do so when he was ready and it would be a clear sign our relationship had taken a significant step forward. When that happened, I knew I would regard it as the highest honour he could pay me.

I collected my scrambled thoughts. "I meant to ask, do you know of a guy called Jim Mason who's recently moved into Kapiti? Late-forties, property developer, extremely charismatic.

I met him last night."

"The name rings a bell, but I can't say I know anything significant. Why?"

"At the end of the evening he had quite an argument with a protester."

"Probably part and parcel of his working life," said Jack. "Developers tend to ruffle people's feathers."

"Yes, but this protester was found dead this morning on Arawhata Road. Not that I would think Jim had anything to do with it, but it's an odd coincidence."

There was silence while Jack absorbed the facts.

"Have the police said what the cause of death was?"

"Not yet, although it's being treated as a homicide. The news report said police were searching nearby properties for possible evidence. I've been wondering whether I should tell them I saw that argument. What do you think?"

"From what you've said there were plenty of other witnesses," said Jack. "It's not as if you could add anything to what they'll report."

"I thought the same, but I didn't want to be failing in my civic duty."

"I don't think you need to worry about that." Jack sounded amused.

"Speaking of duty, I took Pete for a flying lesson today."

"Pete? You're joking. God, you don't want to let that lunatic loose in a plane."

I laughed. "Nah, he was fine, although Roger warned me to keep him firmly under control."

"Your boss is right." I heard Jack's rich chuckle. "I'd better warn Pete to be on his best behaviour, otherwise he'll answer to me."

"Are you saying I can't cope with him?"

"Hell, no, I'm not that stupid." Again I heard his warm laughter. "But those planes are very small. I'm not sure I like the thought of him being in such close proximity to you."

I shrugged away Pete's ambiguous comment earlier in the day and grinned at the thought of Pete trying to make a pass at me. "I'll make sure he keeps his hands on the joystick, if that's what's worrying you."

"It's *precisely* what's worrying me," he said.

"I'd rather have my hands on your joystick," my voice softened, even as I smiled. "The nights are boring here without you."

I realised I was horny as hell, and missing my man.

"Ditto," he said. "I miss you. Here I am, on a tropical island in an exquisitely beautiful part of the world, and no one to share it with. I lie awake at night and think of what you and I could be doing."

My legs had parted, and without conscious thought my hand slipped below the waistline of my PJ's and slid into my sex. I circled my clitoris.

"If it *was* your joystick I had my hands on, what would you do?" I asked softly.

There was a pause. I knew he'd understood the question and the context. I could imagine him assessing the situation. This was a new experience for us.

"I'd be kissing your breasts," he murmured. "Then, when those nipples were erect and hungry, and your body starting to move against me, I'd go further down, kissing every inch of your skin as I went. I'd circle your navel with my tongue and move to your tummy. Then I'd go lower still. I'd touch you. I'd taste you and I'd have you begging."

I gave a little gasp. My frantic rubbing was garnering results. I could feel my overstimulated body ready to release.

"What would I be doing?" I whispered.

"Oh, you'd be returning the favour. With fingers and tongue you'd be working your way down."

I nearly lost it as I absorbed his words.

"And that would please you?"

"Oh baby, it would please me greatly. And then ... ." In his seductive voice he continued detailing the wanton acts we would perform. My breathing grew ragged as I visualised our shared pleasure.

I was concentrating so intensely on his words and the

stimulation of my own release, I'd no room for anything else. Between them I crescendoed and felt the spasms take me over the edge.

"Was that good for you, baby?" he asked after I'd been quiet for a few moments.

"I miss you," I said wistfully.

It was hard to return to the reality of my aloneness. I was, in a sense, satisfied. I'd never tried Skyped sex before, so it was another box I could tick. I could report that it was a pleasant means of release, but sadly, it couldn't replicate the real thing.

"I miss you too," he replied.

"I miss you and raise you one," I sighed. "Still, it's not long now and we can make up for lost time when you get back."

"Count on it," he growled.

* * *

The *Kapiti News*, another local newspaper, had been dropped off by the paper boy and lay on the floor of the office. I picked it up and opened it to the report about Andrew Camborne's death.

After a short paragraph confirming what had been on the news the night before, the article carried on:

Andrew Camborne was well known in the Paraparaumu community as a reporter and investigative journalist for the Kapiti Observer. *A committed member of the Green Party, he worked extensively with local ecological groups and their interests. Terming himself an eco-warrior, Andrew was an active participant in moves to ensure development within the Kapiti area was managed in compliance with the highest ideals of care and preservation for historical and ecologically sensitive sites.*

"How's it going?"

Maria had arrived.

"I'm just reading this piece about the guy whose body they found up the road."

"I hear it was a hit and run, and the police think he was deliberately targeted."

"I hadn't heard that," I said surprised.

"It was on the radio this morning. How true it is, I don't know. Poor man. So young to have your life taken away. It's very sad."

I nodded. "Yeah, it is. It gave me a turn when I saw who it was, because I spoke to him the night before last, at that bun fight Roger made me go to."

I flicked through the rest of the paper and a reference to Paraparaumu Airport caught my attention. I turned back to it and was surprised to see an article written by one of our students.

Tim Andrews had recently achieved his pilot's licence with us and apparently had written a blog about the experience. The newspaper had chosen to publish a snippet. It was a well-written, light-hearted piece and I laughed as I read it, remembering how I'd tried to teach him to stall the aircraft, and how terrified he'd been.

I'd known Tim had something to do with journalism but hadn't connected him with our local newspaper. I wondered whether he'd known Andrew Camborne. I made a note to ask next time he came in.

I went outside to help Nick pull the aircraft out of the hangar.

"Are you enjoying the students?"

"Hell, yeah." Nick's face beamed with enthusiasm.

"So no-one's tried to kill you yet?"

"Not yet," he said. "So far so good."

I chuckled. "Just remember what Roger always says: 'Better intervene too early than leave it too late and come unstuck.'"

It was one of Roger's mantras, and Nick quoted the line with me.

"Yeah, I know," he assured me.

There are some things an instructor has to learn for themselves, and how to cope with high-risk situations a student can cause accidentally is the hardest lesson for a new instructor. Failing to recognise danger quickly enough can have lethal consequences.

"Fore-warned is fore-armed," I said. "You're flying with John Morgan this morning. He's got a nasty tendency to put his feet on the brakes as he's landing. Remind him to keep them up on the rudders, otherwise he'll burn out the tyres."

Nick looked alarmed. "Why does he do that?"

"I think it's nerves. He's scared of landing and tries to brace himself on the brake pedals. If you remind him to keep his heels off the floor and use the rudders, he's OK. He'll get over it as he gets more confident."

"Thanks for the tip," said Nick.

I flew with my own student. Morris held an English pilot's licence that was out of date and he wanted to renew it, or at least achieve one which would allow him to fly in New Zealand. I'd flown with him before, and knew that his technique and procedure, though slightly different to standard New Zealand methodology, was essentially sturdy.

I'd wanted one more flight before signing him off because his grasp of radio work was still erratic for New Zealand conditions.

He started the engine, and I hastily removed my headphones.

"Clear prop!" he yelled, full volume, into his headset.

The first time he'd done that I'd had my headphones on, and the volume of his shout had nearly shattered my ear drums. I accept that, in the early days of aviation and in an open cockpit, a yell of that kind was appropriate to warn bystanders - the volume of his shout made sense if you had to be heard over the beat of the engine: however, in an enclosed cockpit, with a live radio circuit connecting the occupants, such a war cry is not only unnecessary, it's a public health hazard. I'd tried to explain the problem, but I'd failed. One day a passenger would either deck him or have a heart attack.

When we completed the flight I signed him off. He was sufficiently competent, and his radio calls had improved enough to make him safe in New Zealand skies. He went away happy, although I suspected he thought me inordinately highly strung and not up to the full rigour of cockpit work.

I wandered out to the balcony and watched Nick and his student land safely. If Nick had had problems during the flight, they didn't show. The landing and roll-out was smooth and efficient.

"All good?" I asked as Nick waved goodbye to his student.

"Yeah, it was fine, but I'm glad you warned me about the foot issue."

"It struck again?"

"Yes, but I got onto it early enough so it wasn't a problem."

I smiled. "Well done. You live to fly another day."

He looked at me cheekily. "How's your hearing?" I'd told Nick and Greig about Morris's habit.

I laughed. "I've learnt from experience, and took my headphones off," I admitted.

When I walked back into the waiting room I gave an involuntary start. Roger was entertaining Jim Mason. The man had been so much on my mind since I'd met him that I almost felt I'd conjured him up.

"Hardcastle," called Roger, "come over here. Jim here has a proposition for you."

"Oh, yes?" I approached the pair of them with a considerable sense of misgiving.

Jim stood as I joined them. His latent charm was in evidence as he shook my hand and smiled.

"Good to see you again," I said. "How can I help?" Never think I haven't taken on the trappings of customer service lingo.

"I came in to see your set-up," explained Jim. "I was impressed by what you were both saying the other evening, and I thought I'd check it out. I also wanted to ask whether I could organise some flying lessons for my daughter over the school holidays."

I glanced at Roger who was nodding enthusiastically.

"If she wants to learn to fly, we'd be happy to start her on the programme," I said.

"Jim asked if you would be her instructor," said Roger, "and I said you'd be ideal for the job."

I looked at Jim, wondering whether this was as simple as it sounded.

"Sure," I said. "When would she like to start?"

"Would tomorrow be OK?" asked Jim.

I lifted the bookings sheet off the counter. "I'm free between ten and eleven o'clock tomorrow if that suits. Bring her in just before ten, and we'll go from there." I pencilled the booking into the page. "Tell her to wear flat-soled shoes."

"Excellent, I know I leave her in safe hands," said Jim.

"What's her name?" I asked.

"Melody."

I entered the name on the sheet, straightened up and smiled at him. "We'll see her tomorrow, then."

"I'll bring her in and introduce her," he promised.

I watched him leave and turned to Roger.

"What was all that about?"

"A solo dad who doesn't know what to do with a teenager during the holidays?" he hazarded. "I don't care what you do with the girl, Hardcastle. Just remember her dad has plenty of brass and could be good for our business. Don't piss either her or him off."

"Gee, thanks," I said as offensively as I could. "What happened to the 'you must be always in control' routine?"

"Of course you're in control," smirked Roger. "Just be in control and make the girl happy."

I gave a snort.

"Did Jim say anything about the body found in Arawhata Road?" I asked.

"No," said Roger. "Why? Should he have?"

"I recognised the guy who was killed on TV last night," I told him. "He was the man Jim had the argument with."

"Is that right? No he didn't say anything about it." Roger grimaced. "No doubt the police have it all well in hand."

CHAPTER
FOUR

JIM AND HIS DAUGHTER ARRIVED EARLY. I came back from my first lesson of the day to find Jim leaning on the counter, chatting to Maria and Roger. If he knew Andrew Camborne had died only a few hours after their argument, he seemed extremely relaxed about it. There was no shadow to his smile as he charmed his way into Maria's good books.

I waved my departing student on his way, and turned to them.

Jim greeted me with a big smile.

"Good morning," I said, looking at Melody. "I'm Claire, and you'll be flying with me. Are you looking forward to your first lesson?"

"Yeah," she said. A nice, well-spoken voice, I noted, even though she didn't sound enthusiastic. I gave her an assessing look.

Roger had told me she was sixteen, but she could have passed for a couple of years older. She had that sheen only the privately educated seem to acquire – an aura of cleanliness and grooming the rest of us fail to reach. Her face was pretty with a warm peaches-and-cream complexion. I looked at her glossy fair hair and wondered how she got it so bouncy. It could have been in a shampoo commercial.

Her casual clothes were age appropriate, but I'd swear all came from Top Shop or some other designer stable. Whatever their provenance, they were several strata higher up the fashion ladder than Dress Smart or Glassons.

I turned to Jim. "I thought, to start the process, I would take Melody up today for a combination trial flight and first lesson so she can see how she likes it. Is that OK?"

"What do you think, Pumpkin? Does that sound good to you?"

She shrugged. "Fine," she said flatly.

I had a feeling she was her daddy's pampered little princess and I was going to have a load of work to get any excitement or engagement out of her. I smiled at Jim and Roger, and escorted Melody out to the aircraft.

I got her seated and strapped in and we taxied out.

I tried a few conversational gambits. "Where do you go to college?" "Are you enjoying your holidays?" "Have you ever been in a small plane before?"

I needn't have bothered. As soon as we were out of sight of her father, Melody gave up pretending the slightest interest in aviation.

Once airborne, I showed her the basics of turning and yawing the little Cessna. She put her hands where I told her, and used her feet as directed, but nothing I did penetrated the fog of boredom. She showed not the faintest interest in, or appreciation of, the spectacular scenery outside, and made it clear that the worn interior of the little trainer was beneath her dignity.

We certainly hadn't bonded. I got the impression she considered a woman who earned her living pushing machinery around the sky was a lower form of life.

Mindful of Roger's instructions, I persisted with her far longer than I would have with any other rude brat with attitude, but I was coming close to slapping her.

When my nieces complain they're bored, my sister Kate tells them that "only boring people are bored," and finds them some particularly unpleasant chore to do. I rather thought Kate would handle Melody more successfully than I was

"Would you like to go back now?" I asked at last.

A sulky lift of her shoulders was all I received by way of reply. Clearly radio work was going to be a problem for her as well if she wasn't prepared to talk. I felt a surge of frustration with the spoilt, sulky brat.

A little attitude is in fact desirable in pilots. You need to be tough, self-reliant and confident to fly an aircraft. What I couldn't handle was her determination to be miserable in spite of her father's attempts to please her. Self-indulgent moodiness doesn't amuse me.

We'd been up in the air for thirty minutes, and I'd kept the aircraft steadily climbing. We were now three thousand feet above the sea. Without warning, I lowered the nose of the aircraft to build up speed.

"I'll show you a couple of aerobatics to finish off with," I said as I raised the nose, pushed through to full power and pulled us up, over and around into a loop.

I heard a startled squawk from her and glanced over as I levelled out.

"What did you think of that?" I asked, before entering, without pause, into a barrel roll. It was a cracker, and I was pleased with the manoeuvre as the aircraft rolled around the horizon.

I levelled out again and turned to check how she was.

"You OK?"

She gave me a wary look and nodded.

The boredom had been wiped from her face and she had colour in her cheeks.

"Shall we try a couple more manoeuvres?" I asked.

She took a deep breath, and I wondered which way she would jump and how intact her attitude was now. I'd either scared her half to death or given her the most thrilling experience of her young life.

"Yes, please," she said.

"Good girl," I said approvingly. "You're doing well."

I flew us up into a stall turn. She squealed as we hung in the air for the moment before the aircraft cartwheeled. I levelled out again.

"Still OK?"

She nodded.

"Would you like to do a loop again, but this time you fly it with me?" She nodded again, and gave me a slight smile of anticipation.

This was a different girl. She put her hands on the yoke and followed through with my movements. I got her to push the throttle in, then guided her to close it later as we floated upside down over the top of the arc and down the other side.

"Well done," I said. "Did you enjoy it?"

There was something close to a grin on her face as she nodded.

"Most people love flying loops," I said. "They're the easiest of manoeuvres, but also the hardest to get completely correct."

I looked at my watch. "We'd better head back," I said and turned for home.

I set it up for her, but this time she controlled the flying until we were close to landing, and then I let her follow through with me on the controls as we touched down. I thought she'd had enough so I taxied us back to the hangar.

By the time we'd parked, she'd reverted to something closer to her earlier demeanour, I suppose in preparation for meeting her dad. She probably made his life hell.

Still, she thanked me for the flight and said good-bye politely. I felt we'd made progress.

"Well, Hardcastle?" asked Roger once Melody and Jim had left. "What have you got to say for yourself?"

I wasn't sure how Roger was going to react when I told him what I'd done. I hadn't actually done anything illegal, or too unprofessional. But equally, I'd certainly exceeded the training brief I'd been given.

I looked Roger in the eye – I knew him well enough to know boldness was my best defence.

I explained what I'd done.

"You owe me one," I said in conclusion. "That was incredibly hard work, but I think in the end I got through to her."

Roger gave a grunt of amusement, and I relaxed. I wasn't about to be bollocked.

"That's a very unusual first lesson," commented Greig who

was lounging on the sofa. "A sort of *Effects of Controls* on steroids."

"Thank God I remembered we were in the aerobat," I said. "I don't know what I'd have done otherwise. Still, it'll be interesting to see if she comes back for another go."

*   *   *

Roger answered the phone after lunch. I was still attempting to complete the pilots' files. As I'd suspected, Roger had simply returned his own file to me with instructions to bring it up to date. I was busy trying to track down the date of his last medical.

"You've been in to Waitaria Bay, haven't you?" Roger called across to me.

"Where?" I asked vaguely, my mind occupied with the conversation I'd been having with the frustrated practice nurse who was trying to find the date of his last medical appointment.

"Waitaria Bay – you know, in Kenepuru Sound? In fact, I know you've been there. I took you in there myself to check you out on the strip."

My brain re-engaged. "Oh, you mean Nopera airstrip? Yeah, I've been there a couple of times."

"There's a charter tomorrow – probably a long one. The clients are flying down to see a property they want to buy. They need to be dropped off. You'll have to wait for them while they're there. Then you fly back again after they've seen the place. They assume the time on the ground will be about two hours so you'd better take a good book. They'll be here at ten."

I automatically glanced outside through the large waiting room windows. The weather had been good for the last couple of days, but that was no guarantee it would continue.

I nodded. "Thanks."

I smiled inwardly. If I'd had any doubts about whether Roger approved of my actions with Melody that morning, I now had my answer. Charters of this sort are the cherry on the top for pilots. If he had been angry with me, the flight would have gone to Greig.

I just prayed that the weather would stay stable.

* * *

The phone rang mid-afternoon.

"Hi, it's Jim Mason."

"Oh, hi," I said, wondering if he was phoning to complain about the lesson.

"I just wanted to say how much Melody enjoyed the flight this morning. That was inspired thinking, to throw in a couple of aerobatic moves," he enthused. "I could tell Melody was really impressed."

"Well, I'm glad to hear that. I thought she might enjoy them."

"She said you were a brilliant instructor, and from her, that's very high praise indeed. So thank you."

"Well, thank you for saying so," I said. I was pleased. I glanced across at Roger on the far side of the office. "It's all part of our service." I made sure I looked as sanctimonious as I sounded. I saw Roger's eyebrows rise.

Jim laughed. "Whatever it is, could we book again for a lesson in a couple of days? With you, obviously, as the instructor?"

"Sure, but I'm off for the next two days. Will early next week suit?"

"Fine." I pencilled the booking in.

"A happy customer," I said to Roger. "Melody is coming back next week."

I saw an odd look cross Roger's face.

"Well done," he said eventually. "You handled the whole thing very well. Very well indeed."

I was still buzzing with his praise when I got home. Roger is a good and generous employer, but it was more usual for his approval to be shown obliquely, such as the charter to Nopera, than it was in actual commendation.

CHAPTER FIVE

I FUELLED THE CESSNA 172, CHECKED THE meteorological reports and prepared the flight plan for the trip. Fortunately, the weather remained fair, with a light north-westerly and high cloud.

"Hi, I'm Glynn Edwards, and this is my nephew Steve."

I registered the English accent and smiled as I greeted my passengers. Glynn, was a small, tough-looking man. I placed him in his forties, but he could have been younger. He had the wizened face you sometimes see on jockeys who've spent too many hours shedding weight in the sauna. He was dressed in jeans and a polar fleece jacket.

Steve was tall, lean and about my own age, in his mid-twenties. He was a good-looking man, wearing a stylish long trench coat with rolled-up sleeves over a pair of dark jeans.

Something about the pair tugged at my memory, although I couldn't recall ever having met them before. There was no obvious family resemblance between them, Glynn being clearly Caucasian, while Steve could have passed as Maori.

"Hi, I'm Claire," I introduced myself. "Looks like we've got a nice day for it. If you're ready, we'll get you into the aircraft. Is that all your luggage?"

They each had substantial backpacks which I made them put on the scales to check the weight. They were heavy, but within limits. I reached to lift Steve's off the scales, but he grabbed it quickly.

"No, it's much too heavy for you to carry," he smiled at me a little too intently as he lifted it away.

I was immediately wary. There are some guys who find the idea of a women pilot sexy and act accordingly. I've learned to be cautious around them.

Steve fairly oozed an animal form of magnetism and I suspected he was used to having a good deal of sexual success. He may have been wiry, but there were lean, powerful, muscles in his arms. I automatically imagined he'd be a good man in a fight and some edge to his personality made me think he'd require that ability quite often. He projected an unsettling air of roughness and danger, at odds with his slightly too smooth, ingratiating, manner. I thought he probably fancied himself and the smile he gave me openly suggested his expectation I'd fall for his charm. I nodded my head with chilly professionalism, and saw his eyes narrow as he absorbed my rejection.

I got them loaded into the aircraft. As I showed Steve how to buckle himself into the seat belt, I noticed he had five dots, arranged like the five side on a dice, tattooed on his left hand. It was a surprisingly primitive sort of tattoo, and I wondered what it signified and whether he'd marked it on himself.

We taxied out but had to wait as a commuter Air New Zealand flight came in to land. As it rolled past us, its size made our own C172 seem tiny in comparison.

"I'm surprised something that big can land here," remarked Glynn.

"There's a kilometre and a half of runway," I replied, "so there's plenty of length. It's just relativity that makes everything else on the airfield look small."

Once airborne, I steered for the Marlborough Sounds. It was one of those days when the light made everything in the distance seem closer. Far across the Strait we could clearly see the snow-capped peaks of the Seaward Kaikouras.

"Have you both been in small aircraft before?" I asked.

Glynn shook his head. "No, this is a first for me. For you too, isn't it, Steve?"

"Well, you could hardly have a nicer day for your first flight," I said as we flew over a couple of the smaller islands guarding the entrance to Queen Charlotte Sound. I pointed out the Cook Strait ferry in the distance.

"What's that in the water?" asked Steve, pointing towards the coastline.

I looked down at the neat rows of lines in the bay below.

"Mussel farms," I answered. "There are heaps of them in the Sounds. I think they also farm salmon and trout in some places."

"What part of England are you from?" I asked Glynn.

"Croydon," he replied. "My sister came to New Zealand thirty years ago, when I was just a kid and has been here ever since. She settled down, married, raised a family, and kept pestering me to come out and join them. At last I got around to it. I've been in New Zealand five years now. I just love it."

I turned to Steve. "You're a Kiwi?"

"Born and bred," he smiled wolfishly. "I'm the one without the funny foreign accent."

We crossed over the ridge into Kenepuru Sound. There was a variety of water-based activity in the sheltered stretch of water ahead. A fine-looking yacht lay at anchor in a bay off the point on our right. I admired her twin-masted beauty. The dark blue and white of the boat, the sandy beach, the whole framed by the hills behind her, was a pretty enough scene to be on a postcard, or a photograph for Tourism New Zealand. Beneath us, small pleasure craft bobbed about on the water. It would be a lovely day to be fishing, or indeed on the water taxi that was cutting a trail across the sound beneath us.

"Whereabouts is the property you're looking at today?" I asked.

There was a marked silence. After a moment I glanced at Glynn who was staring down at the water.

"I couldn't tell from here," he said at last. "All these bays makes it confusing, and I don't know the area. We're getting picked up from the airfield and driven there."

I started our descent and steered across the sound to Te Matau a Maui Bay. Nopera strip is set on a slope which runs up from the shoreline towards the hills, and the usual aviation rule of taking off and landing into the prevailing wind was superseded here by the requirements of the terrain. Nopera's particular geography dictates landings have to be made uphill from the bay, while all take-offs leave in the opposite direction, gathering speed during the run down the slope towards the water.

Even though I knew Roger had phoned for permission to use the strip, I circled it counter-clockwise, checking for stock before starting the descent that brought us in to land. We touched down at the seaward end of the strip and taxied up the slope. I turned around at the top and parked. The slope fell away so sharply towards the bay that sitting in the pilot's seat I couldn't see any of it in front of the cowling – just the sky and the tops of the hills on the far side of the sound.

"The eagle has landed," murmured Steve.

I saw a car waiting at the gate to the strip. "Looks like your lift's arrived," I said, as I climbed out of the aircraft.

Glynn went across to greet his driver, and I turned to get the backpacks.

I opened the hatch and Steve grabbed them both. "I've got them," he said as he manoeuvred them out of the hold.

I watched as he carried both packs across to the waiting car and realised why the sight seemed incongruous. Steve's light sports shoes and trench coat were out of place with the serious tramping packs he was carrying, which conveyed a mixed message about their plans for the day. I shrugged. Maybe they had boots inside the packs.

I waved as they drove away. I'd dropped a cushion on the grass and settled down to enjoy the peace and solitude before I suddenly realised where I'd seen Glynn and Steve before - they'd been the two men standing behind me watching Jim's altercation with the protesters on the night of the cocktail party! I supposed it wasn't such an unlikely coincidence. Roger had probably met them that evening and encouraged them to charter a plane to their meeting. I recalled the younger one, Steve, had said something offensive, but I couldn't remember what it was.

It might be winter, but it was warm enough in the sunshine, and I was wearing my jacket. I expected a protracted wait so I'd packed myself a couple of sandwiches and a bottle of water. I leaned back against the wheel cowling and prepared to study.

Although I never intended to become an airline pilot, I had recently started studying towards my ATPL licence, simply to improve my overall level of aviation knowledge. The Airline Transport Pilot Licence is, as the name says, the base qualification to fly for airlines. Although the subjects are essentially the same as pilots study at private and commercial level, the technical information is lifted to a whole new degree of sophistication.

I'd decided to start with the most basic of papers – Human Factors – as a warm-up before I tackled the serious subjects of Navigation and Meteorology. Human Factors is the study of how people and planes interact, and of the unexpected hazards the aviation environment can impose on human beings. I'd passed the commercial pilot's level of the subject with full marks, and I hoped to repeat that standard with the ATPL exam.

With Jack away, my evenings and days off were free of distraction and I intended to sit this first exam the following week. With any luck I'd pass and it would be something else to celebrate when he got back.

I worked steadily for an hour, then stopped for lunch. It was warm. I took off my jacket and rolled it into a pad behind my back. It was a lovely view, and from where I sat, I looked across the bay to the hills on the far side of Kenepuru Sound. Protected by the encircling hills from the worst of any wind, the blue water stretched in front of me as smooth and shiny as glass. The beauty of the Sounds is exceptional, and once again I reflected on the perks of my job.

After I'd finished my sandwich I stood and walked down the strip towards the bay. As a matter of habit, I counted my paces down the hill. If I stretched my stride out so I covered roughly a metre with each step, it gave me an idea of the strip's length. I noted a heavy fence post used as a strainer to anchor the fence line. I knew I'd be able to identify it again at the two-thirds point. That marker was significant - as we passed it on our take-off roll we would either have sufficient speed to ensure a safe take-off, or I'd have to abort the run. Mind you, stopping might not be that easy. The slope was steep at that point, and it would be a hell of a job to pull up.

I didn't really have any doubt about being able to successfully get out of the strip. I'd been here before. The weather was cool and crisp, the tail-wind was light and we weren't weighed down by too much in the way of luggage. It was simply good practice to double-check the figures once I'd climbed the slope back to the plane and confirm we were good to go.

It was three o'clock before Glynn and Steve returned. I'd got in an extra hour of studying and was pleased with my progress.

Glynn strode across to the plane as I rose to open the luggage hatch for him. I gathered up my own stuff while Glynn shoved his pack into the hold and pushed it towards the tail.

I was bent over, shoving my gear under the pilot's seat, when I was nearly knocked in the face as the front of the aircraft lifted abruptly.

"Shit!" I looked up, startled.

The weight of Glynn's pack in the hold had altered the balance, making the tail end of the plane drop significantly.

"What the hell have you got in there?" I asked. "Rock samples?"

Glynn didn't reply.

I moved to the back of the plane. "You can't leave it like that," I told him. "That pack's got to come forward otherwise we'll be completely out of balance." I went to shift it but Glynn was already pulling it up from the tail. "Wedge it against the back of the seats," I said.

With the weight of the bag brought forward, the aircraft settled back on an even keel. I watched suspiciously as Steve walked towards us carrying his own pack.

"Is that going to be as heavy as yours?" I asked Glynn.

"Probably," he muttered.

"Then it's going to have to go on the passenger seat beside

you. We can't put it any further back," I said firmly. I made them manoeuvre the pack onto the seat and strap it in with a safety belt. At least the aircraft was now level.

Finally, I got Glynn and Steve seated and strapped in to their seats. I made Glynn, the lighter of the two, take the back seat to even out the weight of the luggage. He looked cramped beside his inanimate companion, but I wasn't sympathetic.

"I'm sorry to make an issue about it," I said, "but in small aircraft we have to be very careful about the weight we carry, and even more careful about how it's distributed." They nodded politely. I doubted if they understood, clients rarely do, but their safety depended on our plane being airworthy. Being overweight and unbalanced are classic causes of accidents.

I revved the engine to full power, released the brakes and accelerated into our take off run. I watched the airspeed climb as we headed down the hill. Even so, we'd only just hit take-off speed by my two-thirds marker. When I eventually raised the nose and allowed the plane to fly off the strip, I noticed the boundary fence at the end of the runway uncomfortably close below us. I kept low over the water as we flew across the bay and allowed airspeed to build before setting her into a climb.

Most of the pleasure craft had already packed up for the day, but the yacht I'd seen earlier was still sitting at anchor in her bay.

"She's a pretty sight, isn't she," I said, pointing her out to Steve.

His eyes were fixed on the boat. "Mm," he said noncommittally.

"What was the property like?" I asked.

"Fine," he replied. His curtness was just short of being rude, and I was aware again of the edgy tension that seemed part of his personality.

I concentrated on flying. Neither passenger seemed talkative, which suited me. It was a lovely afternoon to be in the air, and I was happy enough to let them doze off.

We were just south of Paekakariki when Glynn stirred in the seat behind me.

"Can we fly north for a bit?" he asked. "Seeing as we're in the air, it would be great if we could fly over our work site and see it from up here."

"Fine," I said. "Just let me know where you want to go so I can let the tower know."

"Just north of Waikanae," said Glynn, "between the coast and the new motorway. It's not far."

I radioed in our intentions and headed up the coast.

With Glynn guiding me, I flew over the Waikanae River mouth and north along the line of sand dunes.

"There," said Glynn, pointing.

I circled around the area he indicated. I could see a few parked vehicles, and a digger operating.

"What's it going to be?" I asked.

"A retirement village," he said.

"Another retirement village? I'd have thought Waikanae had plenty of them already."

"This one's going to be different," said Glynn. "Jim's designing it on a European model for people with dementia and Alzheimer's. It's going to be a whole, enclosed village, fully staffed with carers, where it's safe for the patients to wander around freely, go to the special shops and so on. It will cater for ordinary clients as well, of course. He's got big plans."

"Jim?" I asked.

"Yeah, Jim Mason. The property developer. He's my boss."

"You work for him?" I was surprised.

"Why, do you know him?" he asked.

I shook my head. "No, not really. I met him at the Kapiti Businessmen's do a few nights back. I think you and Steve were there?"

There was a silence so absolute you could cut it. I actually tapped the mike on my headset to see if it was still working. When I realised it was, I turned to Steve who was now very still. As he didn't seem about to answer, I swivelled to see Glynn in the back seat.

"I'm right, aren't I? I thought that was where I'd seen you both."

"Yeah, that's right. We were there. It was where we met your boss and he talked us into flying with you." I thought the words from Glynn sounded forced.

"Well, there you are," I smiled. "I met Jim Mason that night, and his daughter came in for a flying lesson." I looked down at the site below us which seemed to be undeveloped scrub land. "Was this the development the protesters were demonstrating about that night? I can't see too much of a problem with it myself. Is there something specific they object to?"

Glynn snorted. "No. They are just generally opposed to progress. Stupid idiots. If they're not fussing about the aquifers or the wetlands, they're protesting about Maori history, graves and every other bloody thing. If we listened to them we'd never get anything done."

"What about the reporter who was with them? He died the other day," I said. "He was the guy they found on Arawhata Road."

Steve made an abrupt movement beside me. I looked at him.

"Sorry," he said. "My leg jerked. I've got cramp."

"I don't know anything about the reporter," said Glynn. "He was probably just writing about another bloody protest."

I turned for home.

After a few minutes Steve asked, "Was that you flying the morning when the police had the road cordoned off? I noticed a plane circling."

I nodded, and mindful of Roger's concerns about Paraparaumu Aviation being implicated in police activities, added, "One of our students wanted to check out the excitement from the air at the end of his lesson."

"I thought I recognised the plane," said Steve.

We got back and unloaded. I was tempted to ask Glynn to put the packs on the scales just to see how much they weighed, but decided it wasn't worth the hassle. I waved them on their way and watched as they carried the heavy loads out to their car.

Greig and Nick were busy shifting planes around the hangar with Roger. For no particular reason, Roger has a rush of blood to the head every few months, and decides he can arrange aircraft more efficiently in the hangar. In fairness, it's an art-form managing the placement of high-wing, low-wing, bi-plane and helicopter aircraft and ensuring that no 'hangar-rash' dings or denting occurs as each one is manoeuvred in and out within the limited space.

Roger once told me that our hangar had been designed by an architect who'd modelled scale versions of each aircraft and placed them into his little model of the hangar. Each plane had fit snugly and safely into its assigned place. Unfortunately, he'd achieved this happy result by lifting the roof off his model and placing the aircraft in from above. He'd never considered the real world, where we had to stack aircraft into a limited space by guiding them through hangar doors and turning them so they could fit. Helicopter rotors had to stack above high-winged Cessnas, and the bi-plane was a pain to fit beside anything, in particular the low-wing Pipers and Grummans.

I'd taken one look at Nick and Greig, sweating under Roger's direction, and hastily followed my clients into the office, abandoning the aircraft where I'd parked it on the apron. I saw Greig give me a bitter look as I decamped. I cited paper work as my excuse and smiled sweetly at him. Sometimes you win, sometimes you lose.

Maria and I were sitting in comfort, sipping cups of coffee.

"That was very odd, and I'm not sure it wasn't actually dodgy," I said.

"Those two?" she asked in surprise.

I tried to explain my unease.

"You know they told Roger they were flying to Nopera to look at property? Maybe they were, but some things just don't add up. They arrived this morning with tramping packs large enough for a week's camping trip. But they were wearing light weight, city-casual shoes. Those packs were heavy on the way out, but much heavier on the trip back, so they picked something up while they were over there. I'd love to know what it was. Whatever they had was more than a picnic lunch, that's for certain."

Maria was silent for a while. She's an intelligent lady, and I respect her input. I was content to drink my coffee, mull over the discrepancies I'd noticed during the day and wait for her opinion.

At last she said, "It would be unlikely they'd carry a load of stuff out on a trip and then add to it." She paused, then followed her argument through to its conclusion. "Surely it's more likely they swapped something they took out, for something they brought back?"

I was startled by the clear logic of the thought. "I don't know. Do you think it was a trade of some sort, and they didn't let us know?"

Maria shrugged. "I'm not sure, but from what you said, then … maybe? It could be that whatever they were up to isn't strictly legit."

I thought of how protective both Steve and Glynn had been of their packs.

"It makes sense in a bizarre sort of way," I said, "except I can't think of anything of value they could have picked up at Nopera." I leaned back against the couch and ran through the events of the day. A thought struck me.

"You don't think they could have brought mussels back with them?"

"Mussels?"

"You know, the green lipped sort they farm. Steve asked about the farms as we flew over. Perhaps they brought back an illicit stash of them."

Maria shrugged her elegant shoulders. "Maybe. If so, I don't think you have a lot to worry about. I don't see buying a few shellfish represents a crime."

The guys came and joined us.

"Nicely relaxed after your trip, are you?" asked Greig sarcastically.

"Yes, thank you," I chuckled. "I'm feeling much better after my coffee." Greig threw me an evil look and I laughed. "I even managed to get in a couple of hours study while I sat in the sun and waited for my passengers. It's been a very productive day."

Nick grinned at the expression on Greig's face. "She's just trying to wind you up, mate."

"She's succeeding," said Greig as he flung himself back on the couch.

"What have you been up to, Hardcastle?" asked Roger, settling himself in his chair. "Did you have a good trip?"

I reprised the conversation I'd had with Maria.

"That's a bit odd," commented Roger. "You should have asked what they had in the bags."

"I didn't like to," I confessed. "I don't usually ask passengers for a manifesto."

"You're the pilot in charge," he said firmly. "If you think something is wrong it's your responsibility to check it out. You'd look silly if they'd been carrying gas cylinders or something, and they blew up mid-flight."

"She'd not only look silly, she'd be dead," said Greig. He was more cheerful now I was getting it in the neck.

"I forgot to add that they work for Jim Mason," I said, hoping to turn the conversation. "At least Glynn said he did. I assumed Steve does as well, but now I think of it, he didn't actually say so. We flew up over the site Jim's developing."

"Oh yeah? What is it?" asked Roger.

"A retirement village." There was a concerted groan from them all.

"I said the same, but apparently it's some special kind of facility where they can look after people with dementia and Alzheimer's."

"It's still going to be another factory where they battery-farm geriatrics for profit," said Roger forcefully. "They've made it illegal to put chickens and pigs in cages, so why is it OK to shut old people up in institutions?"

I hadn't thought of it that way before, and I was startled by the anger in his voice. I looked at Roger and Maria who were probably the oldest people I knew well, and tried to imagine them incarcerated in a home. It was a troubling thought, and I could see why Roger rejected it so fiercely.

"Well, there's only ten sand dunes and a digger out there at the moment," I said. "Whatever they're building will take a while."

CHAPTER
SIX

I ENDED UP GOING TO THE PUB with Nick and Greig. "Come on, Claire," said Greig. "It's trivia night, and Nick's not up to your standard. We're dropping in the ratings."

"My brother's up from Otago as well and wants to meet you," chipped in Nick.

"Not another Burrows brother wanting to learn to fly?" I asked.

"Nah," laughed Nick. "But he knows you were my flying instructor."

I was about to turn the invitation down. A long evening of sobriety, sipping tomato juice, and watching my friends get happy wasn't my idea of a great night out. The quiz could get stuffed.

"She's in a difficult mood, boys," warned Roger, before I could speak. "Her boyfriend's away, so he's not tom-catting around putting a smile on her face, and she's not drinking. No wonder she's sour. Hardcastle's not designed for a life of austerity."

Naturally I gritted my teeth and promptly decided to go to the pub. Only a minute later, when I saw Roger's satisfied smirk, I realised how competently I'd been manipulated, but by then it was too late to back out.

I threw my boss the foulest look I could and heard him chuckle.

*   *   *

Nick's brother Duncan was the older of the two siblings by a couple of years. The family resemblance was so strong, it was like looking at a future photo of Nick. The same tall, lean frame, the same reddish hair. I wouldn't have described Nick as a red head, but if his brother was any indication, in a few years' time Nick's hair would be a deep shade of copper.

Nick made the introductions and his brother smiled.

"Hi, he said. "I've been hoping to meet the wonder woman who turned my baby brother into a flying instructor."

"Hi," I replied. "I don't think your brother needed outside intervention. He's a pretty capable pilot."

"That's the Burrows way," he said.

When I'd first met Nick, his chief quality had been a shy, boyish diffidence. Clearly Duncan had a more robust level of self-confidence.

Jayleen joined us and the introductions were repeated. I watched her eye Duncan up and the way her hand automatically moved flirtatiously to sweep the bright blonde hair back off her neck. I felt like telling him it was dyed.

Duncan's eyes narrowed as he looked at her. Jayleen has been Greig's girlfriend for nine months or more, but it's never stopped her being predatory with other men. I'd seen her in action before, and I wondered whether Greig could see what was so obvious to me.

We bought a round of drinks and settled in to the routine of quiz night. Each of us had individual areas of expertise, and Duncan proved to have wide-ranging general knowledge, more than pulling his weight on the team. Jayleen and Nick between them knew every band and DJ in the country. I was startled to find Nick liked Max Key's *Forget It*.

"You do?" I blurted, after he'd answered a question successfully.

He shrugged. "Someone has to," he grinned.

We ended up in second place, which wasn't bad going. The others stayed on for a final celebratory drink, but I made my apologies and headed for home. There was only so much tomato juice I could drink and remain sociable.

*   *   *

Nelson nudged me awake the next morning demanding breakfast. He likes the days I'm at home as he can enjoy a lazy lie-in with me, but equally he doesn't see why my rest should delay his meal.

I grumbled, but dragged myself out of bed to feed him. The cottage was freezing cold, and I could hear rain bucketing down outside. I loaded the log fire up with wood. There were still a few embers glowing from last night so it wouldn't take long to heat the house up again. I brewed the first coffee of the day, then stood clutching my mug for warmth and looked out the window. It was barely light and the clouds hung heavily over the hills. Even if the rain eased, it would still be no day for flying.

To top it off, the wind was blowing from the east, the most unpleasant direction for us at Paraparaumu. In an easterly, the airflow lifts and curls over the hills behind the town, then drops a nasty down-draught over and alongside the airport. The resulting wind pockets may be harmless, but the bumpy turbulence means nervous, inexperienced pilots or passengers do well to avoid such days.

Pilots have a saying: "It's better to be on the ground wishing you were in the sky, than in the sky wishing you were safely on the ground." I grimaced at the day and took myself back to join Nelson in the snug warmth of my bed. I took my text books with me and justified my idleness with some revision for the exam I was due to sit the next day.

The weather hadn't improved later that evening when I drove south for Lisa's house-warming party. The traffic into Wellington was going at snail's pace, and the cars in front of me, in what was purported to be the fast lane, were barely doing 80 kilometres, their drivers apparently terrified of the wet road. I snarled and muttered obscenities as I trailed in their wake.

I'd taken particular care with my appearance for this party and was pleased with the slim-fitting black sheath I was wearing, topped with a small, sequined, shrug.

Once upon a time, when Lisa, Jen and I had flatted together as equally impoverished young students, clothing choices were simple and limited by our meagre budgets. Now that Lisa was regarded as an up-and-coming mega star of finance, her income had increased exponentially. I had an uneasy feeling that the guests at this evening's party would be in a financial league far above my own and be dressed accordingly. At least I knew Jen would be there to counter-balance any elitist snobbery.

I hadn't been to Lisa's new home before. The apartment was set on the Kelburn hill above the university and near the cable car. Space to park was predictably difficult to find, and I ended up parking down a side street, some distance away.

Fortunately, the rain had stopped as I'd driven down the Ngauranga Gorge, so I wasn't going to be forced to juggle umbrella, high heels, tight skirt, bottle of wine and house-warming gift as I picked my way around the puddles.

I had assumed any apartments along this stretch would be in converted old mansions, so it was with some surprise that I discovered Lisa's pad was part of a new block. She opened the door at my knock, kissed me and led me into a large living area, dominated by an enormous window looking eastward over the harbour and the city of Wellington. I stared at the expanse of lights below.

My jaw dropped. "This is your new apartment? You're kidding me. It's a palace, and holy crap, what a view."

Lisa tried to avoid looking smug. "It's a small thing, but my own," she murmured.

I gave her a hug. "You've done good, girl. What an amazing place!"

I turned to look at the rest of the room, admiring its clean, uncluttered lines. It was about as far as you could get, in interior design, from the country cosiness of my own cottage, but it suited Lisa's spare elegance. She had opted for polished board floors and white walls, one of which was decorated with a textured sculpture in the same white. There was no clutter anywhere, just the stark beauty of the room itself and the incredible view. It created a cool, minimalist vibe.

"This place is spectacular," I said honestly. "You must be so pleased."

"I'm extremely proud," she said. "My very own apartment. I own it and I love it."

Jen and her partner Michael joined us. "It's pretty cool, isn't it?"

I nodded. "Heady stuff. Probably goes some way to explaining the confusion caused by Lisa holding a party when we're all in the middle of Dry July."

Lisa grinned. "At least I'll be a sober and respectable hostess," she said.

Jen and I rolled our eyes at each other.

"Whatever," said Jen.

Jen was dressed remarkably conservatively in a black lace dress worn over a deep red slip. With its high collar, short sleeves and figure hugging design, it had a cheongsam vibe. The demure effect was cancelled by the long slits which reached up her thigh and the way the lace clung intimately to her slender curves. Her hair, a gentle auburn at the moment, was parted neatly in the middle and fell in a shiny bob either side of her face. I'd rarely seen her look so lovely, or so sophisticated, and wondered whether this represented Michael's influence. They had been together for about three months, having met when they were both performing in the *Mamma Mia!* musical. Their romance had lasted longer than the show's run, although I wondered how difficult it was for them to coordinate their performing lives. Michael was a dancer, which involved travelling around the country with his company on tour.

Lisa bustled away to greet new guests, and Jen, Michael and I were left to mingle. The room was filling up rapidly. Lisa's guests were an eclectic group, drawn mainly from her working life, with a few old friends like Jen and me to leaven the mix.

"Do you feel we're getting left behind in the Game of Life?"

I asked as we looked around.

"I'm just a poor dancer," said Michael. "Nothing I earn is ever going to get me a pad like this."

"Me neither," said Jen. "Not unless I get a starring role in something. Actually, not even then. I'd need to be on Broadway to command this sort of dosh."

"I'm out of the running as well," I said. "Maybe I'd better marry into money."

"So how is Jack?" asked Jen. "I'd no idea detectives were paid that well."

"They're not," I said, "and Jack's just fine, if missing in action. Another two weeks before he gets back."

"Claire. Claire Hardcastle."

I looked around as I heard my name called from across the room, and smiled as I recognised the speaker.

"Matt," I said with pleasure, as he joined us. "What are you doing here?"

Matt Johnstone and his family were long-time clients of Paraparaumu Aviation. We'd frequently ferried them to and from the bach they owned on D'Urville Island.

"I've known Lisa for years," he said. "She was an intern in our firm while she was at university. I bumped into her the other day, she told me she'd bought her first home and invited me and Jane to the house-warming."

I introduced Matt to Jen and Michael.

"This is a magnificent place, isn't it?" Matt said. "Although I can imagine Jane saying how hard it's going to be to keep all this white clean."

I smiled. "Well, Lisa doesn't have pets, or a family of children, so it's more practical for her than it might be for the rest of us."

"I hear you've had another suspicious death up your way," said Matt. "I take it you're not involved this time?"

Both Matt and I had briefly been suspects in a homicide which had occurred on D'Urville Island three months earlier.

"Fortunately I've nothing to do with this one," I said. "They found a man on Arawhata Road. If the radio is to be believed, the police think it was a hit and run. I don't know any more than that."

I was about to comment that I'd met the victim the evening before his death, when I felt a gentle touch on my shoulder and turned to find Jim Mason and Jane Johnstone, Matt's wife, had joined us.

"Hello, Claire," said Jim. "What a pleasant surprise."

"I could say the same thing," I said.

Jim smiled. "When I moved down to the Kapiti Coast, I hadn't appreciated how alien the Wellington business scene could be for an Aucklander. I employed Buchanan and Johnstone to represent my firm, and Matt's been kind enough to go the extra mile and take me under his wing. He invited me here tonight to meet other people and maybe do a little networking."

"It's our way of keeping all you Aucklanders out," joked Matt. "Wellington's a government town. If you don't understand your way around bureaucratic circles, you'll be lost here."

He introduced Jane and Jim around our group, then added, "We were just discussing the guy who died up your way in Paraparaumu. It's probably not the best way to welcome you to the area."

Jim nodded. "No, it's a very unpleasant business. The worst thing was I'd spoken to the young man concerned the evening before he died. He'd been a protester in a group which turned up at a function I attended."

He shrugged lightly and gave a cynical smile. "They wanted me to know I was a villain, of course - as all developers are. Apparently I was evilly attempting to develop land on the Coast, add value to the property and create jobs for local people." He shrugged. "All of which would be fine, except the dead guy, Andrew, chose to claim he was doing an article about eco-terrorism and it was centred around me and my business. I was furious of course. The police interviewed me about it. I've got no time for the nonsense the boy was spouting, but I feel absurdly guilty about even that tenuous connection to his death."

"He seemed very heated when he spoke to you," I replied.

Jim turned to me. "Of course, I'd forgotten you were there. You're right, he really was wound up and accused me of awful things. I didn't take kindly to his comments, all of which were nonsense. My company abides by the law, and all my developments comply scrupulously with council requirements. On top of that, he was trying to suggest I was laundering money and other corrupt nonsense. I told him if he was writing an article, he should at least come to my office and interview me properly. I've got no time for innuendo and malicious gossip and nor should any ethical reporter. The kindest thing you could say about his statements were that they were libellous.

"I'm appearing at court in Auckland for a corruption case in a couple of weeks' time, involving the Auckland Council. Don't get me wrong. I've no doubt bribery and other forms of gratuity get offered by some of my competitors. Hell, some council projects are massive, and companies are bound to try every means they can to win a contract, but I'm happy to say my hands are clean. I hate the thought of corruption entering New Zealand and fouling our public sector. You only have to travel to see how widespread it is overseas. We don't want our own almost spotless reputation for being incorrupt to be spoilt."

Jim's comments silenced the group for a minute. Inevitably we all wondered whether there were grounds for suspicion.

Embarrassed, I groped around for something to break the tension.

"I flew one of your employees the other day," I said. "He wanted to go down to Kenepuru Sound, and on the way back we flew over your building site."

Jim grinned. "Oh, you mean Glynn? Yes, he said he'd enjoyed it. Then I filled him in on what happened during Melody's first lesson, and I thought he was going to pass out. Apparently he's not as tough as my daughter."

He looked around the group. "You won't believe what Claire did to get Melody's attention when they went up together."

I winced as he narrated an embellished version of the story. You had to hand it to the man, he was a natural raconteur and he had the group entranced and amused, any earlier wariness fading fast. I tried to smile graciously, but as I still felt self-conscious about the episode, I was glad when he'd finished.

Later in the evening I saw Jim moving among the guests. His charm and polish were as engaging as I'd noted the first time we met, and Matt was doing a good job of introducing him to the financial folk of the capital. I imagined that by the end of the night Jim would be a popular fixture.

Any suggestion of scandal would simply add to his dangerous glamour.

It was late when I left Lisa's and drove home. Jen and I had stayed to the bitter end to help her clean up after the last guest had gone.

Before we parted, we sat together over a cup of coffee.

"You'd better have some," said Lisa. "You've got a long drive home."

I accepted gratefully. "You've got a posh group of friends these days," I said. "Sure you're not slumming, sitting here with us?"

Lisa grinned. "It never hurts to have friends in high places. Mind you, a lot were here because Hanratty and Sons, the firm I work for, and Buchanan, Johnstone and Pritchard, are expected to merge. The rumours are rife in the market-place. Many people were here tonight because they wanted to read which way the wind's blowing."

"Isn't that the firm Matt works for?" I asked.

Lisa nodded. "He's a partner there. The plan behind the merger is to make themselves attractive to one of the big four audit companies. Joining with KPMG or Pricewaterhouse Coopers would be a real feather in their caps."

"I don't know about all the financial types," said Jen sleepily. "They seemed like stuffed shirts to me. But the guy you knew Claire, Jim, now *he* is quite a cool character. He's very smooth."

She was leaning back against Michael's shoulder. I saw him raise an eyebrow at her comment.

"Very smooth," I said. "He was open about the guy who died having challenged him the night before and that it's caused gossip. He seemed very relaxed about it all, which pretty much knocked any scandal on the head this evening."

Lisa nodded. "Yeah, I spoke with him and was impressed."

I ginned across at Jen and Lisa. "He's also devilishly attractive, isn't he? When I went to a function recently, women were salivating over him. He's also got a spoilt daughter whom I'm going to have to find out how to amuse when she comes in for her next lesson. I'm not cut out to be a baby-sitter."

"We all have our crosses to bear," said Lisa, with a smile.

I got up early to drive into Lower Hutt to sit my exam. I'd been through the process often enough before, but even so I was nervous, a situation not helped by being tired after the party the night before. I'm always afraid my mind will go blank when faced with an exam paper, so I was pleased when I completed the test competently enough.

I've always made a practice of paying extra to make the marking of the paper instantaneous. If I fail (I hadn't yet), I've always wanted the option of re-booking the exam straight away.

I'd passed, but with a mark of only 90%, which annoyed me - I'd set my heart on repeating the 100% result of my CPL. Still, it was my first ATPL subject and good to have under the belt.

I knew Andrew Camborne's funeral had been held that morning. I'd briefly wondered whether I should cancel my exam booking and go to it, then decided not to. The only connection between us had been a very brief conversation. I was sorry he'd died, but attending the funeral of a man I barely knew seemed voyeuristic.

I drove home, did a few basic chores then curled up with the latest Susanna Kearsley novel and allowed the day to drift away. There are times when having foul weather on my days off is a wonderful excuse for doing nothing very much at all.

Consequently, when I walked into the office on Tuesday morning I was refreshed, invigorated, and ready to go. I was standing at the counter checking my bookings for the day when Greig brushed past.

"Morning," I said and frowned after him in surprise when he failed to answer. I shrugged and went to get ready for my lesson with Pete Funnell.

I watched as Pete went through the pre-flight, checking the aircraft for anything that would prevent you flying it. It's too late, when you're up in the air, to discover that the flaps don't work or that you don't have enough fuel.

I had to hand it to Pete, he was a quick learner. The only thing he forgot was the passenger briefing he was supposed to give me.

I grinned at him. "Not bad, for a first attempt."

We flew. The weather was still marginal, with cloud at about fifteen hundred feet, but it was high enough for me to teach the Straight and Level lesson. One of the joys of flying is that air is such a fluid medium, and we operate in three dimensions. It's like being in water, able to go up, down and turn with equal ease.

"However," I explained to Pete, "unless your intent is to do some aerobatics, most passengers appreciate a flight from point A to point B which goes in a straight line and doesn't porpoise up and down through several hundred feet of altitude, so try and keep the aircraft steady. Hold the compass heading, and the height."

He nodded, his forehead furrowed in concentration. I showed Pete what to look for and how to set the aircraft up. It's useless to try and fly focused exclusively on the instruments as they always lag behind the actuality of what is happening. Good pilots rely on visual clues to set their 'flight attitude' as much as anything else.

It's harder to fly accurately than it looks, but Pete was coordinated and reasonably quick to pick when he was getting it wrong.

We returned to base with no requests for extra-curricular police work.

"Did you get what you needed from the photos you took last time?" I asked.

"Nothing terribly useful," he confessed. "What we don't yet know from our informers is whether the 'big job' we've heard about relates to meth or ice, or something else entirely. The informer thought it was something different, but what else is there? We've busted a couple of small suppliers, but they don't know anything about what goes on further up the food chain. In fact, I want to speak to your boss about using the plane for some listening surveillance work in Pomare. Do you think he'd be interested?"

"I don't know," I said. "As you saw, he's twitchy about our planes getting caught in the cross-fire between criminals and the police. The other day a passenger remembered seeing us on the flight when you were taking photos. I said it was just us being nosy about the body found up the road, which satisfied them, but it goes to show that people do notice."

"I'll ask Roger anyway," said Pete. "He can only say no."

"Have the police formed any idea as to what happened to that guy they found dead, and why?"

"I only know it's being treated as a homicide," said Pete. "The money is on it being a hit and run, but whether deliberate or not is a different matter. The investigating team are still slogging through evidence, and I haven't heard anything more."

"What do you mean by listening surveillance?" I asked curiously, returning to Pete's earlier query.

"We put listening devices on the aircraft and fly over the property we're interested in. The tech guys can pick up an amazing range of stuff through the headphones. Gang's run big businesses these days, and sometimes we get lucky when we pick up early information on their activities."

I left Pete to go and talk to Roger, and wandered across to the hose bay where Nick was washing a plane. I wanted to ask if he knew what was wrong with Greig.

"Hi, Nick," I said cheerfully, before realising from his pallor and averted face that there *was* something wrong.

"Are you OK?"

He nodded, but turned away and fiddled with the hosepipe until I left him alone. It was so unlike the usual cheerful atmosphere that I began to wonder whether someone had died in the two days I'd been away.

I went back into the waiting room. Maria was sitting behind the counter, Roger had whisked Pete away to his office and Greig was somewhere in the small office at the back of the waiting room.

"What's wrong with the guys?" I whispered to Maria.

"Ah." She looked around to check we were alone. "Greig and Jayleen have broken up."

"Is that all?" I said. "I mean, it's sad and all that, but everyone's acting as if it's a funeral."

"Keep your voice down," she urged. "It's a nasty situation. Jayleen got caught having sex with another man."

"Oh, shit," I said. "That's awful for Greig."

"It gets worse," said Maria gloomily. "It was Nick's brother."

I stared at her in horror. "Holy crap! That's terrible," I said. I remembered Jayleen's interest in Duncan at the quiz night. "No wonder everyone looks as if there's been a death in the family. Poor Greig, and Nick, although I don't imagine it was Nick's fault."

"No, of course it wasn't," said Maria, "but he feels terrible about it, and Greig is just devastated."

"Does Roger know?" I asked.

"Yes. It happened on Sunday, so Roger and I found out yesterday. There's nothing Roger can do, of course, but it's going to make the atmosphere here very tricky for the next few days. He asked Greig if he wanted to take some time off, but Greig said no."

I nodded. I'd been in a similar situation a couple of years ago when I'd split up with my ex. I could testify to the healing power of hard work and flying. It's impossible to pilot a plane properly and have any residual mental capacity left over to waste on self-indulgent grief. I hoped Roger could find a commercial flight for Greig that would scare the bejeezus out of him and stretch him to full capacity.

Pete emerged from Roger's office with a grin on his face, and gave me the thumbs up.

"Roger agreed to the surveillance?" I asked.

"Yes. I'll get it set up and then let you know the time we'll need you and the plane."

I found Nick sitting by himself in the briefing room. I grabbed a cup of coffee and joined him.

"What a crappy thing to happen," I said. "Are you OK?"

"I feel stink," he said.

"It's not your fault."

"I introduced them. I never thought Duncan would do something like that."

I looked at his wretched face. "Well, it wasn't just your brother, was it," I said gently. "Jayleen made a choice as well."

Nick nodded. "The weather was shitty, so we closed the hangar doors, checked in with Roger and left work early on Sunday," he said. "Greig and I went around to Jayleen's to see if she wanted to come to the movies with us, and there they were."

"Crap," I said as I imagined the squalid little scene. "What a mess. Poor Greig."

We sat in silence while I wondered what Greig was going to do. We'd known, because he wanted to be an airline-pilot, that he'd leave us one day. It would be miserable if this shoddy affair precipitated his move. He'd be a real loss to Paraparaumu Aviation, and I didn't imagine Roger would be happy about it. Greig was too good a work colleague, and a friend, for it to end like this.

We were a subdued group that afternoon. Greig's usual cheeky and irreverent banter was missing, and the silence reverberated through the office. There was no muted male chat, interspersed with occasional sexually inappropriate roars of laughter between Nick and Greig issuing from the back office. Roger looked tired, and Maria and I, the female contingent, trod softly around this graveyard of male experience.

I was so desperate to escape the atmosphere that I welcomed Melody and her father like long-lost family. I was inordinately pleased when Melody gave me a small smile as I greeted them.

"That was a good party, the other night," said Jim in greeting.

"Yes," I agreed.

I saw Roger look at us curiously. Let him wonder, I thought, meanly.

I showed Melody into the briefing room and shut the door

firmly behind us.

"Right," I asked. "What do you want to do today?"

"I thought you were going to teach me to fly," she said, looking confused.

"Is that what you want? Only last time, you didn't seem very interested until we did the aerobatics."

She shrugged, so I carried on. "So, do you really want to learn, or is this just your father's idea to pass the time in the school holidays? I'm happy to take you up and fly with you, but if you want to learn, then it's hard work. Pilots earn their licences. They don't come in cereal packets."

She stared at me, and I hoped I wasn't bungling this. Eventually her eyes slid away and she looked abashed. After our last flight I'd put some thought into how to handle her attitude and decided my best approach was to be direct.

"I didn't know if it would be any good," she said. "Now I want to learn." Her tone had reverted to sulky, but I decided to ignore it.

"OK," I said. "Fair enough, let's get started."

I decided to take her last statement at face value, so we went through the 'straight and level' briefing, then I took her outside and showed her how to pre-flight a plane. She was at least compliant until I showed her how to open the engine cowling so she could check the oil level and take a fuel sample.

"It's too difficult," she whined, as, having showed her what to do, I made her do it herself.

"No, it's not," I said briskly. "It's not difficult at all."

"It is," she insisted. "It's too hard. I can't do it." Her voice had pitched up into a wail and I stared at her in amused disbelief.

I couldn't help myself, she was so ridiculous and OTT that I had to laugh. Even so, I couldn't relent.

"Well, if it's too difficult for you, then I guess your flying lessons end here," I said bluntly. "If you can't do the basic chores involved by yourself, then you've no business flying, as I couldn't possibly ever send you solo."

She looked at me in genuine horror, but I was unmoving. Eventually she gave a deep, put-upon sigh and complied. But I was subjected to her hunched shoulders and miserable mouth for the rest of the pre-flight routine to impress on me the degree of grief I'd caused her.

I picked she was at that tedious stage of adolescence when it's seriously un-cool to be enthusiastic about anything. Her attitude was ungiving, but at least she'd cooperated. Round one to me.

By the time we were airborne she'd relaxed a little, and the rest of the lesson was pleasant. She was bright enough, I thought, and had potential, if she could just get over herself. It amused me her father, who had such overwhelming charm, had such a sulky daughter.

I booked her in for another lesson later the next day. Jim waved and Melody gave me a slight smile as she left. I felt we were making progress and allowed myself a small glow of self-satisfaction.

I sat down beside Maria to fill in my time sheet as Roger watched the pair leave.

"You went to a party with Jim?" he asked, the second they'd exited.

I smiled to myself. I'd known he'd be curious.

"He was a guest at a party I was invited to," I corrected. "That's not quite the same thing as going to a party *with* someone. He was there to meet and greet the financial suits of Wellington."

Roger looked thoughtful.

"Don't fuck with him, Hardcastle," he cautioned. "He's not a toy for you to play with."

I was startled, and I heard Maria give a shocked little gasp.

"Well, as I don't intend to fuck with him, in any sense of the word, that shouldn't be a problem," I said tartly. I was grateful there were only the three of us left in the office. Greig and Nick had slunk home to nurse their separate miseries.

I wasn't sure whether to be warmed by Roger's concern, or offended by the suggestion that, with Jack away, I'd consider Jim Mason sexually. Whatever, as with so many of Roger's comments I decided to shrug it off. The alternative was too complicated to contemplate.

"There's already a lot of talk going around," he said.

"Pardon? Who the fuck is talking about me?" If someone had been spreading dirt about me, I was going to be seriously angry.

"Not about you," Roger said impatiently. "I've been picking up some damaging gossip about him," he said. "I've a feeling there's more to Jim Mason than meets the eye."

I stayed silent.

"What have you been hearing?" Maria asked.

"A Rotary friend of mine said he'd heard Jim's fortune was founded on drugs, tax-evasion and fraud," said Roger. "Frankly, I find it hard to believe. He seems a pretty upstanding citizen to me, but then again, I don't know him. I don't like giving credence to third-party gossip, and I wouldn't have bothered with it, except in-so-far as it involves Paraparaumu Aviation."

"Jim mentioned that rumour when we were at the party," I said. "He said he was accused of just those crimes by the protester who died. Jim was pretty angry about it and denied everything."

"Well, he would, wouldn't he," said Roger. "I assume the IRD and the police know what they're doing and will handle any issues if there's a problem relating to his business. It's their job. But with his daughter learning here, I worry we might get caught up in a scandal if there's anything about him that's not kosher."

"I think you're overreacting," said Maria calmly. "We've had several exciting characters turn up for flying lessons before, if you remember, and it hasn't damaged our business at all. If anything, it's added to our glamour."

"I can't see how it can damage us," I said. "Melody's the student, not him. The only scandal I can see is if he can't pay his account with us, and that's not likely. Maria's right. The company isn't going to be ruined by whatever the truth is about Jim."

CHAPTER SEVEN

G REIG AND NICK'S DEPRESSION COLOURED OUR days, and for once the work week seemed to drag on forever. There was no suggestion of quiz nights, karaoke or other forms of socialising. To add to the general gloom, winter had set in, and a stretch of bad weather meant both planes and pilots were grounded for hours at a time, so we were forced to deal with the dreaded paper-work we all tried to avoid.

The only bright spot in my days were Melody's on-going lessons. She'd taken to coming in whenever a brief let up in the weather allowed us to fly and her skills were improving.

Most evenings it was already dark by the time I arrived home, and for the first time I queried the wisdom of living where I did. I'd always enjoyed the solitude my cottage afforded me, but now, in the space between my arrival and the log fire catching and providing heat, it seemed bleak, cold and isolated. Even Nelson's welcome couldn't cheer me up.

I was perceptive enough to know my mood was partly driven by Jack's absence. I'm not normally given to loneliness, but I'd been missing him, and that, combined with the oppressive atmosphere at work, was having a dampening effect on my usually cheerful spirits.

Consequently, when Maria answered the phone and turned to tell me it was Glynn booking in another flight for him and Steve to Nopera, I was less than enthusiastic.

"No," I said. "Not if they're going to have the same amount of luggage. Not in the Cessna 172 at any rate."

"You'd better speak to him then," she said, handing the phone over.

"Hi, Glynn," I said, taking the phone. "You want to go to Nopera again? Will you have those heavy packs with you on the trip this time?"

I heard him laugh. "Yes, we'll be taking our picnic lunch with us again."

I gritted my teeth. Funny bugger. "The thing is, Glynn, when you loaded those packs for the return flight last time, they were incredibly heavy. As it happened, we were lucky with the weather, and there was very little breeze when we took off. But the weather's turned. It's become windy since that day, which changes the whole equation. I'm not willing to try getting off that strip, in a strong tail wind, with a really heavy load. If you're prepared to pay for a larger, more powerful aircraft, then I'm happy to take you. Just not in the 172."

The phone went quiet as he mulled this over.

"How much?" he asked at last.

I told him; there was silence. I could almost hear his brain cells doing the calculations. I gave a mental shrug. It was no odds to me whether he accepted or rejected my terms. I had the responsibility of ensuring his safety and given my crabby mood, I didn't really care whether I made the flight or not. Glynn might not have appreciated it, but those extra dollars were a form of life insurance for him and his nephew.

"OK," he said. "You win. Take the bigger plane."

"That's good," I said. "It's wise to keep the odds always in our favour."

I booked the flight in for Thursday then went and checked the long range-forecast. It didn't look promising, but there were forty-eight hours to go, and the weather patterns might change in that time.

Pete phoned first thing Wednesday morning to confirm the surveillance flight for eleven o'clock that day. The cloud had lifted, and there was a brisk wind blowing. If, as I gathered, Pete's plan was to fly over the middle of the Hutt Valley circling the suburb of Pomare, then I hoped he and his team had strong stomachs and were prepared for the bumps and turbulence which would make their lives interesting.

I phoned the Wellington tower to let them know I'd be doing a commercial flight in the valley and would probably need to circle there for a while. It always pays to keep onside with the guys in the control towers. They can make a pilot's life very easy or can really muck you about if you've annoyed them.

I'd been slightly surprised that Roger hadn't stepped in and poached this project from under my nose. He's always liked bright shiny things, and I imagined he'd be fascinated by the police procedure involved.

I said as much to Maria as I leaned against the desk and waited for the cops to arrive.

"He wouldn't do that," she said. "Pete's your client, your flight. Mind you, if you were talking about a chopper charter, it might be different."

I grinned at her. Maria has a fine grasp of our strengths and weaknesses. I'd asked her once why she hadn't got a pilot's licence herself.

"Why would I do something silly and expensive like that? I get all the excitement I need watching you lot. Why should I risk my neck?"

She had a point.

I explained to Pete's team the likelihood of encountering a few bumps along the way. I didn't imagine Pete would be fazed. He had a robust approach to life, and although I'd seen him scared silly when we'd encountered a paranormal situation earlier in the year, I didn't think simple weather phenomena would worry him.

I wasn't so sure about Jake and Don, his team mates. I don't know the physical criteria for being in the police force, but I doubted these two would make the cut. Their lack of social and interpersonal skills marked them as computer geeks. They barely managed to make eye contact when Pete introduced us, and their complexions suggested they rarely saw the light of the sun. I was amused to see them turn even paler when I described wind pockets to them.

"We'll be fine," Pete assured me, with cheerful confidence.

I shrugged, showed them where the sick bags were, and ensured their seat belts were done up firmly across their laps. Their equipment was more of a problem. I didn't need to have a large box of electronics flying around the cockpit if we hit a rough patch. We solved that eventually by wedging it behind my seat, and strapping it in. It meant the two electronics engineers were cramped for leg space, but at least we were safe.

Pete was carrying his camera again. "Make sure you hold on to that like grim death," I said. "I don't want to be knocked in the head if you lose it."

Pete grinned, and promised me he'd take care of it.

I kept out to sea and away from the hills as we flew down the coast. There was no sense encountering trouble before we needed to. Predictably, as soon as we turned inland towards the Hutt Valley, we started to get shaken around. One nasty air pocket saw Pete's headphones fly off his head, but true to his word, he kept a tight grip on his camera.

While he retrieved the headphones, I glanced behind me at the two engineers and saw them hanging on to their equipment with white knuckles.

"You two OK back there?"

I got a mumble in reply, so I carried on tracking towards Pomare.

Once in the Hutt Valley itself, the winds swirled unpredictably. Flying was like manoeuvring in an agitator washing machine. It was impossible to position ourselves to avoid the bumps. I carried on trying to read the wind patterns and keep the flight as smooth as possible, but it was hopeless. I expected moans and complaints from the two in the back, but to my surprise, once over the target, they were all business.

Apparently the fascination of their work obliterated any other concerns, and they worked steadily, twiddling knobs and reading information from the dials on their equipment.

"Getting anything?" asked Pete.

"Yeah," answered Jake. "But it doesn't help that the platform is so unstable," he complained.

I took that as a reference to my flying. "I'm trying my best," I protested, for which I received a distinctly irritated glance.

Pete pulled out his camera and took pictures as I circled over the properties he'd pointed out.

After half an hour of tossing and heaving in the currents, it was a relief when I got the all-clear to return home. I was unwillingly impressed with the engineer's dedication to their science. Even I was tired with the effort of trying to keep the aircraft as steady as possible for them. I was amused when we landed to watch Jake climb out and collapse to his knees, kissing the ground.

"Hey, get up, mate," said Pete, laughing. "You're letting the side down."

"I don't care," said Jake. "That was the most terrifying experience I've ever had."

"I did warn you," I said. "I thought you all did very well, managing to work in those conditions. Did you get what you needed?"

"We won't know until we get it all back to the office," said Pete, "but we've certainly got some interesting material."

I helped them unload the big box we'd jammed in.

"What is it with flights these days?" I said. "This is the second one I've done recently where we've had to wedge gear in."

Pete cocked an eyebrow at me, so I explained about the flight to Nopera.

"Whatever it was they came back with, it was bloody heavy," I said. "I thought it was rock samples, but Maria thinks it was probably mussels from the local farm."

"Do you think they were up to something dodgy then?" asked Pete.

I shrugged. "They said they'd gone down there to look at

property, so I've no reason to doubt it," I said. "It was just an odd thing, so I noticed. Usually people go home lighter than on the journey out. Anyway, they're booked in to do the same thing tomorrow, so I'll see if it happens again."

I booked Pete in for a lesson the following week and waved them away.

"I know it's only two pm, but I'm knackered," I complained, stretching my back out before slumping down on the waiting room sofa.

Greig obligingly moved over. He wasn't saying much these days, but at least he was still with us.

"Bumpy?" asked Maria.

"It was wicked," I said. "Try turning perfectly shaped circles around an object in those conditions. The wind was pushing us from all directions. But the guys did better than I expected. Not one sick bag used."

"Are you complaining again, Hardcastle?" asked Roger.

"Just saying it like it was," I said. "I don't know if they got what they paid for though. It seemed an odd way to be listening in on people in a modern world. You'd have thought a good bug would have done the trick, or hacking their iPhones."

I revived after a couple of cups of coffee and a sandwich. I looked across at my file-covered desk and decided to flag it away.

"Come and give me a hand," I asked Greig. "No one else is going to go up today. Help me put the planes away."

I saw Greig glance at my desk and give a faint grin.

I'd been double-checking that all our commercial flights had been recorded properly. We've got a series of boxes to tick that should make the process easy, but Roger was convinced we'd have an audit within the month and was making me check and double-check every entry. In spite of the care we'd taken, I'd still found a couple of errors. One charter didn't have a proper weight and balance form attached, while another was missing the meteorological information. Pilots are doers, not natural paper-pushers, and I count myself among that number.

"Plane pushing it is," he said.

We manoeuvred the aircraft up the slight slope and into the hangar, swept up the leaves that had blown in, and pulled the heavy sliding doors shut.

"Are you OK?" I asked at last.

Greig shrugged. "I guess. Yeah, I suppose so." He paused. "You knew, didn't you?" he asked.

I was shocked. "About Duncan and Jayleen? No, of course not."

"No," he said. "I didn't mean that, but I saw you watching her at times, when she was flirting with other guys."

"I thought she was a bit inappropriate sometimes," I said carefully. "That's all."

Greig nodded. "I didn't ever acknowledge it," he said. "I'd notice Jayleen giving other guys the come-on look, but I ignored it. I suppose it was only a matter of time before something like this happened, and I'm better off without her."

I nodded. "When I broke up with Dave, I was the breaker, but I also knew he wasn't the right one for me. I don't think Jayleen was the right one for you either. Not long term."

He shrugged again. "It's done."

We said nothing else.

It was Nick's day off. What had happened between Jayleen and Nick's brother was most surely not Nick's fault, but his consciousness and guilt had been adding to the gloomy atmosphere. I imagined Greig was as grateful as I was to have a couple of days without him so he could process his own emotions.

It was dark when I arrived home. I dumped the mail on to the kitchen bench, turned the lights on, drew the curtains and started the fire. Nelson wasn't waiting to greet me, but he usually arrived back as soon as he saw the lights come on in the house. I had half an ear open for his call as I put his dinner out on the bench, made myself a cup of herbal tea and started to open the letters.

There was the usual complement of bills, bank statements and the like, as well as a small parcel packed in a New Zealand Post box. My first thought was that Jack must have sent me a present but then realised it was domestic mail. I wasn't expecting a delivery and there was no return address.

I sliced through the seal with a vegetable knife, pulling out the bubble-wrapped contents, then unrolled the package on the bench. I had trouble identifying the object which fell out, and had to stare at it for a couple of minutes to make sense of what I was seeing.

Lying on my kitchen bench-top was a severed, coiled-up tail. My hand went to cover my mouth in an instinctive need to still my scream as I studied the hideous thing. The tail was long, smooth and sleek, a warm mocha brown in tone, with no other markings. Very much like the tail of a Siamese cat. More particularly, of my *own* Siamese cat, Nelson.

I gave a moan of absolute horror. Who could have done such a thing? Who would have tortured or even killed an innocent animal? And why?

Eventually I picked up the box again and looked inside. I pulled out a folded piece of white paper.

'CURIOSITY KILLED THE CAT. KEEP YOUR NOSE OUT OF OUR BUSINESS, BITCH.'

My knees gave way. I sank back onto the kitchen stool and sat there staring in complete shock and disbelief.

Please no, please no, please no. I played the phrase over and over again, as if repeating it could magic the horror away. At last common sense reasserted itself. Perhaps the tail wasn't Nelson's. Perhaps some other unfortunate animal had been sacrificed to send this message.

With that thought, I thrust myself from the chair and rushed to the door. It was still very windy outside, and the noise of the branches, tossed and slashed by the gusts, drowned out any other sound.

"Nelson!" I screamed into the darkness. "Nelson, *Nelsoooon.*" I stood for ages, calling into the night. There was no reply. Just the incessant sound of the wind. I told myself it needn't be significant. Nelson came and went as he pleased, and it wasn't necessarily unusual that he hadn't come home yet.

I left the door open, although the wind blowing in was freezing, and returned to look at the ghastly package. I tried to think logically. The tail was long, and thin, just like Nelson's but there was nothing else special about it. I couldn't have sworn to any particular markings on it so there was nothing conclusive identifying it as being his.

I felt a childish wail build inside me before I realised I needed the police. Jack, I wanted Jack. He had managed to comfort me through previous horrors. Why wasn't he here with me now? I wanted him to comfort me on a personal level, but I realised it was as a policeman I needed him most.

In his absence, I had to report this immediately.

I called 111, a process I was becoming far too familiar with, and was put through to the duty officer. I went through the details, and she promised to send a car up to interview me as soon as she could.

I looked at the cup of tea I'd made and rejected it. Dry July or not, I was having alcohol. I poured an enormous slug of wine into a glass and went to sit in the doorway while I waited for the cops. I called Nelson again and again. Nothing. I began to torture myself, imagining scenes of what might have happened.

Had he been killed? Had someone done this while he was still alive? Was he lying somewhere wounded and in pain with no way to get to me? I sickened myself with my visions. My alcohol tolerance hadn't been helped by three weeks abstinence, and the wine was hitting my blood stream like a sledge hammer. I was in shock, shivering in the cold wind funnelling through the front door, and rapidly getting drunk.

Through the fog of misery, I heard a persistent noise which I finally tracked to my tablet. Jack was Skyping me.

I hit the connect button, and as soon as I heard his warm voice I blurted out the whole story.

To his credit, he didn't falter. "Go through it again for me, Claire. You've called the police? Good. OK, you have no way of telling whether this belongs to Nelson or not, so let's not think the worst. Start at the beginning."

I went through the steps, explaining that I'd picked the mail up from the box, and how I'd opened it on the kitchen bench.

"Why?" I ended my explanation. "Why? Who would want to

hurt Nelson?" and I burst into hysterical tears.

"It's not about Nelson." Jack's voice was quiet and steady. "Someone wants to frighten and hurt you, Claire. This is very personal, and designed in the nastiest possible way to get your attention. Who have you been upsetting, babe?"

"Me? I haven't quarrelled with anyone," I said. "How could I? I'm living like a nun and until tonight hadn't had a drink in weeks."

I heard the smile warm his voice. "Well, maybe you haven't pissed anyone off in your personal life, but what about work?"

"God, no-one at work would do this. Can you seriously imagine Roger or Greig cutting the tail off my cat?"

"No," he said. "Of course I can't, but have you dealt with any dodgy people at work?"

"I've done a couple of jobs for Pete," I said, and explained about the flight over the gang house in Paraparaumu and the eavesdropping flight today. "Would you describe Pete as dodgy?"

"I'll fucking kill him," said Jack chillingly. "Dodgy is the least of what he is. Plain fucking stupid doesn't even come close. Claire, I'm going to ring off now. I want you to stay there, make a cup of coffee and keep calm. The police will be with you soon, and remember, this doesn't yet prove anything's happened to Nelson. I'm going to phone Pete to see what he has to say for himself. If he's put you in harm's way, he can get around there and sort it out."

He cut the connection abruptly, with none of the 'you hang up, no, no, you hang up' silliness that usually concluded our calls.

I pushed myself upright and found I was swaying rather dangerously in the doorway. I clutched on to the door frame to steady myself. Jack had ordered coffee. I staggered to the kitchen and brewed myself a strong cup.

By the time the police drove up, I was at least more coherent, and the warmth of the drink had gone some way to helping the bone-chilling shock. I'd called Nelson repeatedly. Once I thought I'd heard him, but had to admit it was probably wishful thinking. My ears had been straining so hard for his call, I'd begun to imagine things.

The police took down my statement and removed the parcel and its contents for investigation. My fingerprints would be all over it so I doubted they'd get any useful information.

The police had just left when my phone went.

"Claire, are you OK?" I recognised the voice of my landlord and neighbour.

"Hi, Ken," I said.

"I was driving home when I saw a police car come down and turn into your place. Has something happened?"

"It's my cat." I explained about the horrible parcel I'd received, and that Nelson was missing.

"That's terrible," said Ken, horror clear in his voice. "Who on earth would do such a vicious and disgusting thing? Do you want to come and stay up here for the night?"

"No thanks, Ken," I said. "If Nelson is still alive and OK, he'd come back here. If he's dead, then there's not much I can do. I don't suppose you've seen anyone hanging around here? Whoever sent this must have known enough about me to know I had a cat, so they either know me well, or they've been watching me. It's not information I automatically share with everyone."

But Ken had seen no one. He tut-tutted a lot, expressed his concern and repeated his offer of a bed for the night.

I declined, but thanked him for the kind offer before ringing off. At this point I didn't care much for my own safety. If Nelson had been tortured and killed, I couldn't think of anything worse anyone could do to me.

I went back to the door and called again for Nelson.

I was still standing in the doorway when Pete arrived. I moved to let him in and shut the door.

"Hi, Claire," he said. "Jack phoned me to say you had a problem. I passed the police going the other way. I take it they've been here?"

"Yeah, they've been. They took a statement from me and removed the box and its contents." I wondered if Jack had actually used the phrase "'a problem'" to describe the situation.

Pete nodded. "Good. That's good." I thought he looked uneasy.

"Do you want a cup of coffee or something?" I asked. I was

still feeling the effects of the alcohol. On the other hand, if I had another cup of coffee now, I'd never sleep.

"What? Oh, no thank you."

Pete shuffled aimlessly around my kitchen for a few minutes before turning to me.

"Look, Claire, I'm really sorry about this. Jack reckons I should never have used you for those surveillance flights. He's really bollocked me for putting you in danger. I'm lucky there's an ocean between him and me at the moment, or I think he'd have beaten the shit out of me over this. I never thought the flights would have this sort of repercussion."

I remembered Roger's concerns about using the aircraft for police work. "Oh, shit," I said, stepping past Pete to get to my phone. Pete looked startled.

"It's OK, Pete. You weren't to know, but I've just realised I'd better phone Roger. If someone was out to get me, they might also have attacked the office."

Roger picked up on the fourth ring.

"Hi, it's Claire," I said.

"Hardcastle? What do you want at this time of night?"

I looked at the time. It was gone eleven.

"Sorry," I said, "but I thought you ought to know what's been happening." I took him through the events of the evening.

"Jesus and Mary! That's terrible, Hardcastle. Are you all right up there in your valley?"

"Yes, fine," I said. "It's just occurred to me, though, that someone might target the hangar if this problem's been caused by those flights I did for Pete."

"I haven't heard any reports of trouble," said Roger.

Pete signalled to me. "I could drive past and have a look."

"I've got Pete here," I said. "He can go and have a look if you like."

"Holy mother of god, Hardcastle. Have you got another policeman up there? They must be recruiting a whole division just to look after you."

"Very funny. Pete will swing by the airport on his way home."

I hung up. My nerves were too raw to tolerate any attempt at humour. For once I was in no mood for Roger's comments.

"Do you want me to stay?" asked Pete. "I mean sleep on the couch, that's all," he said hurriedly. "Just to make sure you're OK?"

I shook my head. "No, Pete, but thank you for offering. Right now I want to be alone. I'll carry on calling for Nelson. If he's still here and alive, he probably won't come in until everyone's gone."

"OK," said Pete. "I hope he's fine and comes back. I'll drive past the airport - and once again, I'm really sorry about this."

I shrugged as I saw him out. I was too tired and overwrought to be kind and say it didn't matter. I needed time to process what had happened, try and find Nelson, and maybe eventually get some sleep.

Tomorrow was a working day, and I had the flight to Nopera to organise.

CHAPTER EIGHT

I HAD A WRETCHED NIGHT. EVERY HOUR or so I got up and called for Nelson. Between times I tried, in vain, to get some sleep. I got up at three and went outside with my torch, scanning the bushes and calling until my voice cracked, but saw and heard nothing. I returned to bed, achingly aware of the empty space beside me where Nelson usually lay. Eventually, an hour before I was due to get up, I dozed off. When the alarm woke me, I felt like I had a monstrous hangover.

I knew it was important to keep going, so I drove myself through the tasks that make up my usual morning routine. I made a sandwich to have for lunch down at Nopera and filled a thermos with coffee.

I forced myself to eat a couple of slices of toast and marmalade. I'd eaten nothing the night before and knew I had to have some food in me to cope with flying that day.

The food I'd put out for Nelson last night sat untouched. I left the cat biscuits, but threw the tinned food away and washed the bowl. Then refilled it. I knew I was probably fooling myself, but if there was the slightest chance Nelson was still alive, I wanted him to come home to fresh food.

Roger had arrived at work before me and called me into his

office.

He looked me over. "You look terrible, Hardcastle," he said with brutal frankness.

"Thanks," I said. I couldn't even summon the energy to be sarcastic.

"You've got the charter to Nopera today?"

I nodded.

"Are you capable of flying?"

I opened my mouth to answer and he interrupted me.

"Don't give me bullshit, Hardcastle. I need honesty. I want you to tell me whether, in your professional judgement, you should make that flight today. I'll let you make the call, but I want you to think about it carefully. I'm not having you or your passengers at risk."

His words came as a harsh wake-up call and snapped me out of my inertia. I'd never lied to Roger, and I wasn't about to start, so I did consider how capable I felt.

"I'm good to do the flight," I said at last. "Yes, I'm upset and rattled, but it's nothing that will affect my flying. I may not be my usual cheerful self with the passengers, but that's about the worst of it. The weather's OK. A bit windy but otherwise fine, and I'm going into a strip I'm familiar with. Frankly, I need to be busy today. If I have too much time to wallow in my misery, I'll go nuts."

Roger looked at me closely. "OK. That's what I thought you'd say, but I wanted you to be aware of what you're doing and why you're making those decisions."

"I am," I assured him.

I used the quad bike to pull the C206 to the fuel pumps and positioned steps under the wings so I could climb up and fuel her.

It's a fiddly job, pulling a fuel nozzle along behind as you climb and the tension on the line pulled me off-balance backwards, but I got to the top and wedged myself securely as fuel flowed into the tank.

Roger came out with my passengers. I nodded good morning

and watched Roger show Steve and Glynn where the luggage pod was beneath the body of the plane. He opened its door for them, then came to hold the hose for me as I climbed down and shifted the steps around to fill up the tank in the other wing.

I'd started to climb when Roger's mobile rang. He thrust the nozzle into my hand as he grabbed the phone out of his pocket, then turned and walked away, leaving me to haul the hose behind me again as I clambered up.

Steve was bent down beside the pod trying to force his over-large pack into the space. One of the clips must have been loose, because as he shoved it in, the flap opened and a packet fell onto the tarmac.

The hose snagged behind me. I turned to free it. By the time I turned back, Steve had the packet hidden and the pack stowed away in the pod. I saw him glance over at Roger, who had missed the incident, then shift his attention to me. A speculative and somewhat challenging expression crossed his face.

I ignored him, made it to the top of the steps and carried on filling the tank.

Roger had ended his conversation by the time I was finished, and returned to take the hose as I climbed back down. I said nothing to him, but I wondered what had been in the packet Steve had needed to hide so quickly. If it hadn't been so improbably dramatic, I'd have said it looked like wads of bank notes.

It was a bizarre thought and just showed how unsettled I was after the horrible night I'd spent. Quite obviously I'd been watching too many thrillers and my over-active imagination was working overtime. It was far more likely they were promotional pamphlets for some business venture.

The clouds covered the sky, but were high enough not to be a problem. The flight to Nopera was uneventful, although we had a strong westerly pushing us sideways all the way across the Strait. The sea was choppy and there were no pleasure craft in the Sounds. I wouldn't be sitting out in the sun today while I waited.

"Gusty old day," observed Glynn. I nodded. They had been quiet for most of the flight and not stretched my small reserves of conversational courtesy for which I was very grateful. I certainly didn't feel like chatting.

As we approached Nopera I caught sight of a boat, safely moored within the protection of a bay. I wondered whether it was the one I'd seen the week before. The colouring was similar, but yachts are itinerant so it seemed unlikely.

As we taxied up the strip I looked at the windsock. It was showing about fifteen knots of wind – on our nose as we'd landed, but it would be behind us for take-off, and it was forecast to rise. I was grateful I'd insisted on flying the C206. The additional horse-power made a considerable difference to our safety margins.

As before, a car was waiting for the two men. I settled back inside the aircraft. At least there was plenty of space to stretch out. I pulled my phone out of my pocket and saw I'd missed a call which had gone to voicemail. Reception can be dodgy in the Sounds, but when I dialled the message service, it went straight through.

"Hi, Claire, it's Ken." I smiled as I heard my neighbour's voice. "I bumped into Fred and June Taylor this morning, and told them about your cat. June said she saw a van pulling out of your driveway yesterday afternoon. There was a man in the front, with a large dog on the front seat beside him. She thought it might have been a pit-bull terrier. I don't know whether that's any use to you?

"I asked if she remembered anything else; there might have been writing on the van, but she wasn't paying any attention. She thought it was a tradesman as she knew a nice girl like you wouldn't be the sort to have a boyfriend with a pit-bull. That's all. Phone me if I can give you any more help. Bye."

I gave a wry smile. That's the best and the worst of living in the country. Neighbours speculate about your private life, and make sweeping judgements. Equally, they care and involve themselves in helping out when you're in trouble.

I didn't know anyone with a pit-bull and I hadn't called on the services of a tradesman. It was very likely that June had seen the villain that had either killed or kidnapped Nelson. I know a cat is a pet, not a person, but I was achingly sick when I thought how terrified Nelson must have been. He knew his home territory intimately, but a determined, cat-killing, dog could have made short work of him if he hadn't managed to get to safety in time.

I took out my Kindle and tried to read to take my mind off my worries, but my eyes kept closing. I'd had very little sleep the night before, and within minutes, I'd dozed off.

The sound of a car door slamming woke me. I checked my watch. Steve and Glynn had been gone barely an hour. I hadn't even unwrapped my lunch. I scrambled off my seat, opened the door of the aircraft and went to greet them.

I saw immediately something was wrong. Glynn at least nodded as he approached, but Steve shoved past me and busied himself stuffing his pack into the pod. Glynn dropped his beside Steve to stow for him.

"Get us the fuck out of here," ordered Glynn as he climbed into the passenger seat and belted himself in.

Their early return had caught me on the hop. I did a quick walk around the plane to check all was well. I finished behind Steve who was tucking Glynn's pack away. As I watched him work I realised what was different today. He was having no trouble at all shoving the bags into the confines of the pod. There was no extra material this time to weigh the plane down.

He saw me watching him and gave me a threatening scowl which I returned with a glare.

"What do you want?" he snarled.

"Just looking."

"Well, remember that curiosity killed the cat," he said.

I felt a lurch of horror, as if I'd been kicked in the guts. I stood and stared at him in numb disbelief until he turned and made his way to his seat.

It was a simple, clichéd saying anyone might use, but in the context of Nelson's disappearance the words had monumental significance. Did Steve have something to do with the hideous parcel delivered to me, or were his words just a freaky coincidence? I didn't like him, but even though I racked my brains, I could think of no reason why he would want to attack me in such a way.

I chided myself for being emotionally jumpy and unstable. He was just a client, I reminded myself. Just a passenger paying to be taken from point A to point B. There was nothing more personal or complicated than that. I counted to ten to get myself back under control. I was flinching at shadows because I was tired and threatened but becoming paranoid wouldn't help.

I wondered whether there was a correlation between the light packs and the men's foul moods and gave a mental shrug. Whatever had rattled and riled them was no concern of mine.

I phoned back to base and let them know I'd be back early.

"That's good," said Maria. "I've just had a call asking whether you could take Melody for another lesson this afternoon. I said I didn't know when you'd be back, but I'll call them and let them know they can come in at three, if that's OK?"

"OK. She's lucky to have a rich daddy so that she can fly every day," I said. I put the phone away, buckled myself into my seat and started the engine. I glanced across at the car Glynn and Steve had arrived in, which was still parked at the gate. There was no sign of the driver.

I gave another shrug. Life was full of puzzles, but the only two that concerned me at that moment were getting the aircraft safely airborne in the gusty tail wind, and the question of what had happened to my cat.

Even with the extra horsepower of the 206 and our overall light weight, it took ages for airspeed to build. The fence at the end of the runway was uncomfortably close when I felt it was safe to lift the nose and fly off the strip. Ominously, once airborne, we experienced a moment of sink, and the water of the bay came perilously close before I established a positive rate of climb and breathed a sigh of relief.

Once I'd reached a safe altitude and levelled off, I glanced at my passengers.

"All good?" I asked. "The bumps don't bother you?"

Steve barely acknowledged my question. I could hear the heavy rasp of his breath. I glanced at the hands resting on his knee and saw they were clenched in white-knuckled fists. Whatever had riled him had upped his usual edgy tension to something close on explosive. I hoped he'd manage to contain himself until we'd landed safely.

"We're fine," said Glynn from behind me.

That was the last conversation we had. Well, if they were having a rotten day, so was I. I was happy enough to fly them home in silence.

We drew up outside the office and opened the pod so they could grab their bags. I could sense some sort of argument brewing, and once they'd made it onto the verandah I left them to it. They were still mucking around with their packs when I entered the office.

"What have you got to say for yourself?" Roger greeted me. "How did the flight go?"

I explained that it had been a close call taking off in the windy conditions, and he looked at me sternly. "Did you take a risk?"

"A calculated one," I answered. "It was within specified limits. I just like a bigger margin for error."

Roger nodded. "Don't push limits," he warned, "they have a way of pushing back."

Steve and Glynn came across to the desk to sign off the paperwork for their flight just as Jim and Melody entered the office.

"Hi Glynn." The men greeted each other. I'd forgotten Jim was Glynn's boss. I got the impression their relationship was cordial.

Glynn caught sight of Melody.

"Hi," he said. "Here for your lesson?"

She smiled and nodded, but I noticed it was Steve she looked at.

He glanced and looked away, but when I sent her outside to pre-flight the plane, Steve's eyes followed her progress out onto the tarmac. I shrugged. I imagined Jim was going to have his hands full trying to keep Melody safe over the next few years. Guys like Steve were precisely the sort I imagined he would want her to avoid.

I checked my phone. Pete had left a message, asking if I was OK, so I called him back.

"Hi. Thanks for your message."

"Any sign of your cat?" he asked.

"No. I thought I should let you know that one of my neighbours saw a van pull out of my drive yesterday, driven by a man with a large dog. She thought it might be a pit-bull. I wondered if that's any use to the police?"

"Was there any way of identifying the van?"

"She thought there might have been writing on it, but she couldn't be sure. She assumed it was a tradesman working at my place, so didn't pay any attention to it. She was more interested in the dog."

Pete gave a snort of disgust. "Not very helpful, although it gives us a time frame, I suppose. I'll pass it on. Will you be all right tonight? Sure you don't want me to stay over just to give you extra security?"

I smiled. "No, thanks. I've got the neighbours gossiping about a dog. Can you imagine what they'd say if you stayed the night?"

Pete gave a short laugh. "Well, my reputation can stand it if yours can."

"No, I'll be fine," I said and hung up.

I looked out at the tarmac. Melody was still walking around the aircraft. "Would you mind if I left work early, after Melody's lesson, so I can search for Nelson?" I asked Roger. "It was too dark to see anything last night, but by daylight I might find a trace of him."

Nick and Greig had heard the news of Nelson's disappearance and it had the effect of shocking them out of their own misery.

"We'll put the plane back in the hangar and tidy up for you," offered Greig.

Roger nodded. "Yeah, finish the lesson and go home. See what you can find, Hardcastle. Good luck, you never know, maybe he'll be there waiting for you and it will all be OK."

"I hope so."

I was too afraid to allow the seed of optimism to take root. It would be too painful when I had to yank it back out again.

Melody was in a more co-operative mood today, and although the weather was gusty we managed to fit in a creditable lesson. I had to hand it to her, she was no coward, and even when we fell into a wind pocket, and the aircraft bucked around us, she seemed unfazed. At the end of the lesson I complimented her on her progress, and was rewarded with a small grin.

It was odd to drive home from work at three in the afternoon. My progress up Kapiti Road was slowed by school patrols manning the crossings. Children flooded out of the school gates and the road was blocked by mothers picking up kids. I supposed they were then whisked off shopping, or to piano and ballet lessons. I'm employed, and my routines are those of a working person, but this was my sister Kate's world. Two young daughters kept her busy.

It reminded me that I must phone her when I got home. She didn't take kindly to me having crises and not telling her. I wondered how she would react when I told her about this one. She wasn't a pet lover herself, but I knew she'd be disgusted by the savagery implicit in the package I'd received. I'd be in for another lecture about how unsafe it was for me to live alone in such a remote location. Kate is two years my senior, but sometimes that gap feels more like twenty. She's very like our mother and despairs at my less orderly lifestyle.

In spite of bracing myself for disappointment, I felt a surge of pure misery when I opened my front door and saw that Nelson's food remained untouched. It was horrible that a small glimmer of hope refused to die and continued to torment me.

I changed, pulled on my gumboots and jacket and went out to search. At the back of the cottage stood the remains of an orchard of old apple and pear trees which still bore fruit. There was no sign of Nelson there, but I was hoping the row of big macrocarpas along the boundary fence might have given him some shelter, or at least an opportunity to escape a dog attack.

Alternatively, if, as I feared, he'd been killed, I hoped some evidence, or at least the remains of his body, might give me closure. Not knowing his fate was the worst torture.

I called and called again as I searched, but there was no sign of him. Not even a blood smeared branch which might have served as a clue. I went up and down the row several times, peering into the higher branches in case he'd climbed up and got stranded.

Eventually I abandoned the trees, and made my way across the paddocks to the old stock yards. It was a less likely place for Nelson to have tried to hide, but I was frantic enough to clutch at straws. I tramped around the adjacent paddocks, continually calling until night fell and I could see no more.

I went back to the cold, empty cottage. Even when all the lights were on and I'd got the fire burning, Nelson's absence filled the emptiness with an uncharacteristic bleakness.

Dinner was the uneaten sandwich I'd packed earlier in the day for the trip to Nopera. I usually liked the gentle kitchen tasks of cooking. The combination of creativity and technical skill involved in making a meal was a mechanism I used to wind-down at the end of a day. That evening I couldn't face the chore and understood why the aged can refuse to eat. Towards the end my nana had lost interest in both food and living. That night, wrapped in misery, I could understand and identify with her.

I looked at the clock. It was too early to Skype Jack, so I called Kate instead. Her reaction to my news was predictable. She was angry and didn't sound in the least sympathetic.

"I've told you before your job is much too dangerous," she scolded. "Not only do I have to worry about you crashing the plane, but the people you deal with are all dodgy."

"That's not quite true . . .," I said.

She didn't let me finish. "Of course it's true. You had all that trouble a couple of months ago. This time it's even worse. It's not just your cat who might have been killed. This is obviously an attack on you personally, and there's nothing to stop someone murdering you. You live out there, all by yourself. Your nearest neighbours are geriatric and too far away to hear if you scream. You need to be more responsible for your safety, Claire. It's not fair on the rest of us."

Really, five minutes of talking to my sister and I'd begun to feel the whole affair was my fault. If I'd been less depressed I'd have argued. As it was, I let her ramble on and finally got her off the phone by agreeing to visit her for dinner on the weekend.

I poured myself a medicinal glass of wine, and phoned Jen.

"I'm confessing. I've failed Dry July," I started.

"No kidding?" she sounded shocked. "You lousy cow. Why?"

As I started to explain, I realised with a jolt that only twenty-four hours had elapsed since I'd opened that ghastly parcel. I felt as if I'd been in this miserable state for weeks. There was a sudden break in my voice and I couldn't carry on.

"Holy shit! You'll have to move, Claire," she said urgently. "They know where you live. It's not safe for you anymore. Do you know who would do such a thing?"

"I don't have a clue. The note said I'd been sticking my nose into someone else's business, but I haven't. Jack thought it was because I'd been the pilot on a couple of surveillance jobs for the police, but it doesn't make sense to me. It's not as if I know anything. Someone else would have done the job if I hadn't. Surely if someone was that pissed off they'd have targeted the police?"

"It does seem illogical," said Jen.

"Completely screwy," I agreed

"Shit," she repeated. "Look, I'll come straight up to your place. I can stay for a couple of days. At least you won't be alone in the house. I'm between jobs at the moment, so it's no hassle. I'll be there in an hour."

"No, no," I said, torn between laughter and tears. Jen hated country living in all its forms. I could just imagine her grimly picking her way around cow pats, morally fired up with a mission to keep me safe and sane.

"Greater love hath no woman than this," I misquoted. "No, Jen. Truly, I can manage on my own. Whatever has happened is over. If Nelson's dead, there's nothing anyone can do. I've got the message, and so have the police. And Jack's back in a few days. I'm OK, really."

Jen took some convincing, but eventually capitulated.

I phoned Lisa and reprised the conversation.

"I'm sorry I fell off the wagon. I'll make good on the donations

I've screwed up on," I assured her. "I just really needed a drink when I got that parcel." I wondered why I was justifying myself to Lisa. Perhaps the icy perfection of her home had intimidated me.

"Hell, donations are the last thing you need to worry about," she said forcefully. "Someone's got it in for you in a particularly nasty way. I can't think of anything more obscene than sending that parcel. Are the police providing any protection?"

"Nah," I said. "I suppose they've got other things to worry about. And no, before you ask, I'm not going to move out of here. I'm not letting some psychopathic prick terrify me."

"Good for you," she said. "Just don't be foolish, though." She paused for a moment. "How would anyone know who was flying the plane, anyway?" Lisa asked. "It seems a bit odd."

"They wouldn't know," I agreed. I said goodnight and promised Lisa I'd be safe, careful and keep the doors locked. We rang off.

But her question tugged at my memory. Someone had recently asked if I'd flown over the site where Andrew Camborne died. I'd flown with a lot of students over the course of the last few weeks, I just couldn't remember who it had been.

CHAPTER NINE

JACK SKYPED ME AS I WAS getting ready for bed. I grabbed the tablet, snuggled into the pillows and brought him up-to-date with the news.

"So I'm no closer to finding Nelson or discovering what happened to him," I sadly said at last, "and I have no idea who would have done such a foul thing. I can't imagine who the guy in the van was, and I can only hope Nelson wasn't killed by the pit-bull. It's just horrible." In spite of myself I felt tears welling up. I looked at the pattern on the curtain material and willed myself not to cry.

"I've started jumping at shadows. A passenger this morning used the phrase 'curiosity killed the cat' and I nearly accused him of killing Nelson. I'm getting a bit screwy."

"Hell, hang in there, baby. Kia kaha. Only five more days, and I'm home," he said. "I hate being over here when you've got all this shit going down and I'm not there to help you."

"I'll be all right," I said, sternly dismissing both my grief and the lurch of excitement his words gave me. My need for Jack frightened me. Since I broke up with David, I'd been careful to maintain my independence. Dropping my worries into Jack's very competent hands was a seductive thought. Letting him hold me, resting my head against his shoulder while he stroked away my fears, was disturbingly attractive, and I knew I couldn't afford the weakness.

There was no commitment between us. Neither of us had yet used the phrase "I love you." His job was busy, responsible and liable to take him away from home unpredictably. Mine wasn't quite as volatile, but even so, I had commitments to both my students and to Roger. I couldn't just absent myself whenever I pleased.

Hell, Jack and I hadn't even managed the holiday we'd planned a couple of months back which was to have included driving north so I could meet his parents. I deliberately turned my mind away and listened to the rain rattling against the windows.

"You won't like the weather," I commented. "It's cold and crappy."

"I'm sure the two of us can warm it up." I heard the smile in his voice. "I'm looking forward to being cool, anyway. It's beautiful here but so sticky and hot. I'm tired of feeling sweaty all the time."

Melody arrived. Jim had invested heavily in her training, and she'd been in for a lesson almost every day of her holidays.

"Jim not with you today?" asked Roger, looking towards the door.

She shook her head, and the shiny blond hair bounced and landed in stylish falls against her face. I smothered my jealousy.

"Dad's away in Auckland for the week," she said.

"While the cat's away . . . ?" suggested Roger.

Melody grinned. "As if."

I gave a small smile. Melody had long given up being shy around Roger. She didn't give him any other sort of attitude either – not that he'd have stood for it, of course. Roger had a way with him that discouraged bad behaviour. In my time at Paraparaumu Aviation I'd seen a lot of young people, predominantly male, come under his influence. He made them cut their hair, clean up their clothes, their hygiene and their act generally. I suppose it was a measure of the respect most felt for him that he delved into personal areas without creating too much rancour. For some it was probably the nearest thing to effective parenting they'd ever experienced. Of course, he did hold a trump card – access to flying. If you wanted to fly, you had to do things his way.

It seemed Melody's social confidence was growing at the same rate as her flying skills increased. She was a long way from the bolshie girl who'd been dragged in here by her father only a couple of weeks ago. She was close to the point where I'd be sending her solo, so we flew repeated circuits around the airfield while she wrestled with the business of getting the aircraft down onto the runway.

It was windy and my admiration for her grew. She wasn't a quitter but fought for control all the way to the ground. A lot of learners give up and collapse in a nervous heap when they're still a hundred feet above the tarmac. It can make for some interesting, bone-shaking landings.

I complimented her on her tenacity and was rewarded with a warm smile.

"Thanks," she said. She was quiet for a while as she concentrated on the aircraft. "You're a great instructor."

I looked at her in surprise. "Well, thank you as well. I'm just doing my job."

"You don't put me down or treat me like a kid," she explained.

"You're morphing into a pilot," I said. "There's nothing childish about that."

She gave a grimace. "People mostly just see me as my dad's daughter and a route through to him and his money."

She caught my look and added, "It's OK, it's just how it is. Only here, with flying, it's different."

"It doesn't matter who your dad is when you're flying," I said dryly. "You're the pilot in control, and no one else is going to land the plane. It's your responsibility." I tapped on the instrument panel in front of her, "And if you don't take on that responsibility about *now*, we're going to land a kilometre short of the runway."

She gave a slight gasp as she realised how low she was on this approach and abruptly focused on the job in hand.

"More power," I suggested. She thrust the throttle forward and retrieved the situation.

I smiled to myself. The art of teaching aviation is to allow students to make mistakes and learn from them. The trick is to keep them alive while they do it.

I walked with her to the office doors. "How're you getting home without your dad here?" I asked.

"My boyfriend's picking me up." The pride in her voice was unmistakable.

It was the first I'd heard of a boyfriend and I wondered whether Jim knew about this development.

I checked the booking sheet and found Tim Andrews had booked a 152 out for a couple of hours.

"Hi," I greeted him. "What are you up to today?"

"Just a short flight up to Palmerston North," he said. "I want to keep my hand in. Then I was going to talk to you or Roger about getting another rating. Maybe in the Cessna 172?"

"That would be great," I said. "You've clocked up a few hours flying since you got your licence so you're certainly ready to stretch yourself again."

I booked him in for a lesson the following weekend.

"I liked your article in the *Kapiti News*," I said. "It was a very enjoyable piece."

Tim laughed. "I'm glad you liked it. I was afraid you'd come after me with a meat-axe because I'd pissed you off."

"Not at all," I said. "It made for good reading. I didn't realise you worked for the local paper."

"I haven't for long," he said. "I used to work in Levin for the *Chronicle*, but flying was bringing me down here all the time, so I applied for a job in Paraparaumu and was lucky enough to get one."

"Did you know the other reporter? The one that died?" I asked. "Andrew Camborne?"

I watched Tim's face fall. "Yeah," he said. "He was a good mate of mine. We did our training together and we'd been close friends ever since."

"Any idea what happened?" I asked. "The last thing I heard was it was a hit and run."

Tim shook his head. "Who knows? I'm certain his death was deliberate though. He was young, healthy and not the sort of guy to get into a physical fight. He wasn't drunk or drugged. I think someone took aim and bowled him over."

"I met him the night before he died," I explained, "so in a very remote way I feel involved. He seemed like a really nice guy."

"One of the best," sighed Tim. "We met for drinks a couple of days before he died. He was really charged up. I recognised the symptoms immediately. You know, partly horrified, but mainly excited, which is a dead give-away in a journalist. I knew he must be working on a live story."

"Did he say what it was?"

"Nah. We had this odd conversation though. He talked about how vulnerable our eco-system was. Well, that was Andrew, always talking about ecology. He reminded me about the calicivirus disease which was illegally released some years ago. Do you remember it? Some disgruntled farmers wanted to control the rabbit population and imported the virus into New Zealand. It killed a lot of rabbits, which was probably a good thing, but the point Andrew was making was how easy it was for someone to deliberately cause enormous damage to our environment."

"He was worried about rabbits?" I asked, surprised. It might make an interesting story, but I couldn't see a man getting killed over it.

Tim snorted. "I don't think so. I think it was something else, something more important and threatening. I wish I'd paid more attention. Andrew didn't give away too much, but when he died I wondered whether he'd got up someone's nose or found information too sensitive to allow him to live. I just hope, if it was deliberate murder, the rotten bastard who did it gets caught and put behind bars for the rest of his life."

My mind flicked back to the night of the cocktail party, and Jim's confrontation with Andrew. I hoped for Melody's sake that there had been nothing more sinister about that altercation than a businessman pushed a little too far by a persistent agitator.

I hated the thought that Jim might be involved with a vicious murder. I wondered what the police had made of him and whether he had an alibi for the night Andrew died. At Lisa's party he'd expressed righteous indignation about being accused of corruption, but I didn't recall him saying where he'd been at the time of the murder.

I flicked that thought around my head for a bit, and realised that although I desperately hoped Jim hadn't murdered Andrew, I never questioned he'd be capable of such an act if it suited his purpose.

The memory of Roger remarking that Jim was probably a bit of a villain echoed faintly in my mind.

CHAPTER
TEN

TWO DAYS LATER I SENT MELODY on her first solo flight. She had flown three circuits with me and if they weren't perfect, they were at least completely safe. I got her to drop me off at the end of the third roll-out.

"Off you go," I smiled. "You're on your own. One circuit only, OK?"

She stared at me in shock. "You mean alone. Solo?" Of course, she'd been desperate to reach this point, and been increasingly frustrated with herself the last few lessons when her own mistakes had held her back. Still, it's one thing to want to have achieved your first solo, quite a different thing to actually have to do it. It takes a fair amount of courage for a novice flyer to be in that aircraft alone for the first time.

"I wouldn't be sending you off unless I had absolute confidence in you," I assured her. "You're more than ready for this. Just do exactly what you've already done three times this morning. Watch your speed, watch your height. I've got the radio with me, so I'm right here if you need to call me. You'll be fine, I promise."

I watched her taxi out and all the nervous qualms I wouldn't admit to hit me in full. I knew she could land a plane safely,

and she'd completed every exercise to a good standard. But ...
there always is a 'but'. The aircraft engine could suddenly fail;
her nervousness might override her newly learned skills; there
could be an earthquake that destroyed the airport and left her
with nowhere to land ...

I gave a wry smile as that ridiculous last thought crossed my
mind. The truth is that however many times I've sent students
off, it doesn't get easier on the nerves.

I watched the plane fly the circuit and come in to land. She
touched down perfectly. I smiled with relief and waited as she
cleared the runway and taxied over.

She was grinning from ear to ear. Long gone was any thought
of being cool, or too sophisticated to show enthusiasm.

"I did it!" she exclaimed.

I chuckled as I shook her hand formally. "Congratulations.
That was a really good landing."

"I did it," she said again in disbelief. "Thank you." She flung
herself into my arms and hugged me.

She was bubbling with excitement as I led her into the office.

Roger shook her hand and grinned at her. "So, you did OK?"

Melody reprised the whole flight for us on a minute by minute
basis. There are few experiences as intense as a solo flight, and
she was revelling in her achievement.

At last her excitement settled.

"You'll have to tell your dad," I said. "Is he picking you up?
Perhaps he can shout you lunch to celebrate."

"Nah," she said. "He's still away. I'll have to phone him."

"So, is the boyfriend picking you up again?" I asked.

She gave me a face-splitting grin. "He is, and wait until I tell
him what I've done."

I smiled as I walked her to the door. The boyfriend in question
was smoking, his back to us, leaning against the bonnet of his
car.

Melody called out and he turned.

My eyes narrowed when I saw Steve walking towards us.

"Hi," he said to me. I stared at him in dismay. Steve was the
boyfriend? Holy crap.

"Good lesson?" he asked Melody. He gave me a knowing smirk as he bent to kiss her lightly on the lips.

My heart sank. I watched her glow with pride as he smiled at her.

"It was sooooo good," she beamed. "I went solo." She was truly a girl on fire. Her excitement was overwhelming.

"You did? Good job," he said. It was a fairly cursory smile, considering the magnitude of her achievement and elation. I hoped he didn't put a downer on her spirits.

She gave me an excited smile and followed him to the car.

As they drove away she waved.

I wondered what was going on. Surely she was too young to interest Steve? I'd put him as mid-twenties, and although that wasn't a prohibitive gap, it was significant for a sixteen-year-old. I also fancied Steve inhabited the rougher end of the social scale and led the sort of colourful life Jim wouldn't consider suitable for his daughter.

I didn't think Melody would be Steve's type either, not unless the overriding attraction was her daddy's wealth. Melody was funny, acidic, cynical and charming, but Steve didn't strike me as a man who appreciated quirky women. There was something feral about him, the sort of guy I imagined more suited to the late, unlamented Jayleen.

I tried to remember whether Steve was also employed by Jim. Glynn had said he worked for him but I couldn't recall whether that had included his nephew. I hoped Jim wasn't going to be away too long, and I desperately hoped Melody wouldn't get hurt or led into inappropriate situations. I wouldn't trust Steve to look after her or make allowances for her inexperience.

Jim phoned a couple of hours later. Roger answered the call, then passed the phone to me.

"I just wanted to thank you for sending Melody solo," he said. "She called me up to tell me all about it and must have kept me on the phone for half an hour. She's one excited girl."

"She did very well," I said. "She should be proud of herself. It's quite an achievement."

"I'm certainly very proud of her," said Jim. "And very grateful to you, Roger and the team. She's a different girl since she started flying. It's given her confidence in herself."

I smiled at that. "Well, we're happy she went so well. She's a pleasure to teach."

I realised I meant it. She might have been a tedious brat when she started flying, but I'd become fond of her cheekiness and her sardonic humour.

"I'm back tomorrow," said Jim. "Can I shout you all a round or two at the bar to celebrate? Melody can't drink, of course, but she'll be happy to party on V or something."

If Jim was back, I thought with relief, he'd be able to handle the boyfriend issue with Steve.

I checked with Roger, who nodded. "That would be great," I said. "We'll have the glasses lined up on the bar when you arrive."

We'd almost wrapped up work for the day when a couple of guys walked in. I'd started tidying up the waiting room, and left Maria and Roger to receive them. Some idiot had eaten potato chips and spilt them across the floor. I sighed and went to fetch the vacuum cleaner.

When I returned, Roger called me over to join them. Something in his manner seemed rattled, and I didn't need introductions to realise these were police. Someone once told me you could always recognise a cop just by their bearing and attitude. He'd been right.

"Detective Sergeant Trevor Jenner and PC White."

I shook hands.

DS Jenner was a big man who was showing early signs of running to seed. Once he'd been tall and solidly built, but now, in his late forties, muscle mass had turned to flab and hung around his waist-line. His hair had thinned and faded to an unattractive shade of beige. I knew I shouldn't judge by appearances, but everything about him was depressing, and engendered an instinctive dislike.

His side-kick was young and fresh faced with a complexion that still had a boy's flush. I'm sure there's a minimum age for joining the force, in which case PC White had met that criteria by barely a week. I realised abruptly I was channelling my late mother who'd made comments about doctors and policemen being too young to be taken seriously.

I was still smiling to myself as DS Jenner addressed me.

"We understand you piloted a flight into Kenepuru Sound the other day? To Nopera air strip?" he asked.

"I did. Yes." I flicked a glance at Roger who had presumably provided this information, and wondered where this was going.

"I understand your clients were...," he checked his notes, "Glynn Edwards and Steve Freeman?"

I nodded.

"Tell us about the flight." I noticed there was no "please", and no explanation for the request.

"Why?" The word tumbled out, an automatic knee-jerk response I have to officiousness.

DS Jenner looked irritated. "We are following lines of enquiry."

Apparently he wasn't used to being questioned.

I looked across at Roger who nodded. "Better tell them anything you know, Hardcastle."

I opened my mouth to protest, then shut it as I saw Roger glare at me.

I capitulated, and gestured to the empty seats.

"OK," I said as I sat down. "It was windy, so we had to fly fairly low. Otherwise it was fine." I'd flown clients into a strip, then flown them home. They'd seemed in a foul mood. What else was there to say?

"What more do you want to know?" I asked.

I could tell I was getting up DS Jenner's nose, but without some indication of the content or context of his question, I didn't know how to answer him.

I cast myself back to the misery of that day. Nelson still hadn't returned, and I'd started to realise he never would. The misery was a constant bruise on my psyche. I tore myself from my pain and concentrated on the men facing me.

DS Jenner drew a deep breath through his nose and skewered me with a glare.

"Ms Hardcastle, we would appreciate your cooperation in recalling as much detail as you possibly can about the flight and the men on it. This isn't a game. I hope you understand that." His tone dripped sarcasm.

Yup, I was definitely getting under his skin just as much as he was getting under mine. Well, if he wanted detail, that's what he was going to get. I started with putting fuel into the aircraft, the tedium of climbing up the steps to the wings. That memory triggered another detail.

"Actually, it might be nothing," I said, "but the younger one, Steve, dropped a package of some sort while I was refuelling the plane. I don't think he wanted me to see it, so I pretended I hadn't."

"What was in it?"

"I don't know," I said. "As I say, it wasn't mentioned again."

"Could you make a guess? Did you see enough for that?" Trevor Jenner was leaning forward, excitement clear on his face. I noticed his lower lip had a dabble of wet spittle, and averted my eyes to look at PC White who was more pleasant to focus on.

I gave a shamefaced smile. "At first I wondered if it was bank-notes, but I guess it wouldn't be. Maybe some brochures? I don't know."

PC White spoke for the first time. "What made you think they might be bank-notes?"

I chuckled. "Probably because the parcel was rectangular and about the right size. I live alone and watch way too many crime movies on TV," I suggested. "No other reason, just an over active imagination."

PC White grunted and added my comment to the notes he was making. I wondered what his first name was and whether he didn't rank highly enough on the police force value scale to merit his own identity.

"What happened next?" DS Jenner asked again, with bare civility.

"I flew them across to Nopera. It was an ordinary enough flight. Someone picked them up when we arrived, and I waited in the plane for them."

"And they didn't say anything about why they were there?"

I shook my head. "When I flew them down the time before, they claimed to be looking at property. I don't know if that's true because they didn't mention it the second time. On that first trip, when they returned to the plane their bags were much heavier than they'd been when we'd loaded them on in the morning."

"Why was that?"

"I don't know," I said irritably. "I teased them a bit, saying they must have collected rock samples. I thought it was more likely they'd bought a load of mussels or something they didn't want me to know about. Anyway, they didn't discuss it with me."

There was a silence while Trevor Jenner thought about it.

"So, the last trip – did they bring back heavy bags this time?"

I shook my head. "No. I noticed the bags were the same coming back as they'd been on the trip down."

"Did they give you an explanation?"

"No," I said. "And I didn't ask for one. Steve saw me watching when he loaded the bags, and told me 'curiosity killed the cat', so I didn't push it further. I just wanted to get them home."

"What did you do while they were away from the airfield?" asked Jenner.

I'd hoped he wouldn't ask this particular question. "I fell asleep," I confessed, looking at Roger. "I hadn't had much sleep the night before, and I dozed off."

Roger managed to stay silent, but from the expression on his face I could see we'd be having words later. Bugger. A thought that made me less than charitable towards the police throughout the rest of the session.

"How long do you estimate your passengers were away from the airfield?" This time it was PC White.

"Not long," I admitted. "They caught me by surprise when they came back. I hadn't even had time to get my lunch out." I recognised the question he was about to ask and forestalled him. "I wouldn't think they'd been gone more than an hour or so. It wasn't much of a nap for me."

I resisted looking at Roger. I suspected he wasn't very impressed with me at that moment, and he was bound to bring it all back to the judgement call I'd made about being fit to fly. Maybe I hadn't been, and that was a nasty enough thought to chew on before I had to factor in my boss's take on the whole situation.

"So, someone dropped them back at the airstrip to catch the plane?" asked Jenner.

"I suppose so," I replied. "I didn't see the driver of the car, but someone must have driven it." I recalled my stray thought at the time that I hadn't seen a driver.

"But you did see a car?"

"I saw a vehicle there. I couldn't identify it because it was partly obscured by the gate and shed. I couldn't see inside it from that angle so I didn't see who drove it."

DS Jenner glared at me again. "Ms Hardcastle, I want you to be absolutely certain about this. Your passengers returned to the plane, waking you up from your impromptu siesta. You saw the vehicle that brought them back but saw no sign of the driver. Is that correct?"

I thought it through carefully. I hate to commit myself to absolute statements like this, but there was no alternative. I hadn't seen a driver, and I'd been asleep when Steve and Glynn returned with the car, so I didn't know who had driven them there, or even whether they'd driven themselves.

I sighed, but agreed. "No, I don't know who drove them back. I didn't see who the driver was. The vehicle was partially hidden, so I only saw its bonnet."

It was as if my agreement freed us all from some web of tension I didn't understand.

DS Jenner stood. "Thank you all for your time," he said. "We'll be in touch if we need any more information or a statement."

PC White smiled at me as he rose and gathered up his notes.

"Can you tell us what this relates to?" asked Roger.

Jenner shook his head. "A man's body was recovered by a fisherman in the Sounds, near Waitaria Bay. We're checking any traffic in the area around the time of his death. Witnesses informed us an aircraft used the strip in the critical period and we managed to track you down."

That was all we managed to get from him, and without a backward glance he and his side-kick left us.

Roger, Maria and I stared at each other.

Roger stood up, and I flinched, waiting for some acidic comment. "Go home," he said to Maria, then turned to include me. "That means you as well, Hardcastle. We'll talk about it tomorrow."

He stomped off to let Greig and Nick know we were closing up.

"Here we go again," said Maria, slumping back into her seat behind the desk.

We all remembered the last police investigation we'd been party to.

"Not bloody likely," I replied.

I felt a spurt of real anger. "No-one's going to draw us back into all that crap."

CHAPTER
ELEVEN

I WINCED AS I WALKED THROUGH MY front door and saw Nelson's bowl of biscuits still sitting untouched on the bench. I knew the time had come to put the bowl away, but still I couldn't bring myself to abandon hope. It felt like killing Nelson a second time, only with me cast as the murderer.

I knew I was beginning to act like an eccentric cat lady, but I didn't care. I'd loved Nelson and mourned his loss as I would a friend.

Maybe Jack's influence would force me to climb out of the emotional mire I was stuck in and engage with the real world. He would be back the day after next.

Pete called as I was lighting the fire. I saw the number as I picked the phone up. Whatever Jack had said had obviously scared the daylights out of him. He shouldered the responsibility of checking up on me and seeing I was OK with alarming thoroughness.

"Hi, Pete," I said.

"Hi, Claire. Any sign of your cat?"

"No, nothing," I said sadly. I perked up as I remembered the events earlier that day.

"Hey, one of your colleagues, a Detective Trevor Jenner came in to see me today. Do you know him?"

Pete gave a short laugh. "T-bone Trev? Yeah, I know him. Large of paunch and short of tact?"

"That'd be the one," I smiled. "I don't think he liked me much. Seems they found a body somewhere in Kenepuru Sound and had heard I'd taken a flight into Nopera about the right time. He wanted to know what I'd been up to. Do you know anything about it?"

"I heard about a body but nothing else," said Pete. "It's not my case, so I don't know the details. Do you want me to find out?"

"Please. I don't really need to be part of another murder investigation, if that's what it's about. Particularly with Jack coming home in the next couple of days."

Pete laughed. "You mean having a girlfriend who's a recidivist suspect might damage his credibility?"

"Something like that," I muttered.

"I'll ask around," he assured me. "Actually, things are heating up with my investigations as well. We still haven't discovered what this rumoured mystery activity is about. We're assuming it's drugs, but hell, it could just as easily be a terrorist attack planning to blow up parliament. We do know there's new product coming into the marketplace. Sales and distribution activity is up, and it's beginning to cause problems with the other gangs. The Head Hunters and the Mongrel Mob aren't on good terms at the best of times. Currently relations are so tense we're expecting a turf war. The last thing we want is drive-by shootings and all the other crap that will go down if we can't knock it on the head."

"Pity I got caught up in it then," I said. I could feel the empty space beside me where Nelson used to curl up on the sofa.

"I'm sorry," said Pete. To his credit he sounded sincerely guilty. "I would never have involved you if I'd thought it would turn so nasty. As it is Jack's likely to have a piece of me over it. I'm considering taking stress leave to avoid him when he gets back. Maybe for a few weeks, starting tomorrow. It might give him a bit of time to chill out."

I gave a reluctant smile. "I think Jack might be someone with a long memory."

"Tell me about it." His tone was gloomy. "Are you sure you don't want me to come up there? I'm happy to be your guard, and it might just earn me brownie points with him?"

"Nah, I don't need a babysitter," I assured him. "Just someone who can use a dowsing stick and find my cat."

Pete hung up, and I spent time sitting, staring into the flames of the log fire. The fire flickered and danced behind the glass door with mesmerising attraction. Too much had been happening recently, and very little of it happy-making, I thought. The pleasure of Melody's success earlier that morning had been subsumed by DS Jenner's questions. Pete's report on an increase in badland activity had been equally depressing. The misery of all that unpleasantness and evil clung around me oppressively. I liked to think of myself as resilient and able to cope with stress. Whatever Nelson's fate, it had struck too close to home for me to shrug it off as peripheral to my life. Evil had entered my own home and it would take me time to recover from its taint.

I hadn't watched TV since Nelson disappeared, but that night I switched it on to see if there was any information about the body found in the Sounds. The report led with news of a suspected foot-and-mouth disease outbreak in the Waikato.

I grimaced. I was no farmer, but I lived in the country, and there couldn't be worse news for the rural community than the possibility of such an infection. We're an island nation, and keep relatively disease-free thanks to an extraordinarily vigilant customs service that prohibits and protects us from imported products that could be infectious. It didn't seem likely that we'd have it, but precautions would have to be taken, just in case. I remembered news reports, when I was a young child, of an outbreak in the UK. At the time, I'd shed tears when I'd realised that all the cows and calves were being slaughtered.

There was a short item towards the end of the programme which stated that the police investigation into the death of a man found in Kenepuru Sound had continued today. The body had yet to be identified. There were no further details.

I flicked the set off. For a woman who led a peaceable life, I was associated with an unconscionably high body count.

Andrew Camborne's death still resonated. Fortunately, I had no connection to the body in Kenepuru Sounds, but even so the police had questioned me about it.

When I'd left work, Maria had looked as distressed as I'd felt. I imagined the guys felt the same. There's a point where what starts off as vicarious excitement turns into oppression. None of us wanted to be associated again with murder. I didn't imagine Roger had been thrilled with DS Jenner turning up yesterday. Roger's business hinged on his reputation for excellence. A steady stream of police investigations at Paraparaumu Aviation wouldn't do anything to enhance it.

I scrambled eggs for dinner, then stood on the porch for a while, calling to Nelson - an exercise which produced no cat but resulted in the temperature of my home dropping by ten degrees. Eventually I gave up and retreated, shivering, to the fire which I had to build up again.

I tried to Skype Jack, but he didn't answer. I knew he was going to be busy over the next couple of days, packing and saying farewell to his students. I'd offered to be at the airport to pick him up, but he'd declined, saying an official party would be meeting them, and the order of programme was a quick trip back to head office for a debrief before he would be free to leave.

I was impatient to see him, but I understood. Work is work – well, up to a point it is, anyway. After that, Jack was mine.

What should I cook to welcome him home? For the first time in days I started thinking about food and its preparation.

CHAPTER TWELVE

"WHAT HAVE YOU GOT TO SAY for yourself, Hardcastle?"
I'd arrived at work a few minutes early because I'd had an uneasy feeling Roger wasn't going to ignore such minor details as me going to sleep while I was on a contract flight. I said something blasphemous under my breath, directed at DS Jenner, and turned to face my boss.

"That depends on what you want to know," I said, combining nonchalance and civility as judiciously as I could.

The phone on the desk rang, and while Roger answered it I seized the opportunity to retreat to the back office and start tidying up. I didn't imagine it would buy me much time.

"I want to know everything about those two contracts." Roger had come into the office, and wasn't going to tolerate evasion. "It's quite obvious to me you thought something dodgy was going on."

"I might have thought stuff was odd," I countered. "Dodgy? I'm not so certain." I picked my words carefully. I didn't want Roger flying off the handle at me, and I could tell he was cranky.

"Everything could have a perfectly innocent explanation. Maybe they were genuinely looking at properties the first time I took them down, and they were offered a couple of sacks of mussels to bring back as a sweetener. Perhaps the second time they didn't get that offer. Maybe the property deal fell through, and everyone was feeling sour. I was too miserable about my missing cat to pick up on every signal they gave out that day."

"What about the body they found in the Sounds?" he asked. "Was that related to them?"

"Why would it have been?" I asked. "People die of drowning every year. It's the Sounds. There's water. People fall in." I shrugged. "Why would it be sinister? T-bone Trev didn't…"

"Who?" Roger's shout echoed through the offices, cutting off my explanation.

"Sorry, but I was speaking to Pete last night, and that was how he described him. DS Trevor Jennings."

There was a dangerous thirty-second silence while Roger absorbed the information, before he began to chuckle.

"Is that really his nickname? T-bone Trev? I guess he's not much liked or respected in the force then?"

"I guess," I said, and began laughing too.

To my relief it eased us over the awkwardness of my less-than-professional-behaviour on that flight.

"I'm sorry, but I hadn't slept much the night before," I said. "I know I shouldn't have … "

"That's not what worries me," said Roger, cutting me off mid-sentence and dismissing my apology.

Relief flushed through me as the weight of guilt lifted off my shoulders. He wasn't angry that I'd stolen an unauthorised nap.

"What concerns me is that I don't want my business to be known as the flying establishment most patronised by the criminal classes. I've said before that trouble has a way of following you around, Hardcastle, and you're running true to form."

"Well, I don't ask for it," I said indignantly. "And we don't actually know Steve and Glynn are villains anyway. I didn't choose them as clients, so it's not fair to blame me."

I could feel my temper rising. Even the suggestion was unjust. Christ, I'd been through enough crap already with cops and crims!

"I know, and I'm not," said Roger shortly. "Instinct tells me there's nothing simple when you're involved. That in itself worries me more than anything else."

I glared at him. I'd have snorted if I could, but knowing my luck, I'd have snotted my face rather than making an elegant statement. I turned and left his office before I said something I'd regret.

To my surprise, that chat with Roger re-energised me. For the first time since Nelson's disappearance I felt a surge of my usual enthusiasm for the day ahead.

I headed out to the hangar and helped Greig and Nick pull aircraft out onto the line. I thought I detected a thaw in relations between them. Maybe soon we'd all be able to go to the pub together and compete in quiz night again. Before Jayleen's fall from grace, I'd taken for granted the good working relationship we all enjoyed. I found I missed the easy banter between us, the camaraderie at work and the social outings of an evening. Now that I had abandoned Dry July, I was ready to resume normal social activities and impatient for my colleagues to feel the same.

There were lessons to be taught, chores to be done and paperwork to be processed, so it would be unfair to say I spent the day thinking about Jack's imminent return, but I couldn't quite suppress my excitement and anticipation.

"He's back tomorrow?" Maria's voice registered.

I turned and she grinned at me. "You've been sitting there, smiling vacantly into space for the last five minutes. I assumed you were thinking about Jack?"

I felt a flush warm my cheek.

"Oh," I said, embarrassed to have been caught daydreaming. "I suppose I was. He arrives in Wellington tomorrow, although I don't know whether I'll get to see him, but at least he'll be back in the country. He's coming via Brisbane. They arrive there late tonight and stop over for a few hours before flying into Auckland early tomorrow morning. In fact," I checked my watch, "he'll be just about boarding his flight in the Solomons now."

"You'll be pleased to have him back," Maria commented.

I nodded shyly. I wasn't used to discussing my love life at work.

Maria saw my awkwardness and smiled again. "Oh, to be young again," she sighed. "Enjoy it while you can."

It was corny, of course, but I spent the evening doing all the things women do when we want to look our best. I plucked and depilated, washed my hair and painted my nails. When I'd finished, I stood in front of the mirror and looked at myself. I'd lost weight I realised. Since Nelson disappeared I hadn't eaten much, and it showed. I wondered whether Jack would like my new sleek look.

Pete phoned in the middle of my preening.

"You know you were asking about the body they found in the Sounds?"

"Hi, Pete," I said, tucking the phone beneath my chin while I carried on rubbing moisturiser into my legs.

"You didn't hear it from me, but it's homicide. The guy was shot at close range and then dumped in the water. From the marks on him it looks as though the killer tried to weight him down but didn't secure him well enough, so the body floated up. He's been identified as Gordon Anstruther. He had an Aussie passport, and had leased a boathouse in one of the bays to use as a base while he wintered over in the Sounds, but he actually lived on his yacht which he moored close by."

"A pretty blue and white boat?" I asked, remembering the one I'd seen.

Pete laughed. "I don't know about that. I didn't get any real details. But get this. The yacht had been used for smuggling. As soon as they started examining her, they found concealed hiding places. The forensic team is having a field day, and T-bone Trev's all excited and self-important. He's got a real murder on his hands. Let's hope he doesn't stuff it up."

"What was being smuggled? Do they know yet?"

"It's not been confirmed, but it's bound to be drugs. They didn't find any, but there'll be chemical traces they can identify."

"I suppose T-bone already knew that when he came around to see Roger?" I wondered why he hadn't made me sign a formal statement. No wonder he'd wanted to know about my flight into

Nopera.

"Shit." I started putting two and two together. "It does look as if the guys I flew down must have been involved somehow. I thought they were dodgy. And if they were smuggling, it would explain the weight in their packs on the first trip."

"T-bone will need to wait for confirmation from forensics," said Pete, "but your passengers surely have some questions to answer. Anyway, I won't keep you, but I thought you'd like to know."

"Thanks," I said. "I'm glad it's all in the capable hands of the police."

By the time I went to bed the house was tidy and I was groomed. As a final act, I wiped the kitchen bench down, tipped Nelson's bowl of biscuits into the rubbish, washed up and quietly put the bowl away.

I slipped my newly de-fuzzed, pampered and moisturised body into pyjamas and snuggled into bed. I reminded myself to change the sheets in the morning, then grinned. Jack had better make all the preparation I'd done worth my while.

His plane would be close to Brisbane by now, I thought, as I turned out the light. I'd assumed anticipation would keep me awake, rather like a child the night before Christmas. Instead I crashed off to sleep as soon as my head touched the pillow.

CHAPTER THIRTEEN

EITHER HE MADE VERY LITTLE NOISE getting in, or I was so deeply asleep I didn't hear. I woke when he switched the light on in my bedroom.

I was disoriented. The transition from sleep to waking was so immediate that reality and dream were indistinguishable. I rolled over and pushed myself until I was propped up on one elbow. It took appreciable moments for my eyes to focus in the sudden light and recognise who it was. It took even longer for my brain to process the monstrous reality that Steve Freeman was standing in the doorway of my room with a gun pointed directly at me.

"Get up."

The order was so curt I almost missed it, but the gesture with the gun was clear.

I sat up.

"What the fuck are you doing here?" I asked. "Steve? What do you want?" I was incredulous, but the shock was rapidly being replaced with anger. I hadn't yet processed the threat from the gun.

"How did you get in?" At least my brain was beginning the process of coherent thought. I'd had an intruder in my house three months ago and subsequently installed security locks. I knew I'd locked up securely before I went to bed. The horrid parcel I'd received had ensured I was extra careful. I was furious he'd broken through my safety net.

"Get up," he said again. "You won't like it if I have to haul your ass out of bed. Get up and get dressed. You're coming with me."

That woke me up completely.

"Like fuck I am," I exclaimed. "I'm not going anywhere with you. How dare you break into my home." I hadn't begun to consider the gun. I suppose I simply didn't believe anyone would use such a weapon outside American TV thrillers.

He crossed the room in two strides and slapped me hard across the face with his free hand. My head snapped back, and before I'd recovered from the first, he delivered another, equally as vicious.

My hands flew to my damaged face in response. I felt my cheek swelling from the blows, and tasted blood. I ran my tongue around my mouth. No teeth were damaged, but my lip was split and my nose had started to bleed.

I groped on the bedside table for a tissue to staunch the flow and gaped helplessly at him.

I was badly shaken and, for the moment, cowed. I'd never realised how personal an affront a blow to the face was.

"Get up, you stupid bitch." Steve stripped the covers off me. "If you don't want a real hiding, get dressed so we can get out of here."

He yanked one of the hands from my face and used it to pull me to my feet.

"Put your clothes on," he ordered.

I stumbled to the pile of clothes I'd discarded when I went to bed. Gathering them up, I moved towards the bathroom.

"Where're you going?"

"To the bathroom to get dressed."

"Don't fucking move. You're not leaving my sight. Put your clothes on here, where I can see you."

"But ....," I stared at him, realising the necessary removal and replacement of garments, the simple shame implicit in what he was demanding. "I need privacy to change."

"No. You change here. You think I'd let you lock yourself into a bathroom or try something dumb like climbing out the window?" he said. "Fuck that. Get on with it. If you don't, I'll hit you again."

I saw my plight amused him. He was sucking pleasure from my humiliation, and it was that knowledge that strengthened me. I wasn't his to use in any sense.

I had simple cotton pyjamas on. Changing into bra and knickers was going to involve exposing some skin. I studied his implacable face, reading both his intent and his lascivious gratification. Well, fuck you too, I thought. I've seen, and been seen in, the nude before.

I turned my back, but knew he watched every move I made, and every intimate fold of skin I exposed as I drew my PJ pants down and replaced them with lacy knickers. I knew he could see the curve of my breasts as I hooked up my bra. I clenched my teeth and climbed into jeans and a sweatshirt.

I turned and stared him down. His eyes travelled over me slowly. At least this time I was decent, and his appraisal fed my anger.

"Shoes," was all he said.

"Where are we going? How do I know what sort of shoes to put on?"

Why don't men understand this? Shoes are important. There are shoes to go tramping in, shoes to go dancing, shoes to impress your friends, shoes to slop around the house in. They're not interchangeable. Why can't they get this?

"The shoes you wear to work."

So, we weren't painting the town red then. I sat on the edge of the bed and laced up my brogues. I reached for my phone, but he stopped me.

"Leave it."

I didn't go anywhere without my phone. Who does? I picked it up – not so much in defiance but in a simple disbelief anyone would expect me to be without it.

He gave a grunt of frustration and slapped it out of my hand. The phone flipped in mid-air, and I saw it fall down the back of the bedside table and disappear out of sight.

Its absence enhanced my vulnerability.

Steve checked me over and hauled me to my feet. "Take a jacket."

"It's on the hook in the porch."

He took a step towards me and, against my will, I flinched. I read satisfaction in his expression as he grabbed my elbow and frog-marched me outside. As we passed the porch, he paused to collect the jacket before forcing me down the steps towards the car.

I struggled to get my arms into the sleeves as he pulled me across the drive. I only got my right arm in once he'd released it to open the car door. I looked at the dark interior of his vehicle and baulked. He wasn't getting me in there.

He felt my resistance and swung me around so I faced him. "Listen, you bitch, I'd be very happy to kill you. Your only value to us is if you're useful. Get in the car, and you live, at least for now. Refuse, I shoot you here, and you're dead. Understand?"

I looked at his face, accepted he meant what he said, and bent my head to allow him to guide me into the back seat.

I was already half-way in before I realised the car had other occupants. I automatically recoiled, causing Steve to give me an impatient shove, which sent me sprawling.

The car engine started up as I scrambled into position. Steve climbed in beside me and sat, resting his gun in his lap, the barrel pointed towards me. The dashboard's light allowed me to recognise Glynn behind the wheel. I was behind the passenger, so couldn't see her face, but even in the faint illumination the bouncy blonde hair was unmistakeable.

Melody said nothing, and I wondered what she was doing here. Surely she hadn't teamed up with her boyfriend for some nefarious purpose? Or was she also a hostage?

The night was fine, with the smallest crescent of a new moon showing. Enough to be picturesque, but not enough to shed any light. The clock on the dashboard read 1.15.

Where were the police when you needed them? An encounter with a handy booze bus would have been really great. Instead we drove unchecked through deserted streets. We turned off Kapiti Road into the residential streets that led to the airport. Glynn parked outside the office.

Steve opened his door, climbed out, and looked around. He listened, but nothing disturbed the quiet of the night. He bent towards me.

"Out!" I was aware of the gun pointed at me so I slid across the seat to him obediently.

"You too," he said to Melody. "Keep hold of that one," he said to Glynn before gripping my arm and manhandling me towards the office door.

"Open it," he said, pointing towards the key pad.

Until recently we'd had a key and an ordinary lock on the front door, but in the interests of greater security, Roger had replaced the old locks with an electronic system. There was irony here. With the old system I could at least have said I'd lost the key. Now, all I had to do was push buttons in the right order. I looked again at the gun and knew claiming an onset of amnesia wasn't an option.

"Don't try and be clever," warned Steve. "Just open the door."

I punched in the numbers, let us into the office and switched on the lights. Steve's mobile rang, and he pushed past me, walking through to the front of the office before answering it.

"What…." I heard him ask before Glynn, who'd been dragging Melody behind him like a dog on a lead, indicated the door to the briefing room.

"In there, you two," he said urgently.

He shoved Melody through, and I followed her. He shut the door behind us, leaving us alone. The door was thin and unlocked. I put my ear against it trying to hear what was going on outside. I could hear Steve's voice, but it was too indistinct to pick up words. I glanced at Melody, who said nothing, so I took the risk of gently turning the handle.

The phone conversation was still in progress.

"Nah. We're OK," said Steve, "but if we hadn't been tipped off they'd have picked us up tonight when they raided the place. It was fucking close. Now we're out of here."

I wished I could hear the other side of the conversation.

"Where they won't find us, mate," replied Steve. "We'll lie low for a while."

There was another break before I heard Steve say, "Yes, we've got the stuff with us. Don't try calling again. They'll probably track my number. I'm getting rid of the phone anyway."

I assume the call ended then, because I heard no more. Steve and Glynn were talking, but their voices were low and I couldn't hear any details.

I eased the door shut and leaned against it.

I wondered where the airport security guards were. With any luck they'd notice the lights on in the office and come and investigate.

I turned and looked at Melody. The light was harsh, so neither of us looked our best, but she looked terrible. Her face, usually so animated, was drained of colour; her eyes, enormous in her tight, miserable face, had panda-like circles beneath them. I checked to establish this was from shock and terror, and not the result of trauma. The bruising made her look very young. Any suspicion she might have been party to this night's work evaporated. At least she appeared unharmed.

As if she followed my thoughts she looked at me and winced. "What happened to your face?" she asked.

"Steve hit me," I replied. "Are you OK?" I didn't want to dwell on my own hurts. The cheek was hot and puffy, my nose felt enormous and my lip stung.

She nodded shakily.

"How did they get you?" I asked.

"Steve phoned and asked me to let him in." Ugly colour flooded her cheeks. "I opened the door for him. I knew Coral was asleep and wouldn't hear me."

"Coral? Who's she?"

"Coral looks after me when Dad's away. She's sort of a housekeeper."

I didn't comment. Melody's drooped head and shamed face said it all. I imagine she'd expected cuddles and romance when she'd unlocked the door for Steve. Instead, she'd been abducted.

The silence built between us. "Bastard," I said at last.

She nodded. Her lips quivered, and I saw she was fighting back tears.

I went to her, put an arm around her shoulders and hugged her. "Don't fret. We'll get through this," I said as confidently as I could.

Steve opened the door. "Come through here."

They'd left us long enough for Melody to recover a semblance of poise, and for me to wonder why the hell we were there. I'd tried listening at the door again, but it was futile. I'd heard the rumble of conversation but couldn't pick out what they were discussing.

Steve grabbed at my arm as I walked past, but I was fed up with being handled like a side of meat, and twisted away.

"Get off me," I hissed.

He made a guttural noise that might have been laughter as I followed Melody out.

"If you don't like being pushed around, you'd better do as you're told."

The office seemed bleak and unfamiliar. The heating was off, of course, so it was cold and unwelcoming. The large front window framed the black night outside, against which the LED lights inside were harsh and unforgiving. I shivered, less from the cold than the unsettling feeling of being a stranger in an environment so familiar and loved.

Glynn was leaning against the counter at the front of the office.

"What do you want from us?" I asked.

"You're going to get us a plane and fly us out of here," he said, "and you're going to do it fast."

I glanced at the window. The black expanse of the runway lay between us and the distant street lights.

"There's a curfew until six am," I said. "I can't fly until then. Where do you want to go?"

"We don't give a rat's arse about your curfew," said Steve. "You'll get the plane and fly us out now, and you'll be quick about it. We'll tell you where we want to go when we're airborne."

I stared at him. "Don't be stupid," I snapped. "You can't treat a plane like a car and just say 'follow the road'. If you want to fly somewhere, I need to work out the heading to get there. I have to know how much fuel we need, and whether we need to stop somewhere to refuel. I need the right charts too so I can navigate. I need to know these things *before* we get in the air, because I can't work them out while I'm flying."

"Use the bloody GPS," said Glynn.

"Not all the aircraft have GPS, and anyway, that isn't going to solve the fuel issue," I said scathingly. "What do you think? That I can pull over and park on a handy cloud when we run out of gas? And GPS isn't going to point out the height of terrain we're going to encounter, the weather systems we'll meet or any other dangers. Flights have to be planned, otherwise you tend to die."

The two men glanced at each other.

"Get the plane out first," said Glynn. "Then we'll tell you where we're going. But make it fast."

Steve shrugged.

"OK. Let Melody go," I said. "I'll fly you where you want to go, but let her go."

"Not bloody likely," Steve said. "She's our hostage, you stupid bitch. Stop arguing and get the plane ready."

"I won't take her," I said. "I won't fly unless you let her go."

Steve moved quickly. I thought he was going to hit me again. Instead he grabbed Melody by the hair and yanked her hard back against him.

"If you don't do as you're told," he said, "she gets hurt. And if you waste more of our time arguing, she gets hurt. Do you understand? I can damage her a lot and still leave her useful as a negotiating tool. Maybe I can put a cut or two on that pretty face?"

His casual viciousness was all the more sickening because of the warm smile which accompanied it. I realised then that Steve liked cruelty for itself. He'd take pleasure in causing pain.

Melody gave a low moan of distress and writhed in his grip. I saw her terrified face and knew I was beaten.

I took the key to the hangar from the hook, and went to get the plane.

Once outside, I looked back through the office windows and saw Steve release Melody. She dropped, like a discarded rag, into a seat.

Glynn came out and joined me.

"I can manage," I said.

I disliked leaving Melody alone in the office with Steve. I reckoned Glynn was the more stable and less violent of the two men.

Glynn shook his head. "We need to move quickly. It'll be faster with two of us."

He helped as I pushed the heavy hangar doors open and pulled a couple of smaller aircraft out of the way.

"We'll take the Cessna 172," I said indicating KIM.

Steve came outside, lit up a cigarette, and stood watching from the balcony as we pulled the aircraft over to the fuel pump. At least he was where I could see him, and not inside with Melody.

I filled the tanks and checked the oil – not such an easy task when the only light was what was coming through the office windows. I reached inside KIM, ostensibly looking for a cloth to polish the windscreen, and took the opportunity to set the emergency code on the transponder. All aircraft carry these automated transceivers which emit or 'squawk' an identifying signal. I hoped a control tower would pick up the emergency code and register I was in trouble. I didn't think Glynn or Steve knew enough about aviation to be aware of what it meant.

The action only took a second, and I was back outside the plane, climbing up to wipe the windows down – not such a frivolous move as the cold outside temperatures meant they had fogged up.

I climbed the step onto the verandah and walked into the office. Glynn followed.

"The plane's ready," I said as I passed Steve. "Now, where do you want to go?"

They both hesitated, and I suppressed a surge of irritation. I was fed up with their hurry-up-and-wait approach. If they were prepared to abduct and terrorise me and Melody, they could at least be decisive about their plans.

I walked behind the counter and pulled a pile of charts off the shelf.

"Let's make it simple," I said. "Do you want to go north or south?"

"North," said Glynn.

I opened the 1:500000 chart which covered most of the North Island.

"Where? Can you point to the spot."

Steve's finger hovered for a moment, then came down in the hilly country near Lake Waikaremoana. "Here."

I looked at it for a second. "OK, I'll take you to Wairoa. That's your closest option."

The computer on the desk was left permanently on, so it was a matter of seconds for me to enter the SkyDemon program and type in NZPP to NZWO. The programme brought up the route, heading and all airport information for both airfields. I gave a small sniff of satisfaction. Although it was too dark to see outside, at least, once airborne, we'd be flying in clear skies and light weather. I dragged the cursor over the route to change the course we'd take through the Manawatu Gorge. It put a dog's-leg in the track, but would keep us clear of the mountainous area north of Palmerston North. I sent the plan to the printer and looked up.

"Isn't technology great?" I said to the men. I knew I was using sarcasm to hide my fear, but if I focussed on the real mess Melody and I were in, I'd go to pieces. If what Pete had said was true, these guys dealt with drugs, and maybe even murder. I shut the terrifying thought away and concentrated on being a pilot.

The counter between us was a barrier, and the familiar tasks were going some way to restoring my confidence. Knowing the flight would be tracked through the transponder made me a lot more cheerful.

Melody was sitting quietly, watching. She might be scared,

but she wasn't hysterical. We'll get through this, I sent a silent promise across the room to her.

Glynn moved, but it was Steve who broke the silence.

"Nah," he said. "Wairoa's no use to us. There's an airstrip on a farm. We'll show you where it is when we get closer."

I gestured to the view outside the window and the pitch-black night.

"Does your farm strip have lights to guide me in? Because if not, we're not landing. It's dark out there. There isn't even any moon, and if I can't see where I'm touching down, or how to approach it, then I can't land."

"But they did it in the war," protested Glynn. "I've seen the clips of Allied pilots dropping supplies into France, and landing at night behind enemy lines."

"I've seen the same clips," I said dryly. "I think you'll find that a host of friendly partisans marked out the runway with flares, or car headlights or whatever. No pilot can fly and land an aircraft if they don't know what they're flying into. Otherwise the technical term for the manoeuvre is a *crash*."

I allowed my sarcasm to filter through unchecked. My fear was morphing into anger. I recognised they needed me, if only in the short term, as their means of transport. It allowed me some control and consequently strengthened my backbone.

Steve was psychotically unstable. I was tired, my face hurt and I'd been distressed by Melody's terror, but I wasn't about to cooperate with these goons any more than I needed.

Steve's face flushed with anger, and his fist slammed down on the counter. "You little bitch. You'll get in that plane and fly us where we want to go."

I ignored him and concentrated on Glynn.

"Let me explain this really simply. When we are up in the air, we're not going to see anything beneath us that isn't illuminated. It doesn't matter whether we're over sea or land, it's just going to look like a black hole underneath us. I can't bring an aircraft down into that because there could be hills, wires, trees or buildings right in front of us, and we'd never see them until we hit them."

I saw Steve start to speak, and cut in. "You have two choices. You can wait until daylight for us to find your strip and land there, or else, if you're in as much of a hurry as you claim, we fly to Wairoa in the dark and land at the airport where there'll be proper lighting."

"How long's it going to take to get there?" asked Glynn.

"Two hours, give or take," I said.

"There you are," said Steve. "It'll be light by the time we're there. Stop fucking around. Just get in the bloody plane and let's get out of here."

I stared at him. Clearly he was the brawn, not the brains of whatever operation they had going.

"It's July," I explained patiently. "It's the middle of winter, remember? Sunrise isn't until seven or thereabouts. Currently its two-thirty. You do the maths. If we leave now we'll be at Wairoa at four-thirty."

I looked at Steve's blank face. Plainly I was going to have to join the dots for him.

"At four thirty, it will still be dark," I explained. Really, it was like talking to a small child. "We'll be there two and a half hours before sunrise."

"Can't we circle for a while?" asked Glynn.

"The fuel tank only holds enough for about four hours flying at maximum," I said. "We can't circle. We'd run out of fuel before the dawn. If you're really determined to land on your strip, then we need daylight, so if you want to fly directly there, we can't leave here until five thirty at the earliest."

"Fuck. Will nothing go right for us?" Steve's cry of frustration echoed in the small room. He swung towards the windows and looked out. "If we don't get a move on, they'll find us," he said urgently. "We've got to get out of here now."

Glynn gave a sigh. His tension was as great as his nephew's, but his was still under control.

"We fly to Wairoa then. Can you refuel there?"

I nodded.

"After that we'll get airborne again, and you go where I tell you."

CHAPTER
FOURTEEN

"BEFORE WE GO ANYWHERE, I NEED to go to the bathroom," I said, "and if you've got any sense, you will as well. Do you want to join me, Melody?"

"Not so fast," said Steve. "You can go," he said to me, "but she stays here until you come back. If you're not back in two minutes, she suffers for it. Understand?"

I nodded. There was little choice. I performed the necessary, washed my hands and looked at myself in the mirror. The woman looking back from the glass was unkempt, drawn and scruffy. Four hours ago I'd gone to bed feeling like a pampered princess. I examined the bruises Steve's attack had left on my face. They weren't pretty. I'd have given a lot for a toothbrush so I could clean my teeth. I could still taste blood on my lip and my mouth felt foul. I shrugged philosophically. At least my eye hadn't swollen so much that I couldn't see out of it.

I went back to the group so Melody could take her turn. Glynn and Steve had to alternate as well so one of them was left on duty to guard us. In spite of myself, I was amused.

"It's like that old riddle of having a goose, a fox and some corn," I murmured to Melody. "How do you get all of them across the river when you can only take one item at a time? You know, the fox will eat the goose, the goose will eat the corn and so on."

She looked confused for a moment, before she understood what I was saying and gave a giggle. I was pleased to see a little of the misery lift from her face.

"Shut the fuck up, and concentrate on the plane," snarled Steve, pointing the gun at me as he escorted us out to the aircraft. He hadn't let go of it yet. I wondered whether he'd been relaxed enough to put it down in the bathroom.

"Melody and Glynn take the back seats," I directed.

Steve was immediately suspicious. "Why?" he demanded.

"Because I want the lighter passengers at the back to keep the weight as far forward as possible," I explained. I didn't add I wanted Steve where I could see him and not sitting beside Melody.

"You can't bring that gun with you," I said pointedly as he moved around to take his place in the aircraft.

"Fuck off," he replied, ignoring me, and putting it into the aircraft.

I stood my ground. "If you want to bring that gun on the plane, you disarm it, and it goes down the back. I'm not having a loaded weapon sitting beside me. That would be crazy stupid in a small aircraft. It goes down the back or we don't fly." I figured quoting CAA regulations wouldn't rate with Steve, but hopefully common sense would win out.

I thought he'd come around and hit me again, but I wasn't going to increase the hazards natural to aviation by doing something completely stupid. I could just imagine what would happen if we hit turbulence and his finger involuntarily tightened on the trigger.

Fortunately, Glynn intervened before the standoff escalated.

"Stow it, mate," he advised. "You can't use it while we're flying. And she's right. It's not contributing to our safety. Take the bolt out and put it in the back, for Christ's sake, and hurry up, you're costing us time."

That Steve and Glynn were on the run was obvious but so far there'd been no sign of pursuit. I wondered what they were nervous of.

I was annoyed that the airport security guys hadn't shown up. I'd never taken any interest in their activities before, so I had no idea how often, or indeed *if*, they patrolled the airfield at night. I'd just assumed they did their rounds regularly. Without their intervention, there was no alternative but to cooperate with those two jerks.

I climbed into the pilot's seat and put my headphones on. I'd deliberately not brought any out to the plane for the others.

"Where are my ear-phones?" asked Steve.

"You don't need them," I said. "I need to leave them at work. They've got students flying today."

I was right in a sense. They didn't need the headphones for the flight, although they did a good job of cancelling out ambient noise. I wasn't going to talk to them; I didn't really want them talking to each other; and if I fielded calls from Christchurch Control, or any other flight service querying my transponder code, I might have a slight advantage if the others couldn't hear what was going on.

I turned on the small torch I kept for night flying and began the checks. The small beam of light was the only illumination I had.

I thought I'd got away with it, and was half-way through the start-ups before Steve punched me on the arm.

I pulled the earphones off.

"What?" I asked.

"Get us headphones," he demanded.

I glanced over my shoulder at Glynn. "You don't need them," I explained again. "I've got to leave them in the office for people coming in today."

"Why don't we need them?" asked Glynn. "You've always provided a set when we've flown with you before."

"Then you were paying passengers," I said tartly. "This time you aren't, unless you intend to pay for the flight?"

Glynn considered this for a moment. "Get the headsets," he said at last. "You aren't going to make any calls to anyone, so keep the radio off, but with headphones on, Steve and I can talk to each other if we need to."

I cursed silently. It probably wouldn't have made much difference, but I'd liked the feeling of having a slight edge over my kidnappers.

I flicked the switches off.

"Fine," I said. "If you say so."

I wondered whether Steve would insist on coming with me, but they let me go alone.

I entered the office, and bent to get the headsets from the box behind the counter. I knew the men would be watching through the glass windows, so I made a big issue out of lifting each headset out and putting it on the bench. I used my left hand as I groped and lifted. With my right I grabbed a biro and scrawled "To Wairoa," on the desk pad and heavily underlined the words.

I hoped when Roger and Maria arrived they'd see it and understand it was from me and a pointer to where I'd gone. It was only a faint hope the clue would be useful, because the office wouldn't open for five or six hours yet. Roger was usually the first one in, but even he wouldn't arrive before seven thirty. By that time, we could be half way to the farm strip.

I picked up the headsets, which were a pest to carry. The long wires and plugs tangled and dragged as I walked. I returned to the plane and passed them around.

"Can we go now?" I asked.

Steve was busy trying to find the jacks to plug into, so he ignored me. I checked over my shoulder at Glynn who nodded.

I completed the rest of the checks as we rolled along the taxi way, lined up for the start-up run, and let the plane lift into the sky. For better or worse, we were on our way to Wairoa.

Once airborne, as I'd warned Glynn, the night around us was very dark indeed. Kapiti Island was on our left, and to the right were the peaks of the Tararua Range. Both might as well not have existed, so completely invisible were they in the blackness. We left the lights of Paraparaumu behind us, and headed north. The lights of Otaki township shone as a beacon ahead of us in the distance.

I knew this area intimately, so I ignored the GPS in favour of positioning the aircraft on a safe line. I planned to get as far as Palmerston North flying a path nearer the coastline but roughly parallel to the GPS route, before deviating to fly through the Manawatu Gorge.

The direct track would take us over the Ruahine Ranges, which I was anxious to avoid. Not only was the land below pretty much tiger country and best avoided, even by day, but the range was high, and I didn't fancy negotiating around mountain peaks in the dark when I couldn't see them. If I took the lower route, which I knew well, I'd at least have the lights of the various towns and hamlets as a back-up guide, and I stood a reasonable chance of landing the aircraft on a level paddock if things went wrong.

Predictably Steve pointed to the GPS.

"Why aren't you following the track?"

"Because I want to make sure I'm clear of any high ground I can't see," I explained.

He grunted at that, but let it go.

I found it unnerving being forced to fly with no communication to air traffic control or the towers. I hoped the blip we represented on their radar would ensure they steered other aircraft well out of my path. The local towers would be closed at this time of night anyway, but heaven knew how many aviation by-laws we'd flout on this trip. I'd have to do a bit of explaining to the CAA if I survived.

Fifteen minutes later, when I swung east to cross the ranges at their lowest point over the Manawatu Gorge, Steve interrupted again.

"What the fuck?" he exclaimed as my course diverted at a broad angle, to the GPS line. He tried to grab for the controls, but I held firm.

"Get back the way you're supposed to be going. Are you trying to be clever or something? You'll pay for it, I swear it, if you put us wrong." In the dim lights inside the cockpit I saw him glaring and recognised what little it would take to incite him to violence. Already his fists were balled in his lap.

"I'm saving your stupid neck," I said tersely. "We're crossing where the hills are low, and the only things I have to worry about are windmills underneath us. Up where you'd take us, in the ranges, it's too dark to see the hills around us. What's more, if there's any mist or fog, we won't know until we're stuck in it and can't get out. Now kindly shut up and let me do my job. That's assuming you want to get to Wairoa alive?"

Steve watched suspiciously as we traversed the gorge, and swung north again when we were overhead Woodville.

"See," I indicated the GPS. "We're closing the angle again with the direct track, but over safer terrain. Happy now?"

Steve subsided. I could hear him swearing under his breath but ignored him. I might be operating under duress, but I still had a duty of care for those I flew to deliver them safely.

This side of the range the towns and hamlets were fewer, and further apart. Large tracts of land lay black and empty beneath us as we sped along our northern path. The cockpit was warm, and the night outside so dark and featureless it was easy to become detached and seduced by the warm comfort of the cabin.

I'd experienced the phenomenon before; the curious irrelevance and unreality of everything beyond your immediate confines. As a pilot, I'd learned to guard against its spell, or at least take some No-doz tablets if needed. I glanced over my shoulder at Glynn and saw he had succumbed and was fast asleep, his head propped against the side window. I couldn't see Melody but rather thought she was asleep as well. I hadn't heard a sound from her for ages.

Steve was the last to give in. I watched his head droop several times in the early stages of surrender before he'd realise and snatch himself awake again. Eventually he, too, drifted away in sleep and I had the aircraft to myself.

I'd been wondering what the best course of action would be if I found myself unsupervised. I had the option to change direction and fly to a more populated area. Ohakea Airforce Base was less than an hour's flight behind us, and I imagined the military there would give Steve and Glynn short shrift. Unfortunately, I couldn't assume Steve would sleep long enough for such a manoeuvre to go undetected and the GPS would give me away immediately. The thought of a psychopath rampaging in a tiny aircraft was too terrifying to contemplate. Steve was the sort to act first and think later. I thought of Melody asleep behind me, and shuddered.

Reluctantly I decided my best course was to continue to Wairoa and hope Melody and I could make a break for freedom after we landed.

Five minutes later Steve woke, and my decision proved wise. He was disorientated for a moment, staring at his surroundings. His gaze fell on me and I saw awareness return as he focused. He immediately checked the GPS and gave a grunt when he saw we were still on track.

"I half thought you'd try something stupid," he said. "Then I'd have had to kill you."

I heard a faint whimper of protest. Melody must have woken. Steve heard it too, and glanced back at her before giving me a cheerful grin. Violence turned him on. There was a sexually charged excitement in his smile.

I concentrated on flying and tried to conceal my revulsion.

*   *   *

It was four thirty when we reached Wairoa. The aerodrome was north of the township, and the night seemed all the darker in contrast to the street lights below us.

"You're going to have to let me put the radio on," I said. "I need it to switch on the runway lights."

"Like hell you're having access to the radio," said Steve. "Who're you going to call?"

"Ghostbusters," I said irritably, "who else? It's the middle of the frigging night and there's no one at the airport to turn the lights on for us. The radio frequency switches on the lights, and I can't land without them. Your call. We can circle up here for the next hour or so until we run out of fuel and fall out of the sky, or you can stop being a dick and let me do my job."

"You'll do as you're fucking told," he snarled.

I wondered whether he'd punch me again and braced myself for a blow, but Glynn intervened.

"Let her switch the lights on," he said. "The sooner we land, the better."

Steve subsided but gave me a look that didn't bode well. I hoped he'd remember he needed me in physically good shape to fly the next leg of the journey. I tried to master my nerves and ignore him as I flicked the radio into life and dialled up the lighting frequency.

The runway lights lit up the airstrip below and guided us down onto the field. I was relieved to have the flight safely behind us, even though I worried about what lay ahead for Melody and me. As I turned the plane to taxi back to the parking area I realised my hands were shaking.

I hated my reaction to Steve. The abuse he'd dealt out earlier had taught me to fear him, and it wasn't just the threat of physical abuse either. Something in the irrational, unstable nature of the man sickened me and lifted the hair on my arms in a purely animal response of rejection. I loathed the constraint it had on me and the knowledge of how easily I had been physically cowed. I was ashamed of my reaction, and felt sullied and as grubby as if I'd deliberately lent myself to some vileness. It was a lesson in humility. I wasn't nearly as proud or as brave as I'd imagined.

I taxied off the runway, parked on the apron and cut the engine.

The silence was immense as we sat there in the dark.

CHAPTER
FIFTEEN

I WAS SHATTERED. I PULLED THE HEADPHONES off, leaned against the door beside me and closed my eyes. I rested my head against the cool glass window for a few moments, letting the chill cut through my tiredness. I opened my eyes and rubbed them until I saw spots.

Eventually Steve moved. "Everybody out," he ordered, unbuckling his safety belt and opening the door.

The draft of cold air into the cabin revived me. I watched as he climbed out and turned to push his seat down so Melody and Glynn could climb out beside him.

"Hurry up," he said to me, as I just sat there. "Move it."

I shook my head. "I'm staying put," I said. "I'm tired. You all went to sleep while I was flying, but I couldn't. If you want me to do another flight, you'd better let me have a nap now or I won't be able to concentrate."

Predictably Steve began to bully and bluster.

"You. Out of there. You'll be sorry if I have to come around and haul your fat arse out myself."

I watched him march around the plane in front of me, a dark shadow silhouetted against the night sky, and regretted I didn't still have the propeller spinning. An aircraft can be a powerful weapon if used ruthlessly.

As it was, Steve reached my door and yanked it open, grabbing for my arm to pull me free.

"Leave her," Glynn called. "She won't have had much sleep. She's got a point. Let her be. We're going to need her until we're safe in the hills." Glynn at least could be relied on to use his brains.

"I need sleep," I reiterated, "and then I need coffee." I thought I might as well make the most of my reprieve. "The town's just a couple of kilometres or so down the road. There's bound to be a late-night garage open or something. We can't fly out of here until daylight, which won't be for at least two hours. Why don't you go and get us some food and hot drinks? Even if they're cold by the time you get back, it will be better than nothing."

"What, and have you fly off without us?" Steve sounded incredulous. "You think we're dumb or something?"

He'd dropped my arm, but was still standing by my door. I stared at him for a long moment, not trying to challenge him, but because my brain wasn't able to focus sufficiently to answer his question. If I'd been able to find the words, I'd have agreed. Of course he was dumb. Dangerously dumb.

At last I shook my head, reached forward, and drew the keys out of the ignition.

"Here," I said, handing them to him. "If you take the keys with you, then the plane can't go anywhere. But I need to sleep. OK? You can even use the keys to lock me in if you want to, but if I don't get a nap, we're not going anywhere. As it stands, at the moment I don't think I could stay awake long enough to taxi out to the runway. Got it?"

He grabbed the keys from me then looked across the aircraft to Glynn for guidance. Glynn shrugged, and I heard Steve give a frustrated sigh. I watched him as he moved down the plane to the locker and retrieve his coat and gun. What was it with this guy? Did he think he was Rambo? I wondered whether certain types of men were plain needy. My ex, David, had been inseparable from his mobile phone, so perhaps it was part of a syndrome.

Steve shrugged into his coat and cradled his gun as he walked around to join Glynn. They moved a few steps away and stopped at the furthest reach of light from the aircraft, their heads close together as they spoke.

The passenger door opened, and Melody slipped back in beside me. "I want to stay as well," she said as she shut the door behind her.

I smiled at her in welcome – not such an easy exercise because the bruises had frozen my face muscles. We watched the dark shapes of the two men.

Their argument became heated and at one point I watched Steve punch a fist into the air in frustration. Glynn seemed able to control him for now, but I feared what would happen if Steve ever decided to strike out on his own.

At last they returned to the aircraft.

Glynn opened my door to speak to me. "We'll lock you in," he said, "and go and find some food."

I nodded, but Steve interrupted. "For fuck's sake. At least take Melody. That one won't make a run for it if we've got blondie," he said, gesturing towards me. "Otherwise we'll have her flying out of here the second our backs are turned."

"I can't fly if I don't have the keys, and I won't be able to fly at all if you lose them," I said.

I supposed, if push came to shove, I could try swinging the prop to fire up the engine, but I didn't fancy it and I wasn't about to suggest the idea to them. I didn't even know whether it would work on a 172.

"We've been through this," said Glynn. He sounded tired. "Coffee and food is sensible, and we've got the time. If we take one of them with us as hostage, and they cause a scene with people around, then we're stuffed. It's safer to leave them here. Just lock them in, and be done with it." He fumbled in his jacket pocket. His keyring had a small torch attached that he passed to Steve.

"You can see to lock up with that."

"We should at least tie them up."

"What with, and why?" asked Glynn. "They'll be locked in a small capsule. They can't get out, they can't start the engine -

what do you think they're going to do? For fuck's sake, turn the bloody key and get on with it. I'm going to find a shot of coffee and something to eat."

He turned and started walking towards the distant street lights. Steve gave a muttered curse.

"You'd better still be here when we get back."

"You'd better bring back coffee. A lot of it," I replied.

He glowered at me and slammed the door shut. I heard the key turn. He walked around and locked the passenger door. I wondered whether he'd forgotten the luggage hatch, but he locked that as well. As a parting gesture, he slapped the body of the plane hard enough to shake the whole aircraft. Just a friendly reminder of his violence.

I watched him walk into the night. The darkness was so intense I completely lost sight of him once he was a few metres away. The little torch was so faint it was virtually invisible. Some moments later I saw a small flame glow and realised he'd stopped to light a cigarette. I tracked his progress across the apron by the intermittent flare of its tip before he turned the corner and disappeared from sight.

It wasn't a comforting thought to realise that, cigarette excepted, he'd be able to return to the aircraft and I'd have no warning of his presence until he stood right beside us.

We sat in silence for a few minutes, both Melody and I enjoying being free of the men. We might be in the claustrophobic confines of a very small cockpit with no means of exit, but to me it felt like freedom.

"Are you OK?" I asked.

"Yeah, I'm fine. Do you really want to sleep?"

"Yes, I'm so knackered I can barely keep my eyes open."

"Do you want to move to the back seat?" she asked. "There's more room there for you to stretch out."

I glanced at her. Her features were shielded in the darkness, but her voice was firm and confident. I admired her poise.

"Nah, I'm fine here. I can lean against the side and shut my eyes."

"OK. I'll move then. That way you get more room here."

I nodded, although she couldn't have seen me, and moved to let her scramble over the seats to the back.

I settled my head back against the glass, closed my eyes and let myself drift.

I woke to the sound of scratching. It had woven into my dreams then forced itself into my conscious mind. I opened my eyes, registered where I was and that I had a stiff neck. The scratching sound continued, and I looked towards the back seat.

"What are you doing?" I asked. My voice sounded groggy and unlike me. I coughed to clear my throat. My face was numb where it had been pressed against the cold window.

"The axe," whispered Melody. "I'm trying to free it. Sorry, I didn't mean to wake you."

"The . . .?" Full consciousness returned. All small planes carry emergency equipment and an axe is standard, along with a fire extinguisher. For some reason, it's always referred to as an axe, even though it's actually a hatchet, useful for smashing a way out of the aircraft in an accident, or alternatively, for chopping firewood to make a signal fire to alert rescuers.

"Good thinking!" I exclaimed. It said a lot for my own state of mind that I'd completely forgotten we had an axe in the plane.

"I can't work out how to get it loose," she complained. "I can't see anything, and my hands can't find out how to free it."

"It's got a split pin holding it," I said. "Wait, I'll put my torch on for a second." In this darkness the smallest pinpoint of light would be a beacon, so I shielded the glow as I shone the light down and illuminated the pin that held the hatchet in place. "Pull that out," I said.

She fumbled a bit before working out which direction to pull the pin. Even knowing, it was a fiddly procedure to get a grip on the small pin, and I heard her swear as a fingernail ripped.

Eventually she loosened the pin, tugged it out and freed the axe.

I turned the torch off again.

"Well done," I said, with genuine admiration.

"What do we do with it?" she asked.

"Good question," I said. "We either cut our way out now and

make a run for it, or we hide the axe somewhere on ourselves and use it later." I tried to think logically.

"How long was I asleep?" I asked.

"Ages," she said.

"Yeah, but it would be great if we had something more specific," I said. "A lot depends on how close those thugs are. There's not much point in us trying to escape if they're already walking across the apron towards us."

I peered at the window, but it was worse than useless to see outside. Not only was it still dark night, but our breath had covered the windows with an opaque mist. We were in our own little bubble.

"I'd check my watch," she said, "but I can't see it. It's too dark. I need the torch."

"You wear a watch?" I asked in surprise. I'd given up wearing mine two years ago when smart phones became really smart.

I felt rather than saw her shrug. "It was my mum's."

"Your mum left you?" I realised I knew nothing about Melody's background.

"She died."

"Oh crap. I'm sorry," I said. Now I felt awful. I'd assumed Jim was divorced. It had never occurred to me he was widowed.

"When did she die?"

There was a moment of silence before she replied. "Two years ago."

"About the same time my mum died," I offered.

"It sucks," she said shortly and I felt the barriers go up. Fair enough, this wasn't the time for a heart to heart.

"You really have a watch?" I asked again.

"Yeah."

"Bring your wrist down here so I can shine the torch on it then." I switched the little torch on again as she put her arm forward.

"5.35," she said.

"Shit, was I asleep for a whole hour?" I was shocked. I must have been tired.

I estimated the airport was no more than three kilometres

from the town. Possibly it was less. The two men were fit, unburdened, and there'd be no reason for them to linger once they'd found somewhere that sold food. More than enough time had passed for them to have reached town and started back. I looked at the window again. It was still blackest night outside without the faintest hint of a coming dawn. A whole army could be encamped outside and we'd never see them.

"If we'd thought of it earlier, just after they left, we'd have had time to get out and away. Now, I think it might be too risky," I said. "I don't even know how long it would take to cut our way out, and I don't like the thought of getting caught in the act. We'd be sitting ducks for Steve and his gun, and we wouldn't see him until he was right on top of us."

Even as we spoke, I thought I caught a slight gleam of light. It disappeared. I cursed and rubbed my sleeve over the window hoping to clear the mist. There it was again. Just a faint spark that flared and quickly faded as the smoker inhaled. If the night weren't so dark, I'd have missed it. Steve and his cigarette.

"Shit, I think that's them," I said. "Quick, we have to hide the axe."

"I've got it," she said.

I heard rustling from the back seat.

"I've shoved it up the sleeve of my jacket," she said.

"It'll fall out," I said.

"Nah. There's a strap around the cuff. I've tightened it around my wrist. I reckon it'll hold. I put it in handle up, so the head will fall into my hand when I need it. I think I can get it out quickly."

"Good thinking," I said. My admiration for her grew, laced now with apprehension. If she was caught with the hatchet, I didn't imagine Steve's reaction would be pleasant. It was too late to insist she pass it to me.

We tracked the pair's progress across the tarmac by the glow of Steve's cigarette. It was like watching a tracer beacon, and I acquired a new and unexpected fondness for cigarette smoking. The lit tip far outshone the fading glow of the little torch carried by Glynn. Without that warning light, Melody and I would have been caught completely by surprise.

I felt my muscles tighten as my breathing quickened. We'd had a peaceful interlude, and I'd been lucky to get some sleep, but I had no illusions how dangerous the men approaching us were. We'd been safe so far because they'd needed us, but there was no telling what we would encounter in the coming hours, or even whether Melody and I would survive. I felt fear squirm in my stomach and schooled my face to hide it, as Steve unlocked the doors.

"Out," he said. Food and caffeine didn't appear to have improved his attitude.

I climbed out and straightened my spine, letting the cramp and cricks ease out. Melody and I had made the inside of the aircraft snug with the warm fug of our breathing. Outside the air was wickedly cold. Much colder than it had been earlier when we left Paraparaumu. I shivered at the sudden change in temperature.

"Did you get food?" I asked. "And coffee?" I rubbed my hands together. The cold chilled my fingers and I knew my breath vaporised in front of me although I couldn't see it. The sky carried a myriad of stars in a sweeping canopy above us, a promise of a beautiful day to come.

"Here." Glynn passed a paper bag to me and another to Melody. It held a cooling meat pie and a paper cup of tepid coffee. I leaned back against the cold empennage of the plane and scoffed both as if I'd never seen food before. I realised I'd been running on empty. I was so hungry, even the cooling, congealing, pie filling didn't repel me.

I watched Melody to see if she betrayed the presence of the hatchet up her sleeve as she moved, but she was admirably cool. I wouldn't have guessed anything from her mien. She stood beside me as she swiftly demolished her pie. Her nose wrinkled at the taste of coffee.

"Yuk," she said. "I don't drink coffee." But she swallowed it anyway. "Anything else?" she asked Glynn.

"Nah. That's it. Back into the plane." He took the empty bag from Melody and reached to take mine.

"I need to pee," she said.

He was in front of me, the empty bag of food in his hand, and

I felt him stiffen.

"Again?"

"Yes. Again." Melody invested the phrase with the sort of scorn and derision only a teenager can fully express. "The last time was three hours ago, and anyway, who's counting?"

"Fuck," I heard him mutter under his breath. "OK, you'll have to go behind the plane. In the dark we won't see you."

"What, squat? Out here in the middle of the tarmac?"

"There isn't anywhere else. Take it or leave it - that's all there is on offer."

Melody hesitated.

"Do you want me to come with you?" asked Steve. He sounded amused. "I could hold your hand or something?" His tone made it clear the comment was obscene.

Melody gave a disgusted snort. "Fuck off, jerk," she said and walked away to the rear of the plane.

"I need to follow her," I said.

"Not until she comes back," Glynn replied. "Then you can go."

While I waited I lifted my hand and ran it over the leading edge of the wing above me. It was as I thought. The surface was rough, cold and hard beneath my fingers. I drew my hand away and wiped it on my sleeve before shoving both hands into my pockets to warm up.

Melody returned and I took my own trip behind the plane.

I suppose Glynn and Steve at least had the decency not to follow, or shine their torch on us as we squatted inelegantly on the tarmac, but it felt unpleasantly vulnerable to be bare-bottomed and peeing within a few metres of them. I was glad to draw my jeans back up and return, fully dressed and decent, to the aircraft.

"You can get back inside. Put that gun back in the hold, Steve." I noticed that at some point during the men's trip to town Glynn had assumed the role of speaker. Apart from lascivious leers and under-the-breath mutterings, Steve was keeping quiet. I wondered if Glynn had told him to shut up and stop harassing us.

"Only an hour to go until sunrise," he said once we'd resumed our places in the plane.

I wondered when I should tell them that there was another problem looming. Now, so they could get used to the idea, or at sunrise, when they expected to be able to leave? Either way, I expected a difficult reaction.

"At least it's a clear morning, and there's no cloud to block the sun," I said cautiously, "but there is another issue to consider."

"Seriously?" exclaimed Steve, turning to me. "What the fuck now? You're just trying to delay us. It's one bloody excuse after another." His explosive anger was palpable and barely restrained. Involuntarily I flinched back from him.

"Steve!" Glynn's snap of command was instant and had the desired effect of shutting Steve's tirade off although his glare would have melted me where I sat if he'd had his way.

"What sort of problem?" asked Glynn, "and as Steve says, you'd better not be trying delaying tactics just to piss us off."

I shook my head. "It's been a cold night. There's ice on the wings. We can't take off until it's melted. We'd kill ourselves trying to fly as it is at the moment."

"What do you mean, ice?" asked Glynn, peering out into the still, dark night. I got the impression he expected to see an iceberg of Titanic proportions.

"I felt it when I touched the wing just before. There's a hard layer of ice on the wings. Unless you've got hot water to start the melting process, we need to wait until the sun warms the wing up and the ice falls off."

"But you flew us out of Paraparaumu OK," Glynn objected. "There were no problems. Why's there a problem now?"

"The plane had been in a hangar when we first got into it," I said. "Now we've been parked out in the open for a couple of hours on a cold night. The temperature has dropped and there's been a dew fall. It's frozen on the wing."

"It's only a thin layer, for fuck's sake," said Steve. "It's not going to make a difference."

"It's a thin layer of water," I countered. "It's probably increased the weight of the aircraft by fifty per cent. Water's heavy, remember? And even if weight wasn't a major factor, which it is, there's no saying that there's an equal distribution of ice on each wing. If one side is heavier than the other, then that wing is going to be dragged down and we won't be able to fly. It's a sure-fire way of crashing."

"She's making it up," Steve said to Glynn. "I say we go anyway, as soon as it's light enough."

The men were silent, and neither Melody nor I had anything to say. The window was too misted for us to look at the stars outside for distraction. Under other circumstances it could have been restful to have sat in such a quietly meditative mode. As it was, the unspoken words were terrifying, building up like a tidal wave behind our silence, before the inevitable moment when the wave's momentum would rise up and swamp everything.

I was acutely aware of Steve sitting beside me, every inch of his frame radiating tension. I could hear his breathing, harsh and noisy, his breath too swift for a sedentary man.

Glynn, outwardly at least, seemed relaxed, and I began to ponder the relationship between the two. Glynn clearly provided the brain-power but I had no doubt he'd use Steve as a tool to control me if he felt the need. When I'd mentioned the ice, his eyes hadn't left my face as he weighed both my words and why I'd said them. There'd been a cold, clear eyed assessment in his gaze.

CHAPTER SIXTEEN

I CLOSED MY EYES AND ALLOWED MY mind to wander to a happy place. Jack would be onboard the plane from Brisbane. I imagined our reunion, the pleasure of his company, the sweet, slow smile he gave me when he was happy. For a moment I felt safe, warmed by my memories.

Steve moved beside me and woke me from my reverie. There was a possibility, I supposed, that if things went wrong, I might never see Jack again. My mind flinched away from the pain of that thought, and I looked outside. The windows were misty, so I rubbed a small corner and peered out.

Steve's restlessness was both annoying and worrying. I watched him from the corner of my eye. It wasn't so much that he fidgeted, it was the tension that radiated from him: the abrupt movements, the clenched fists and the restless leg.

The sky was changing. On the eastern horizon the deep blue was showing a border of paler colour. It wouldn't be long before that faint line smudged light into the rest of the sky and the new day and its adventures - or horrors - would begin.

I imagined it must be shortly after seven o'clock. Soon Roger would be at the office and registering that there had been illicit activity last night. He'd find the premises unlocked, the hangar doors open, and one of his aircraft missing. I wondered whether he'd see my scrawled note, understand it's meaning, and call the police.

I was, in fact, very disappointed no helpful policeman had come to check on us already. I'd hoped air traffic control would have registered the transponder code I'd used on our flight and would have organised someone to investigate. Either we hadn't been flying at sufficient altitude for radar to have been able to monitor us, or Wairoa didn't have enough locally available police resources to respond. I had no idea how long it would take to send reinforcements in from Gisborne or Napier, but of one thing I was certain: if we weren't intercepted before our next flight, it would be much harder to track us into a remote farm strip up in the mountains.

And time was running out.

The aircraft rocked as Glynn moved behind me.

"It's almost light," he said.

"'Bout bloody time," replied Steve. He attempted to stretch, a difficult operation in the confined cockpit. "Shit," he swore, as he banged his elbow against the door frame. "I'm going to stretch my legs."

There was a blast of ice-cold air into the plane as he opened the door. I reached over and shut it behind him. He hadn't gone two paces from the aircraft before he'd hunched over, shielding the flame with his hands as he lit the inevitable smoke.

"At least he's consistent," I said.

There was a muffled snort of laughter from Melody.

Steve was visible now as a dark silhouette against the lightening sky. He reached up to the leading edge of the wing and ran his hands along the length.

"I'm picking he didn't trust my word about the ice," I said scornfully.

"What do you suggest we do next?" Glynn asked.

I shifted in my seat so I could turn and talk to him.

"I'm serious about the ice. Until it's off the wings, it's not safe for us to fly. And I mean *completely* off, not just roughly scraped off in patches. You either find hot water from somewhere, or we wait for the sun to warm up. Then I want to fuel the plane up, and you need to show me where you want to go so I can plan the route."

He said nothing for an appreciable while, but just looked at me as if trying to divine the honesty of my words.

"Let me out," he demanded at last.

Out towards the sea the light was strengthening. It was going to be a glorious day. I opened the door and climbed out so he could follow me. The chill morning air felt lovely against my skin - a sudden wash of cleanliness and refreshment. I breathed deeply, enjoying the new day. I felt a sudden surge of optimism. Melody and I would come through this. Why did problems always seem easier to deal with first thing in the morning?

Melody followed Glynn out and stood quietly beside me as he walked across the other side of the plane to talk to Steve.

"OK?" I asked.

She nodded. "Are you putting them on about the ice?" she whispered.

I shook my head. "No. We're in trouble if Glynn doesn't listen to me. I daren't take off with the wings covered."

She gave me a wry look. "We're in trouble anyway," she said tartly. "I don't know what Steve meant when he said I was a hostage, but it didn't sound good."

I agreed. I didn't imagine any scheme Steve dreamt up was going to be pleasant for either of us. I wasn't even sure, once my usefulness as a pilot ended, whether they'd bother to keep me alive. If Steve's plan was to put Melody up for ransom, then I stood no chance. I'd be valueless. There was no wealthy daddy available to redeem me.

I sighed. Some of the optimism had just been stripped from my morning.

"I guess we just hang in there and see what happens next," I said. I meant it to sound encouraging, but for all my efforts the words hung flat between us. There were too many intangibles for us to make plans, and that damn gun of Steve's skewed everything.

There was an argument going on between the men. Although

they were on the far side of the plane from us, their words carried clearly.

"She's lying."

"Do you seriously want to take the risk?" Glynn asked. "We're nearly safe. Let's not stuff things up now."

"We're not safe until we're in the hills, and that bloody bitch is just being difficult and slowing us down."

"For fuck's sake. We don't know we'll be safe even then. How do you know your family will take us in? What's up there for us?" Glynn's voice had risen in frustration.

"They'll take us in." Steve's voice was confident.

"We're on the run, why should they?"

"You wouldn't understand," said Steve. "We're Maori. It's a whanau thing. Anyway, I don't intend to tell them we're on the run. I'm going to appeal to the Maori sovereignty crap they all believe in. You wait and listen. I'll pitch it so we have them begging to look after us."

"What the fuck's our mission got to do with Maori sovereignty?"

Steve gave a short laugh. "I can join the dots up for them. I learnt a lot of stuff when I was inside and I know how those guys think. Why do you think the Mob were so keen to get involved distributing the stuff in the Waikato? It wasn't because I've got a pretty face."

Glynn rubbed a tired hand over his face. "I hope you're right, mate. In the meantime, we've got to get there safely. We get the ice off the wings, and that's final."

The men walked round the aircraft towards us.

"I'm going to find some hot water," said Glynn. "Steve will stay here and keep an eye on you both. While I'm away you can get the fuel into the aircraft. Understood?"

I was less than thrilled to be left with Steve, but I accepted that fetching water was a concession to my advice and shrugged my shoulders. I didn't understand what they'd been talking about, but I figured it wasn't any immediate concern of mine.

"OK." I looked at Steve. "I'll need the keys back so I can taxi over to the fuel pumps."

His hesitation was due more to natural contrariness than any real threat implied in my request, but it made me wonder if I could get Melody on board and simply power down the runway without him. Gun or no gun, ice be damned, I'd be prepared to take the chance. Of course, my bravado was based on complete ignorance of what a bullet could do to a small aircraft. I wouldn't even have to take off. A spinning propeller is a powerful weapon and I wouldn't hesitate to drive the plane straight at him.

He handed the keys to me and beckoned to Melody.

"You can come across with me," he said to her as he looked at me. "That way *she* won't get any stupid ideas," he told her. Melody flinched as he pulled her towards him and forced her to walk in step with him.

I sighed in defeat, fired the engine up, and obediently taxied to the pumps. As soon as I'd got the propeller spinning it sent a blast of freezing air back over the plane, fogging the outside of the windows. I had to open the door and lean out to see where to go, which meant I got the full blast of polar air in my face. It was a slow trip, and I was cold, cross and grumpy by the time I'd got the aircraft to the pump and dug out the swipe card to unlock the fuel.

By the time I'd climbed down from filling the tank in the second wing a car pulled up and let Glynn out. He walked towards us, his body on a slight lean as he balanced the weight of a full jerry can in his hand.

"I found someone up early at a house nearby who was prepared to lend me a can for a few minutes," he said, nodding towards the waiting vehicle. "Let's get these wings clean so we don't have to keep him waiting. And you two girls stay just where you are. No silly business, OK?"

Steve gave Melody a little shake to reinforce the advice.

I looked across at the vehicle and cursed all helpful people. I'd hoped to gain another hour on the ground at Wairoa before Glynn got back. I didn't dare risk running to the car while Steve held Melody.

"How do we clear it?" asked Glynn, indicating the wing.

"Have you got a credit card?" I asked. "You climb up using

that step there, and put your other foot on the strut. Then pour some water on a patch of ice and use your card to scrape it clean. Keep working until the whole surface is clear on both wings, but don't damage the paint."

I stood at a safe distance, making it quite clear I didn't intend to do the work myself. Glynn gave me an irritated look, but handed the tank to Steve.

"Here, you do the pouring while I scrape. Just make sure you don't waste the water. I don't want to have to do another trip."

Steve dropped Melody's arm and she flinched so sharply she almost jumped apart from him. I could read her revulsion, as if contact with him sullied her. I thought of the laughing, shining girl she'd been on the day she'd gone solo, and grieved for her.

Between them the men worked methodically. I ran my hand carefully down the wing to check their work. It was so cold a mist formed over the wing surface almost as soon as they had cleared the ice. In a perfect world there'd have been a towel to complete the drying process, but at least the thick sheet of ice had gone. Once the propeller was spinning, the rest would blow off.

I looked up towards the hills. It was clear daylight now - the start of a beautiful day. Wisps of mist clung on some of the ridges. I hoped they'd burn off before we had to worry about landing.

Glynn returned the jerry can to the helpful Samaritan and waved him away. I watched the car drive off, wondering whether, by dithering, I'd lost the only opportunity we'd get for rescue. I began to see why victims became compliant in their own abuse. Fear was a powerful form of control.

"We're ready to go." Glynn walked back towards me.

"When you show me where I'm flying to," I said, and watched with resignation as Glynn spread the chart out on the engine cowling.

Steve's stubby finger pointed to a spot on the chart.

"There!" he said.

I looked where he was pointing, and saw nothing.

"What do you mean, *there*? There's nothing. Not even a

township or village. How do you expect me to find it if I don't know what I'm looking for? Are we looking for some clearing in the bush or something? Because in that country we don't stand a shit show in hell of stumbling onto it if you don't know exactly where it is."

"We'll find it," said Steve with admirable confidence.

He pointed at the blue shape of Lake Waikaremoana.

"We fly up through there," he said, "and follow the road."

CHAPTER SEVENTEEN

ONCE WE WERE AIRBORNE THE SUN was behind us - picking out, in high definition, the hills and shaded valleys. We flew west, towards the high country. The clarity of the light made everything it touched below us glow in colours of fresh green and gold. As we climbed further, into territory where the valleys were deeper and the ground more rugged, the mist thickened in the hollows and covered the lower ground, filling the space between the hills.

"It looks like a bucket full of eels," said Melody suddenly.

I flicked her a surprised glance and saw she was looking out the window. I looked down again.

She was right. The bush-covered ridges below us emerged from the surrounding sea of white cloud like dorsal fins on some monstrous, antique creature. I shuddered. I don't mind eels, but we were high in the Ureweras, flying over Ngai Tuhoe country, a land steeped in myth and legend. It wasn't beyond belief that a fabulous monster, such as the mystical taniwha, lurked below, protecting the land from invaders. I only had to glance out of the window to see why its people were known as the "'children of the mist'".

Steve was sitting beside me again, this time acting as navigator as we followed the line of road up towards Lake Waikaremoana. I could sense his tension and frustration as the road came into view, only to be hidden by the next drift of mist.

"Unless we're very lucky and the mist burns off, or you've got some better way of navigating than just following the road, we're going to lose our route soon," I observed as yet again the shroud of cloud covered the land beneath us. "Are you sure you don't want to turn back to Wairoa, and give it an hour or so for the mist up here to lift? I know how long this stuff can hang around in the hills. Even if we stay safely above it, and fly overhead your destination, there's no way I can go down through the cloud and land."

"We keep going," said Glynn from the back seat. "Take our chances that we can get in to the strip OK. If we can't, then we'll discuss where to go next."

I shrugged lightly enough, but had plenty of concerns I thought best to conceal from the men. I'd kept the aircraft climbing steadily since we'd left the airport so we ourselves were in no danger of being surrounded by cloud. Even so, this wasn't territory I was familiar with, and in the absence of clear visibility beneath us, and with no GPS coordinates to follow, it would be easy to get lost. Steve's instructions were dependent on being able to see the road below, contact that could be lost irretrievably in less than a minute should cloud roll in.

"Where now?" I asked as the road disappeared once more. "I can hold this heading, but if we're not careful, I'll overshoot the lake itself without even knowing it. Do you know where we go from there?"

There was a consultation between Glynn and Steve.

"It's your family," said Glynn, "and your idea to come up here. You'd frigging better make this work, mate, because going back home isn't really an option anymore."

Steve threw him a harassed glance.

"I'll find it, I tell you," said Steve. "Just get us to the lake, fly along the edge, then turn up into the hills."

I bit back the urge to point out we were in the hills, and that I'd already mentioned we could well miss seeing the bloody lake.

I picked Steve was close to exploding. Even for a man who frequently exhibited levels of high stress, he seemed abnormally febrile. I had no wish to precipitate a scene I'd have no way to manage within the confines of a small plane.

I gritted my teeth and focused on flying a straight line while scanning every inch of the area beneath us for some break in the mist.

Even so, we'd have missed it if it hadn't been for Melody's excited call.

"It's there, just beneath us," she almost squeaked with excitement. In spite of our predicament I had to grin. This was more like the girl I'd come to know.

"Where?" I asked.

"There," she said, pointing to an area behind my shoulder.

I had to tilt the plane to look down. Without Melody's call I'd have flown on oblivious, but there, framed by the window on Steve's side, was a clear area beneath us where the edge of a lake was clearly visible.

I breathed a sigh of relief.

"OK, Steve. There's the lake. Now where do we go?"

"Lower," he said. "You'll have to take us lower so I can follow the road."

I looked at the chart resting in my lap.

"No way, Jose," I said firmly. "There are mountains all around here, and in this visibility I could well clip one if we get too close in the mist. Look at this one, Mt Maungapohatu – it's enormous." I pointed out the highest peak I could see on the map.

"That's where we're going," said Steve tersely.

"We are? Is there a landing strip there?" I stared at the featureless aviation chart in frustration. It was too large a scale to be at all useful in navigating my way through these mountain valleys. Frankly, in this type of country, I'd have done better with a tramping map. Obviously no one expected light aircraft to buzz around in this territory. I wasn't sure I'd ever even seen a large-scale chart of the area. If one existed, we'd certainly never sold it at Paraparaumu Aviation.

"Just follow the edge of the lake," advised Steve. "I need to pick out where the road up to Maungapohatu turns off. Then we follow that instead."

"You'll be lucky," I snorted. "We'll lose visual contact in a minute." But I adjusted our heading to follow the line of the water anyway.

The misty clouds floated between us and the shore, but there was sufficient clear space for us to track not only the edge of the lake, but also the road that ran beside it. As the border of the lake began to turn south again, I banked the plane and turned to follow the road.

By some serendipitous freak of ambient temperature, the road beneath us stayed clear, and Steve found the intersection with no problems. We made a sharp turn to the north and followed the road – by now little better than a track, - into the hills.

From the air it can be hard to fully appreciate terrain below, and in this case it was worse than usual. Enough to say that the track was almost impossible to follow with its zig-zags and switchbacks and the way it dived suddenly under the cover of the bush overhanging the road, completely disappearing from view for a kilometre or so.

I tried to take a bird's eye view of the landscape and extrapolate our position as we went, but our route led deeper and deeper into the rugged terrain, and I doubted whether any outside agency could track us. I glanced sadly at the completely redundant transponder, still squawking its pathetic emergency code and reflected that, if emergency services had failed us at Wairoa, there was absolutely no chance the transponder could guide any search parties up into these mountains to help Melody and me now. We were on our own.

We came at last to a series of valleys, hard up against the mountain Steve had mentioned before.

"That's it," Steve said, pointing excitedly. "We land down there."

Our present altitude guaranteed our safety, so I looked down warily, unwilling to sacrifice our height unless I was certain of a safe landing site.

"Fuck," I said, as I took in the valley where Steve was pointing.

"There's no landing strip."

"You can land on the grass," said Steve impatiently.

There were a couple of grassed paddock areas that might have been promising as a landing site if it weren't for the sheer cliffs and peaks which encircled them. The geography of the place was so dramatic I couldn't even begin to work out a suitable approach to fly down in there, and if I stuffed it up, I wouldn't have a clear escape route to get us out of trouble. I felt the palms of my hands begin to sweat.

"I can't land down there," I murmured, as much to myself as to the others.

"You fucking will," snarled Steve. "That's the reason we've got you with us, so don't be stupid. I swear if you don't get us in there, I'll take you apart."

I shot him an irritated glance as his words disrupted my concentration. Didn't he understand that the very real danger posed by the terrain was more immediate and urgent than any threat he could utter? I was currently much more frightened by the possibility of down draughts and other mountainous hazards than I was of his bully-boy blustering. The challenge of landing the plane in this valley was sufficiently terrifying without Steve trying to up the ante. I wondered whether anyone had ever landed up here and lived to walk away.

I circled over the valley, keeping a wary eye out that I didn't fly into a cliff or bluff, and tried to work out a possible track. It had been a still morning when we left Wairoa, and I could see no obvious sign of wind activity up here. With no better information, I had to assume – a very dangerous assumption – that conditions up here were the same as they'd been back on the coast.

"Can you all keep a look out and let me know if you see any power poles or electric wires that might get in our way?" I asked.

Steve snorted. "You think they've got electricity out here? If you want it, you generate it yourself. Same as telephones. No fancy mobile phone towers out here. The only contact with the outside world is by radio. Welcome to the real New Zealand, baby."

I could hear the glee in his voice. Another opportunity to bring the townie down.

"Well, phone wires, electric fences across gullies. I don't care what they are. If they're wire, look out for them and let me know if you see anything."

I was too intent on finding a suitable landing spot to pay Glynn much attention, but I heard him say acidly "Great. It's not going to be five-star accommodation then, is it? Thanks a lot, Steve."

Steve swung his head around to look at Glynn. "Well, what did you expect? You wanted somewhere safe to hide out – and there's nowhere as remote and safe as here. Take it or leave it."

Glynn had never struck me as an outdoorsy type of man - more a pallid product of urban Britain. But Steve had said his father was Maori, so this must be his family the men were seeking refuge with.

Under other conditions I'd have been interested, but their chatter disturbed my concentration. I scowled at Steve. I don't know whether he interpreted my look as a message to shut up or not, but he relapsed into silence. I resumed my focus on planning the landing.

Eventually I chose a paddock that looked less bumpy than its neighbours. There were a couple of small, fenced plots along its side, so I'd have to manoeuvre around them on the roll-out, but otherwise it looked reasonable. I took a deep breath, drew the throttle back and started a spiral descent. As we got lower, the steep walls of the valley towered over us, blocking our escape route.

For better or worse, I was now committed to landing.

I was sick with a combination of claustrophobia and terror. There was no margin for error, and I was all too aware that if I got it wrong, in a few minutes' time we could all be dead.

The last turn was the worst. We were low, slow and banked over. The presence of the surrounding mountains was oppressive, and I had no room to overshoot if my judgement was wrong. My hands were slick on the yoke as I rolled the aircraft level for the short approach to the paddock.

We touched down with a bump and bounced across the

overgrown paddock. I was terrified we'd encounter some hidden object that could damage the plane, but luck was with us - there was nothing concealed in the long grass. Once we'd slowed, I swung the plane around and taxied as close to the end of the strip as I could before turning around and parking the little plane, ready to go, in the direction of what passed up here as a runway.

If Melody and I managed to escape and got a chance to fly off here, I would need as much length as I could get.

It was an unlikely scenario but I wanted to stack all the odds in our favour.

I cut the engine and we sat in silence. I could feel my shirt clinging to my skin and discovered I was drenched in sweat. I was completely wrung out and exhausted. I wiped my palms on my jeans. I wondered whether my companions realised how touch-and-go the manoeuvre had been.

I could hear Roger's words running through my head. "'Don't push limits, they have a way of pushing back.'" Well, today I'd pushed my own limits, and come out a winner this time. I felt a surge of euphoric self-pride and elation.

Steve moved first, opened the door and climbed out. The rest of us followed. I, for one, was grateful to be safely on the ground and able to stretch my legs, although it was cold outside. I desperately wanted a shower and fresh deodorant. My shirt was wringing wet and I could smell the rank sweat of fear on my body.

Only now, on the ground and leaning safely against the wing strut, could I admit to myself how terrified I'd been. My legs quivered with the release of tension and I felt shattered.

Glynn rifled through his pack in the hold, pulled out a warm jumper and added the extra layer beneath his jacket. Steve wrapped his heavy trench-coat around him tightly. I watched them jealously. I was wearing my jacket, but it wasn't doing much to keep out the morning chill.

I realised Steve's actions had another purpose when he took his gun from Glynn and pushed it into a pocket built into the lining of the coat. It must lie against the length of his thigh. From the outside at least, there was no sign of the concealed weapon.

A man came roaring across the paddock towards us on a quad bike.

"Hi guys," he said. "You here to see someone?" The words were fine, but the tone made it clear this wasn't the friendliest of greetings.

Then he saw Steve, and broke into a grin of recognition.

"Steve! Hey, is that you cuz? Why didn't you tell us you were coming? What's with the plane, man?"

Steve ran to the newcomer and they proceeded to jostle. There was a good deal of laughter, back-slapping, hugging, hongi, and complicated fist bumps.

"Good to see you, bro," said Steve eventually. "I didn't have time to call up first, mate. This is something of an impulse visit."

He turned to us. "This is my cousin, Tamati."

The man nodded at us as he parked the quad bike beside the aircraft. "Hi, welcome to the mountain. I'll take you up to the house."

"Come on girls," Steve commanded as he and Glynn grabbed their bags from the hold. I locked the plane and followed behind them. The group fell into a natural arrangement of Tamati and Steve in front, Glynn stalking behind them and Melody and I trailing along in the rear.

We followed the track for about a kilometre. As we rounded a corner the village came into view. Tamati pointed out a house on the outskirts of a small cluster of homes, set on a small rise in a valley surrounded by rugged bush-covered hills.

"That's where we're going."

Steve nodded. "I remember it. I had good times there when I was a kid."

I could see a marae at the top of the hill, giving focus to the hamlet and looking out towards the largest of the hills.

Tamati paused and glanced behind at us. When he saw where I was looking he came back to me and stopped to explain. "That's Maungapohatu," he said. "It's our maunga, our sacred mountain."

I nodded. I was familiar with the idea of an ancestral mountain holding paramount place in a Maori tribe's historical, spiritual, ancestral and cultural identity. I liked the idea, even if my imagination could barely scrape at the significance it must hold for a man like Tamati, who, I assumed had been born and bred in the shadow of this mountain.

I smiled at him. "Thankyou. Steve didn't introduce us, but I'm Claire."

He smiled back at me and Melody. "You're welcome. I mean, you're both welcome here as our guests."

Steve looked towards us. His eyes narrowed as he took in the inappropriate degree of fraternisation taking place.

"Hey, Tamati," he called.

Tamati went back to Steve and we resumed walking. I could see Steve talking earnestly to him. Tamati gave an occasional grunt of surprise. Once, I saw, he looked back at Melody and me, as if not certain what to make of us or whatever our current status was.

It suddenly occurred to me that *I* didn't know what our status was either. Such had been the effect of Steve's intimidation when he abducted me, I hadn't questioned whether the relationship had changed since we'd landed here. And yet it must have done: Steve and Glynn were now safe in their mountain fastness, protected by both the terrain and the family Steve belonged to. Presumably there would be no need for either a pilot or a hostage any more.

I felt immeasurably cheered, and turned to Melody.

"Are you OK if I tell Steve we want to leave?"

"What?" she said.

"Well, we've got them here. They're safe, and they can't need us anymore," I said. "I'm going to tell Steve we want to fly out of here now and see what he says."

I saw doubt in her expression, and it emboldened me. The sooner I got Melody away from psychotic Steve, the better.

"Hey, Steve," I called.

He swung around towards me.

"What." Neither his attitude nor his tone were encouraging, but I persisted.

"Seems to me I got you and Glynn here safely, so you don't

need me and Melody any more."

I tried to sound as casual and nonchalant as I could and ignore the vicious anger rapidly gathering on his face. I was counting on the presence of both Glynn and Tamati to control him. Surely he wouldn't want to alienate Tamati, I thought.

"We'll just go back to the plane and make our way home, now that we've seen you safely delivered. Lovely place you've got here, Tamati. Great to meet you."

I'd barely finished speaking before Steve flattened me. He'd shoved passed Tamati and Glynn and took one almighty swipe at my face. I flinched back, which stopped the full force of the blow landing against my jaw, but it connected to my chin violently enough to knock me to the ground.

I tried to scramble away as soon as I landed, but Steve grabbed my hair and yanked, pulling me to my feet again. I cried out at the pain of it as I felt hair rip from my head, but he held me upright with his hand clawed into my scalp and slapped me again.

"Don't try and get clever with me, you bitch." He hit me again as he spoke.

I sagged in his grip, so dazed and disoriented I couldn't even protest at the extra pain.

He dangled me a second or so more before dropping me. I collapsed like a rag doll and landed on my knees, where I stayed, eyes shut, head down, gasping for air. My head was ringing, and the world around me had turned a deep shade of red. I didn't think I could move and was too afraid anyway in case I found something was broken.

The world was roiling, and I wondered whether I would vomit. My hands pressed against the ground, and I leaned even further forward, trying to ease the sickness inside me. I was shaking so badly I could barely even breathe.

Some long minutes later I became aware Melody was kneeling beside me, her arm over my shoulders.

A slight ancillary pain nagged at me, and I traced it to where my hand was pressing against the stones of the track. A sharp piece of gravel was cutting into my palm. The minor discomfort forced me back to consciousness.

"Are you all right?" Melody asked. I realised she'd been repeating the same question for some time. The words had woven themselves into the colours inside my head.

"I'm fine," I tried to say, then discovered the words hadn't come out properly and I'd produced little more than a mumble.

I pushed my body upright until I was kneeling back on my heels. I felt Melody's hands help and steady me. Gradually I forced myself to lift my head and open my eyes.

I flinched at the rush of light. It took a few minutes to focus before I could look around. Melody's face, creased in concern, filled my view. I saw she'd been crying.

"Are you OK?" she asked again. "Don't get up. You probably shouldn't move yet."

Her voice seemed surprisingly distant for someone just in front of me.

I shook my head, which was a bad move. I imagined my brain sloshing from side to side inside the skull cavity. The nausea surged, but I bit back on it, and after a gulp or two it settled.

I looked past Melody. The men were involved in a furious argument which had reached the shoving stage. Soon, I supposed, it would come to blows. Glynn was between Steve and his cousin, and although my hearing felt muffled, I could hear the angry, raised voices and a good deal of swearing.

Melody's gaze followed mine. "There's been a right scene going down since Steve hit you," she said. "Glynn was angry, but you should have heard Tamati. He'd have taken Steve out if Glynn hadn't stopped him."

As we watched, Steve made a grab at Tamati who avoided him by stepping aside. I couldn't hear what Tamati said, but his body language fairly blazed contempt. He stretched to his full height, spat a gob at Steve's feet before turning and surprisingly, running back down the track we'd just walked. I couldn't believe he'd desert me. I hadn't picked him as a coward.

I decided I felt too ill to care what anyone else did and dropped my head in defeat. It was only Melody's sharp intake of breath that made me realise Tamati's defection effectively left both of us at Steve's mercy.

I raised my face to watch the men. Steve stood there laughing, watching where Tamati had disappeared around the corner. Glynn was saying something, but it was obvious Steve wasn't listening. He was too roused and far gone with blood-lust to be accessible to reason any more.

Even as I watched, Steve's gaze focused on me and Melody, and he started towards us with Glynn trailing behind him like the chorus from some Greek tragedy.

I heard a faint whimper of fear from Melody. I tried to scramble up.

"Get away from us, you prick," I heard her say.

I got up on my feet and stood there wobbling, much like a new born lamb. Steve had nearly reached us when I grabbed for Melody's hand to swing her behind me to safety, but at the same moment she turned to bolt and her hand slipped through mine. As her fingers slid away I was left holding a hard piece of metal. I nearly dropped the object before I realised what it was, turned it and tightened my grip on the handle.

Steve's attention was on Melody.

"Come here, bitch," I heard him say.

Fear, pain, anger and a fierce need to protect Melody flowed into an imperative.

As he reached to grasp her I lifted the hatchet she'd brought from the plane and brought it down as hard as I could across Steve's outstretched arm. It was as strong a blow as I could manage, though my hands shook and wobbled.

There was a strangely flat sound when the axe drove into flesh and bone.

Steve's scream filled the valley and silenced every bird's cry for miles around. I looked up to see his face, mouth open in shocked horror, staring down at the partially severed wreck of his right arm. The hand was still attached but hung limply from the sleeve of his coat. Blood squirted down his fingers in a regular rhythm.

"You fucking psycho," I screamed at him. "You try and touch either of us again, I'll bring this axe down through your skull."

Melody still stood in front of him, paralysed by shock, staring at the bloody axe in my hand. The hatchet was too heavy for me and started to slip.

There was a roaring in my ears. Glynn, Melody and I stood frozen in a ghastly tableau staring at Steve. His frantic, guttural cries of shock and pain held us hypnotised.

Then Melody broke free.

"Give me the axe," she commanded, and grabbed it from my unresisting fingers.

The roaring in my ears turned out to be Tamati riding full tilt up the track on his quad bike. He pulled up beside us and stared at the scene.

"What the fuck? I went to get the bike for Claire. What happened?"

Melody took control.

"Steve attacked us again, and was injured." A part of me registered amusement at such a masterly understatement.

"Get Claire onto the bike before she falls over," she ordered Tamati, then turned back to Steve who, no longer frozen, was frantically trying to hold his hand back where it should be, in line with his arm. The cries kept pouring from his mouth.

Tamati took my arm and assisted me to the quad. My knees didn't want to co-operate or hold me up, and Tamati had to support most of my weight as he got me seated on the carrier.

I was deeply shocked by my action. My emotions swung wildly between appalled horror at my violence and an equally deep satisfaction that it would be a long time before Steve could hit another woman. I slumped on the back of the quad and watched the blood spurting from his arm.

"Shut up and stand still, Steve," ordered Melody. "I need to tie something around your arm, and I can't if you carry on being a damn drama queen. You've caused enough trouble already."

She looked towards Glynn. "Have you got something I can strap it up with?"

Glynn, who looked as shocked as I was, shook his head.

Melody was now getting fully into role as senior prefect and gave a small, tut-tutting noise.

"It'll have to be your sleeve then," she said to Steve. He'd been wearing his coat with its sleeves rolled up, exposing the shirt beneath. The shirt had ripped where the hatchet had landed and now she tried to tear it further. This produced further wails from Steve that turned into expletives as her actions jarred his arm further.

"Here," said Tamati, pulling a knife from the sheath on his belt.

Between them they cut a strip of cloth and Melody proceeded to fashion a rough tourniquet.

"Do you know anything about first-aid?" she asked.

He shook his head. "Not much. Just stop the bleeding, I guess, and get him back to the house so we can radio the rescue chopper. They'll have to send a helicopter up for him. I didn't get a chance to tell you guys, but the road is blocked. A slip came down last night, so no one can get up here until it's cleared."

"He'll need a sling," Melody said, and returned to cutting away more of Steve's sleeve which she fashioned into a workable loop.

"Here. If I can get your arm through this and loop it around the back of your head, it will give your arm some support while we get you to the village. You'll have to ride along with Claire."

Steve screamed every time the arm was shifted, but with some persuasion and manoeuvring, Melody got the thing into place. She and Tamati shoved him onto the back of the quad beside me.

"Just follow the road to the first house," Tamati explained to the others as he started the quad. "You can't miss it, and I won't be going fast anyway in case I lose my passengers."

It was true, neither Steve nor I were showing much resilience. I was so feeble the slightest jolt could have displaced me, and Steve, in deep mourning for his arm, appeared equally incapable of helping himself. He hadn't even reacted to my presence beside him.

At least for the moment, his nasty violence had been stopped.

CHAPTER EIGHTEEN

THE QUAD PULLED UP OUTSIDE THE house.

"We're here," said Tamati. He climbed off the bike and reached out his hand to help me slide off the carrier and stand up. I straightened up rather tentatively but found with pleasure that my body obeyed me, and I could stand without support.

I gave Tamati a relieved smile.

"The bumpy ride must have shaken the brain cells back into place," I told him. "I'm almost back to normal."

He gave an amused grunt, but his eyes lingered on my face. Self-conscious, I put my hand up and assessed the damage.

"Does it look bad?" I asked.

"It's not a good look," he replied, "least of all on a pretty lady, but I guess you'll heal OK. I'm picking it's pretty painful right now, but it's only superficial stuff."

I nodded, slightly reassured.

He turned to Steve.

"Let's get this lunatic sorted out."

I thought he intended me to help, but he smiled slightly and shook his head.

"Not you. You get yourself inside," he said. "Hey, Johnno,

come and give me a hand."

I looked around and realised for the first time we weren't alone. Two women were standing in the doorway. A group of men stood watching us from across the track and another, presumably Johnno, had already moved forward to help Tamati.

One of the women came down the steps towards me.

"Come on in," she said. "I'm Krystal." I watched her eyes narrow as she took in the damage to my face but she made no comment.

"I'm Claire," I said. I tried a smile, though my face felt stiff.

"Come with me," she said.

I was gently guided up the steps into the house.

"This is Maia," said Krystal, introducing the older woman. I assumed she was in her sixties, but she could have been older.

"Welcome," said Maia.

"Looks like you had a rough night," she said after a brief look at me. "We'll take you into the bedroom and I'll fix up something for your face." She was a stoutly built woman with short-cropped grey hair, steady dark eyes and a face lined with the sort of creases that came from laughter rather than anger or grief. I studied her and read a comforting mix of competence and compassion in her gaze.

For the first time in hours I felt safe.

I tried another smile and received a pat on the shoulder.

I looked behind to see Tamati and Johnno coming up the steps behind me with Steve.

I'd created a road block standing in the hallway. I allowed the women to lead me deeper into the house.

It was sparsely furnished, the furniture old and worn, but everything was tidy, well-ordered and homely as if the owner didn't have much money, but took pride in maintaining it to the highest standards. There was an overwhelming impression of neatness and cleanliness.

The women took me into a side room and sat me on a chair.

"I'll get you a cup of tea," said Krystal.

I slumped comfortably on my seat, and allowed the world and my responsibilities to fade away as I let these wonderfully kind strangers take care of me. I wondered if I should ask to use the phone, and at the very least contact Paraparaumu Aviation, then I remembered Steve had said there were no phones up here. I relaxed and allowed myself to drift.

Time flowed around me. I was strangely detached, and unnaturally content to be completely passive. I was given hot, sweet, milky tea – a combination I'd usually decline, but its warmth comforted me. I sipped it slowly.

Shortly afterwards, Melody joined me. We were given hot buttered toast and jam. I realised I was famished and Melody and I fought amiably for the last slice.

Maia came back. "Come over here, Claire," she said, indicating a mattress on the floor. Her quiet authority penetrated my apathy and I struggled to my feet.

"Lie down. I want to put this on your face." She indicated a bowl containing a dark green concoction.

"What is it?" I asked cautiously. It looked to me like a mess of cooked spinach, although the smell was pleasantly astringent.

"A mixture of kawakawa, kahikatea and kowhai bark."

"Oh," I said. I had no idea whether it would help my sore swollen face, but Maia was clearly being kind and I didn't want her to feel her help was rejected, so I lay back on the mattress and let her bathe my face with the mixture.

Her hands were firm but gentle as she applied a layer across my cheekbones and down my jaw to the chin. I felt a slight tingle as the mixture went on, but nothing worse, and as the liquid dried, I thought it sucked some of the painful swelling away.

I shut my eyes and gave a slight sigh of relief.

"Is it working?" Maia's voice sounded mildly amused.

"It feels good," I said honestly.

"I'm just about to do it again," she said. "Then I'm going to cover your face with a poultice for twenty minutes. I want you to keep your eyes shut so the mixture doesn't sting them. OK?"

"OK."

My face was bathed again, and then I felt her spread a heavier layer over the top. I kept my eyes shut, and allowed myself to relax. It was like having a facial.

"I want you to lie there and relax," said Maia. "I'll be back in twenty minutes." She covered me with a blanket and I allowed myself to give in. My last conscious thought was a little mental wriggle of elation that I'd managed that tricky landing. I smiled and gave way to my exhaustion. I was asleep, I think, before she left the room.

I woke when she returned and gently wiped the poultice away. Finally, she spread a light cream over my bruises.

"That will do for now," she said. "You'll be as pretty as ever soon."

I smiled faintly at her, but my eyes kept closing. I thought I felt her kiss my forehead, like Mum used to when I was a child.

"Sleep tight," I heard her say.

It was the last thing I knew for a long time.

*   *   *

I woke to find Melody curled up fast asleep beside me on the mattress. There was a moment of disorientation, before memory kicked in, when I couldn't imagine how I'd ended up in bed with a student. I stared at her stupidly before the events of the last twenty-four hours came crowding back.

I lifted my hands to my face and pressed my cheeks tentatively. The tight, stretched skin that had puffed up after Steve's blows had softened and eased, and the swelling had virtually gone. I wondered what I looked like. There was a mirror backing an old dressing table, but it was against the wall on the far side of the room. I couldn't be bothered moving. For the moment I was content to lie where I was, revelling in the comfort, warmth and safety of my situation. The light in the room was muted. I looked at the window expecting to see lace curtains then realised that the mist must have rolled in and blocked out the sun.

Jack would be here in New Zealand by now. I sent my thoughts out towards him, but received no reply. Apparently neither of us were sensitive enough for telepathy, or perhaps we weren't yet psychically bonded. I wondered when he'd realise I'd disappeared.

Roger should have been at work hours ago. I assumed he'd have notified the police that a plane was missing. I wondered if he'd found my note. I was still disappointed that the cavalry hadn't ridden in to rescue Melody and me when we were at Wairoa.

I looked across at her. She slept with the fierce concentration of a small child. I smiled. How different she'd turned out to be from the bolshie, self-absorbed teenager she'd seemed when Jim first brought her in.

I felt a surge of affectionate admiration. She'd had the presence of mind to remember the hatchet in the plane, retrieve it and hide it; she'd been uncomplaining through a difficult night, courageous enough to challenge Steve directly, and competent and self-assured enough to organise our group after I'd hurt Steve.

Melody was growing into one hell of a woman. I tried to remember what I'd been like at sixteen, and failed. I didn't think I'd been as composed or as mature as she was.

I gazed up at the ceiling and let my mind float free. I wondered whether the tea had been spiked, or whether there had been something in Maia's medicines that was a relaxant, but I felt a complete release from stress. I shut my eyes, and opened up my other senses. I could still smell the astringent, woody scent of the lotion Maia had used on my face. It had a sharp potency that was attractive. I tried to memorise the scent, but it was beyond easy definition, so I lay and let it work its magic.

The door opened and Maia came in. She smiled when she saw I was awake.

"How are you feeling?"

"Much better thanks," I said, propping myself up on my elbow. "Whatever was in your mixture seems to have worked a treat. My face is a lot less sore."

She smiled. "It's good stuff for reducing swelling. Do you want to get up? There's a hui through in the other room, and it might be a good idea for you to be there. Remind the silly sods of reality, rather than the macho track they're getting led down."

I could hear the dull rumble of conversation. In fact, I'd been vaguely aware of people talking since I'd woken up, but it was distant and the words had that abstract "'rhubarb, rhubarb'" sound that film directors use to suggest background conversation in crowd scenes. It didn't take a vast leap of imagination to work out the matter under discussion was the arrival of Steve and his assorted hangers-on. The morning's drama would be a juicy topic of conversation, and probably not the usual turn of events when a relative dropped in for a visit.

"How's Steve?" I asked.

Maia pulled a face. "I've made him comfortable, but he needs proper medical attention as soon as possible. Unfortunately, the rescue chopper can't come to get him because the cloud's down on the mountains, and we can't take him to hospital any other way because the road's blocked. I've given him some pain killers to get him through." She gave a fatalistic shrug. "Not much else we can do."

"You need a hand?" She reached out to help me up from the mattress, then took a searching look at me once I was standing. Whatever she saw must have pleased her, because she gave a little nod, as if to say "'you'll do'".

I walked over to the dressing table to check my face out, and gave a horrified gasp.

"Holy crap, I look like a nightmare." The swelling and stiffness may have been eased from my face, but Steve's blows had caused startlingly technicolour results. My cheeks, eye sockets and chin were an extraordinary mixture of colours, ranging from purple so dark it was almost black, through to lighter shades of pink, muddy yellow and grey. It was hard to find a clear patch of skin.

I was both appalled and fascinated. Maia had come to stand behind me and was watching my reaction.

"It's a bit dramatic," I said.

She gave a faint smile. "Fortunately it's only superficial, and the colours will fade in a few days, but yes, it's very dramatic and will tell its own story when you walk into that room."

I looked at her. There seemed to be some meaning I was missing, but she shrugged and said nothing.

I looked at myself again. "My hair's a right mess," I said,

putting my hand up to try and straighten it.

"Ow," I said involuntarily, as I touched tender areas. I checked my fingers. There was no sign of blood but my scalp felt raw where Steve had pulled my hair.

"Sore?" asked Maia.

"No, I'm fine," I said. I wondered whether he'd actually pulled chunks of hair out, and if I'd end up with tufts of hair as it regrew. It was impossible to tell in the dim light.

"Let me see," commanded Maia. She poked and prodded through my hair for a bit while I winced and flinched every time she hit on a sore spot.

"He's left you with a few raw patches. I'm not surprised it's sore."

She let me go. "I'll go and get you something to ease it," she said. "If you want to use the bathroom it's at the far end of the hall."

When I returned, Melody was awake and chatting to Maia.

"Here," Maia handed me a glass containing an opaque, watery mix.

"What's this made of?" I asked. It had never occurred to me to take an interest in alternative medicine before, but I'd been impressed with what Maia's concoction had done for my face.

"It's Disprin," said Maia, and then laughed, like a little girl, at my look. "You thought it was some secret Maori healing stuff I'd gathered from the bush? We do use modern drugs when they work."

I grinned, and slugged back the mix.

"Just asking."

"There are no willow trees up here to make aspirin from," she said, "even if I wanted to. There's nothing wrong with what's in a packet if it works."

Melody went off to the bathroom, and Maia produced a hairbrush and helped me brush my hair. As long as we stayed away from the really sore spots, it wasn't too bad an experience. She tied it back in a ponytail for me, and at least I looked slightly more presentable. There wasn't much that could be done with my crumpled clothes, though.

Melody returned and we exchanged wry glances as we looked over our hastily donned and now travel stained garments.

"I don't stink, do I?" Melody asked, concern in her voice.

I shook my head. "I was about to ask you the same."

"You're both fine," Maia assured us, "and once the meeting's over you can have a shower and freshen up."

"Meeting?" asked Melody.

Maia nodded. "The family are coming around. They've all heard about the trouble this morning. Steve's seriously injured, and the family are confused. He's sitting in there with the young lads, trying to position himself as a hero, some sort of urban terrorist."

"Who *is* Steve?" I asked. "He claimed he had family up here, so what's the connection? Is he a relative of yours?"

Maia sat on the bed. "Well, his grandfather was Poppa's brother, which made him my uncle. His son, my cousin, was Steve's father. So what does that make us? Second cousins once removed? Anyway, Steve is family, although he wasn't brought up here in the mountains. When his dad got married, they lived in town. Steve used to come up here sometimes in the holidays when he was a kid, but we haven't seen him in years."

There was a raucous shout of laughter from the other room, and Maia stood up.

"As if he hasn't done enough damage already, Steve's been trying to get all the young guys fired up. Very convincing he sounds too. You'd think he wanted to start World War Three up here in the Ureweras."

"What do you mean, firing the guys up?" I asked.

"You'll see," said Maia cryptically. "You two ready? OK, come on through."

CHAPTER NINETEEN

MAIA LED US ACROSS THE HALLWAY and stopped in the doorway. This was the family room, and today it was packed. At first I thought the audience were exclusively male, but then I saw Krystal sitting on a window seat, a small child on her lap, behind a group of young men on the floor. She waved when we walked in. Tamati stood beside her and gave us a smile.

Steve sat among a cluster of men in the centre of the room. Most of them looked in their teens. He looked pale, and I hoped he was in a lot of pain. He was still wearing his coat like a dressing gown. His wounded arm, now neatly bandaged, hung in a sling. Maia's painkillers must have been strong, because aside from his pallor, he wasn't demonstrating any sign of weakness. I was fairly certain that if *my* hand had been partially severed, I wouldn't look anywhere near as composed.

He'd been talking – almost holding audience, until he became aware of Maia in the doorway. His head snapped around towards us as we walked in, and I could read the anger in his look. He wanted revenge.

I mentally gave him the finger.

Glynn was in the group of men standing behind Steve. I

thought he looked awkward. As I watched he lifted his hand to his neck and ran his finger underneath the neckline of his T shirt as if it was constricting him. If I read his body language right, he wasn't enjoying his surroundings much.

Serves him bloody well right, I thought.

I realised then that Maia's pause in the doorway was a deliberate act to draw attention to our entrance. After a moment, when she was certain she'd captured her audience, she reached for me and, pushing me before her into the room, announced loudly and clearly,

"This is Claire. The pilot. She flew Steve and his friend up here. I want each and every one of you to look at her face. This is Steve's work. This is the sort of man he is."

She held me there, by the shoulders, for a long minute so I couldn't duck for cover. I felt my face burning in mortification. It's one thing to endure a beating, another to have your shame exposed in public and however I played it over in my head, I *was* humiliated. It wasn't enough to assure myself it wasn't my fault, or that I'd been attacked by a psychopath. The bruises on my face marked me as a victim and, by extension, fair game for anyone else who wanted to bully me.

I wrenched myself free at last. "Have you all had a good look?" I demanded. I glared around the room and noticed a few men drop their heads. Of those who held steady, not one met my eye, but stared off at some indeterminate point, casually distancing themselves from the situation. At the same time, there was a tangible frisson in the room comprised of voyeurism, lechery and excitement mixed with shame. Maia was right, Steve had been firing this lot up.

"This is what your 'cuzzie bro' did to me," I said with all the scorn I could muster. "Take a good hard look at what this 'great man' did. He'd have done more, if I hadn't done my best to chop his hand off. Now, have you all seen enough? Because I'm damned if I'll be a victim for any one of you to gloat over."

I forged a path across the room towards Krystal who was moving across to make space for Melody and me to sit down.

Our arrival, or perhaps my speech and smacked-up face, had

been a catalyst and triggered a pause in proceedings. Men stood, moved around, went out and came back with cups of tea. Others went to the bathroom. The level of chatter rose to a normal level. Steve stayed where he was, brooding. I saw him look at me but I ignored him.

Krystal smiled as we approached.

"How are you both feeling?" she asked.

"Much better," I said. Melody nodded.

"We managed to get some sleep so that's helped. What's going on here?"

Tamati spoke up. "Steve's on the run, right?"

I nodded. "I guess. I don't know whether he's running from the police, the gangs or both. But he and Glynn had to get away from Paraparaumu quickly. That's why they kidnapped us."

"Do you know what he's been doing? Why he's had to come up here to hide?" His voice was incredulous as he asked the question.

I shook my head. "A policeman friend of mine said something last night that made me think it was drug smuggling and that he and Glynn must have been bringing them in off a yacht. It took me a while to work it out. I was the one who flew them down to the rendezvous to pick the stuff up, and I didn't twig until too late. It's possible they've murdered someone down there as well, although that's just conjecture. But drugs, yes, I'm sure of it."

Tamati shook his head. "Ice. Yes, they've been importing P, but that's not the worst of it."

Melody looked puzzled. "What else were they doing?"

"Foot-and-mouth disease," said Tamati bleakly.

I frowned. "What do you mean?"

"That's what Steve's just told us. They've imported foot-and-mouth virus into the country to poison our herds in New Zealand."

I stared at Tamati in disbelief. "For fuck's sake. Why would anyone do that? That's beyond criminal. It's insane."

"It's what Steve's just said," Krystal confirmed. "It's 'eco-terrorism against the government of a colonial oppressor, and Tuhoe should join him in the struggle to overthrow a system imposed on Maori by white, land-grabbing settlers',", she quoted. "He says he wants us to win the land back for indigenous people."

"You're kidding."

"Nah," said Krystal. "He's just a few years too late, that's all. Te Urewera is a legally independent entity, and we Tuhoe are guardians and governors of our own land. Steve doesn't even know that about us. We achieved that for ourselves, without having to act like criminals and destroy the environment."

"He's insane," whispered Melody.

Krystal shook her head. "No, he's not insane, or not in the way you mean. He's just been using too much of his own product. He's off his head on P."

"P?" squeaked Melody.

I echoed her shock. I'd been flying a passenger who was off his face on drugs?

Tamati nodded. "That's why he was so violent this morning. He's unpredictable and dangerous. Look at him now. He's had his arm chopped through, but I doubt if he even feels it that much. Although he's sweating, and his face is pale, I don't think he's aware of his own symptoms."

"How do you know?" I asked curiously.

"About the P?" asked Krystal. "His shirt was ripped up and soaked with blood, so when Maia and I undressed him to bandage his arm, I took it away to wash out. I found his glass pipe along with his cigarettes and a little bag of crystals. I gave them back to him and he shoved them in his coat."

I thought about all the times during the past night that I'd seen Steve smoking. It had never occurred to me the tell-tale glow might be coming from a glass pipe rather than a cigarette.

"Shit," I said. "I don't suppose you got rid of his knife and gun? They were in the coat."

Krystal shook her head. "Nah. I only washed his shirt. The coat wasn't too stained with blood."

I sighed. "I wasn't happy about him being armed before. Now we know he's a druggie, it's even worse."

"What were you saying about foot-and-mouth?" asked

Melody.

Tamati explained. "Apparently the other dude, his uncle, used to work at a laboratory in England where they study the virus. When he moved to New Zealand he kept in contact with his old work mates. Somehow he's managed to get some of the virus smuggled out and brought into the country along with Steve's P. I think he's the mastermind behind the foot-and-mouth part. Steve's just a druggie."

"But why would Glynn want to import foot-and-mouth?" I asked. "It doesn't make sense. He's got no interest in Steve's crackpot revolution. And I know that's just a front anyway. I heard Steve discussing it. Steve's not interested in being a revolutionary, he just saw it as a way to curry favour up here. As for Glynn, he's a Pom. I doubt if he'd ever heard of the Tuhoe before today, let alone worried about Maori sovereignty. It's an incredibly dangerous thing to smuggle a disease like that into the country. It could wreck our economy."

Tamati shrugged. "You'd have to ask him," he said. "I thought he looked surprised when Steve was talking about a Tuhoe uprising. I'm picking it was the first he'd heard of it."

"Why has everyone met here?" asked Melody. "I wouldn't have thought Maia would have wanted a meeting like this in her house. Why hasn't she chucked them out?"

Tamati grinned. "Maia will be thinking that it's best to hear all the talk that's going around, rather than finding out about it later. This way she stands a chance of controlling what happens."

"Is this Maia's house?" I asked surprised. "I thought you'd said it was yours?"

"It is," said Krystal. "Maia is Tamati's mum. This is her house, and Tamati and I live with her when we come up here into the valley. She looks after us and the grandchildren and we look after her."

"You don't live up here then?"

"Nah. We come up here regularly, but supplies need to be brought in from outside, so not many people live up in the valley."

"Where is Maia, anyway?" I asked. "She seems to have

disappeared."

"She's gone to fetch Poppa," said Tamati. "She'll be back."

"Who's Poppa?" asked Melody.

"The old man?" Krystal grinned. "He's Maia's dad, and in the same way that she's Aunty to everyone in the village, whether they're related to her directly or not, the old man's the boss of everything. Not much happens up here in the valley that he doesn't know about."

Tamati's friend Johnno came over.

"We weren't introduced properly before," he said. "Are you two OK now?"

"Yes, thanks. Maia looked after us well," I said.

"Good," he replied. "Would you like a drink? There's tea or beer I could get for you?"

He was talking to me, but I could see his real interest was in Melody. The looks he gave her were admiring, and she was responding. Fair enough. Johnno was a good-looking man.

"Tea would be great, please," I said.

Melody nodded. "Me too."

Clearly her words broke the ice because Johnno now addressed her directly.

"You're OK? You were very calm when you arrived considering everything that had happened."

"She was bloody brilliant," said Tamati. "Stopped Steve's arm bleeding. Ordered me around. Got everyone marching ...."

"Oi! I did not," Melody protested, but she was laughing.

"You were amazingly brave," I agreed. "You took control of the situation like a pro."

"What happened to the axe?" asked Tamati.

"Uh, I've no idea. I can't remember." Melody looked startled, as she realised Tamati was laughing at her.

"I can't think of everything, you know," she said cheekily.

"It's on the quad," said Johnno. "I saw it there."

"It'll need to go back to the plane," I said. "It's part of the emergency gear."

"Well, it came in handy when we needed it," said Melody, "but I don't know that I'd have had the nerve to chop Steve's arm off."

"I was too scared to do anything else," I admitted. "I hadn't planned it, it was a reaction when he went for Melody."

"Hey, who knew city girls could be this tough?" Johnno said to Tamati. He grinned at us. "I'll go get the tea."

People were coming back from the kitchen in groups of two or three at a time. Some were chatting earnestly, and I assumed they were discussing Steve's proposal. I wondered what they really thought about what he'd been saying. Surely they wouldn't buy into his crazy scheme? They were polite and friendly, but I didn't see any sign they were about to set him up as a prophet to lead them into a grandiose nationalist campaign of terrorism. If anything, I thought, they were wary.

Someone had handed Steve a can of beer. The majority were drinking soft drinks or tea. As a group they seemed nearer a sociable sports team than a likely band of guerrilla fighters.

Johnno brought the tea to us just as Maia came back in.

"Good timing, eh?" he said as he handed over the hot drinks.

I nodded, and Melody smiled her thanks as I studied the man who had walked in with Maia.

In his youth he would have been tall, but age had bent him. Now he stooped, leaning on his ornately carved walking stick as he moved slowly into the room. Maia walked beside him, and several older people followed behind.

He was painfully thin. The flesh he'd once carried had been devoured and refined by the ageing process to reveal the planes and hollows of the skeleton beneath the skin. Tendons and sinews, which once supported muscle mass, now ran as stringy lines through his arms and hands.

A tweed jacket, fawn trousers, collared shirt and a knitted waistcoat gave him a quaint formality which alone would have made him stand out here where casual dress was the norm. The garments spoke of a time when a gentleman was distinguished by his clothes, and they had the effect of making him appear as if he'd stepped out of some nineteenth-century photograph. He wore a spiral of greenstone wound through each ear lobe. I thought what a fine subject he'd be for a classical New Zealand painter - Lindauer or Goldie, perhaps.

In another place and culture, he might have been relegated to a retirement village.

"'Granddad can't cope'," someone would have said, as they shuffled him away into a home. It would have been a lie.

Aged he might be but there was no disguising the vital intelligence in Poppa's face. His eyes were unclouded, aware and fierce. Behind the thin disguise of frailty this man was as proud and as wilful as he must have been fifty years earlier.

"'The boss'," Krystal had called him. If so, his dominance was not based on physical prowess but on the sheer force of his personality. The charisma of all he was clung to him like a cloak. There was no mistaking him as a leader, and it made the younger men in the room look like mere children.

A chair was pulled out for him and the women seated him comfortably. An extra cushion was brought to support his back. One of the men gave him a cup of tea.

There was a great air of ceremony as they carried out his care - a willing investment of time and affection for his dignity and wellbeing that was at once touching and spoke volumes for the man who could command it.

At last he was settled and Maia turned her attention to the rest of the gathering.

"Hey, boys," she called to men leaning in the kitchen doorway. "You'd better leave it clean and tidy in there. I don't want to be cleaning up your mess."

There was some grinning and muttering, which I read as amused affection for Maia. The man nearest the door looked back into the kitchen to check.

"It's OK, Aunty," he called. "They've done a good job. No mess."

"There'd better not be," Maia sniffed, and took a seat beside her father. "Steve, you come up here and pay your respects to Poppa."

Steve rose, helped to his feet by the man beside him, and made his way to the front of the room. I was amazed at how steady he was on his feet. He'd lost a lot of blood; shock and pain must have affected him, and if Krystal was right, he'd taken drugs. His endurance was phenomenal. He should have been pole-axed. Instead he moved carefully but steadily until he stood before the old man.

"Poppa," he said formally, holding out his left hand for a shake and simultaneously bending his head down for the hongi. They touched noses briefly, and Steve stood back while Poppa studied him.

"You've been wounded." It was a statement, not a question.

Steve nodded. "I'm OK, though."

"We've radioed for the rescue helicopter," said Maia. "It will arrive as soon as the weather allows. The mist is almost gone now, so with any luck it will be here soon, and he can get properly treated in hospital. He's going to need surgery if there's any chance of saving his hand."

"I don't need to go," said Steve impatiently. "I'm OK. Maia's looked after me. I don't want to leave here when I've only just arrived."

"Don't be stupid, boy," said Maia. "You can't risk losing your hand. The longer you leave getting your arm fixed, the less likely you'll have a usable limb. Of course you're going. You can always come back up here once the hospital has fixed you up."

She turned to Poppa. "It'll be a miracle, even so, if they manage to save his hand."

Steve looked unconvinced, and I thought he was about to argue when Poppa interrupted.

"Why are you here?" he asked. "And why have you brought these people with you?"

His eyes travelled around the room and I felt the flick of his attention as he picked out Glynn, Melody and me.

Steve hesitated, then stood up straighter.

"Glynn and I are in business together," he said. "Through him we've been able to import something into New Zealand that could change the course of our history and restore Maori to their rightful place as tino rangatiratanga. I've brought it here to show you, and to discuss how we implement an attack on the current government system that will utterly destroy it." He paused for effect.

Poppa said nothing, just sat there looking at Steve, his eyes never wavering as he gave his great nephew his full attention.

If Steve was flustered by the lack of encouragement, he didn't allow it to show as he continued his speech.

"You ask why did I come here? Because you are my whanau. You are my people and we share a famous tradition. The Tuhoe are proud, independent warriors who never relinquished their sovereignty over the land. Our rights and our land have been stolen from us, and we must fight to regain what is ours. Who better to be at the forefront of this but you, Poppa? You alone have that rare ability, the mana, to weave our people together, to make us strong and united against the enemy. With you as our leader, how can we fail?"

It was stirring stuff, and I could appreciate the power of Steve's rhetoric, even if it represented sedition, treason and half a dozen other crimes against the state. As a white skinned New Zealander, however, and a stranger here to boot, the subject matter made me deeply uncomfortable. Could a Maori uprising really be planned and instigated by an unstable, drug-addicted criminal like Steve?

New Zealand's modern post-colonial history is short and complicated. We like to consider ourselves egalitarian and non-racist as a nation, but the inequities that are the result of that history are indisputable.

Even so, there must be better ways of addressing the issues than eco-terrorism.

I noticed a couple of young men in the audience nodding their head in agreement with Steve's speech. Most, though, stayed silent, waiting for Poppa's reaction. It was impossible to know what they were thinking.

I glanced at Melody, and our eyes met. She was as troubled and confused as I was by this turn of events.

Poppa sat erect, his hands resting lightly on his walking stick. He had the air of an Old Testament patriarch about him as he studied Steve for a long moment.

"So suddenly you return to your whanau, not just with a mission, but with a weapon for us to use?" The voice was dry, the tone sarcastic.

I saw Steve squirm like a schoolboy.

"It could work, Poppa," he urged. "If we just have the courage to stand up for ourselves, we could sweep to victory."

"What is this weapon that's going to change the world?" Poppa asked.

His tone wasn't encouraging. I had a feeling he already knew the answer - Maia would have told him when she went to fetch him.

For the first time, Steve looked uncertain, and hesitated, but he'd already said so much he could hardly refuse to answer a direct question. Being Steve, he decided that attack was the best form of defence.

"Two canisters of ampoules that contain foot-and-mouth disease," he said. "What we'll do is release the virus at a dairy farm, infect the animals, and that's the end of New Zealand's dairy industry. In two weeks we can bring the economy of the country to its knees, destabilise the government, and force a revolution. They won't know what's hit them, but we'll be prepared. We had a trial run with the virus a week ago in the Waikato. It worked a treat. We only have to spread it in a couple more locations, and the disease will become unstoppable."

He paused, and looked around the room, working the audience with his gaze. "This is a catalyst for change, my brothers and sisters. We have the means to redress endless wrongs to our people, to our iwi, to our family. Let us take it with both hands and walk, unafraid, into the cauldron of social uprising. We will emerge as the winners we were always destined to be. Let us grab this opportunity, and let only cowards and the weak try to sway us from the bright light of our shared destiny."

You couldn't fault Steve's presentation. He'd pitched his message with messianic fervour and conviction. There was passion, enthusiasm and complete self-belief ringing through his words. Even I was swayed and felt a pang of guilt and self-doubt. Had I, all these years, been caught up in a privileged white woman's view of New Zealand society? Should the unthinkable be used as a shock tactic to enforce change in our country? We prided ourselves on being a multi-racial society, and yet Maori tikanga was still as foreign to me as Outer Mongolian. The only time I'd been on a marae was on a trip when I was in primary school. I'd never been to a tangi, never had to recite my pepeha, that statement of identity that connects Maori to their ancestry and their land. I'm New Zealand born and bred, yet I knew very little of the culture of these New Zealanders I'd met today up here in the mountains. I felt my values waiver beneath Steve's fervour.

For a brief moment the only thing that kept me centred was knowing Steve's history and modus operandi. The marks on my face bore witness to his brutality, and I knew in my bones that under no circumstances could he be trusted as a leader of anything. Nor did I, for one minute, believe Steve cared for Maori sovereignty or any other high ideal. He was an opportunist, using what was at hand to save his skin.

There was some murmuring among the group standing behind Maia. Poppa gave a slight sniff but made no comment on Steve's speech.

"Who are your companions?" he asked. "Introduce that man to me," he said, indicating Glynn.

Glynn made his way forward and shook hands with Poppa, although he noticeably shied away from the hongi and achieved more of a knocking of foreheads than a touching of noses.

Steve explained that Glynn was his uncle.

"You brought the disease into the country?" Poppa asked.

Glynn nodded. "Yes. I did."

"Why?"

There was a perceptible pause as Glynn stared at Poppa.

"Uh …" he stammered, stopped and then turned to Steve for guidance.

"It's like I said, Poppa …, Steve began.

"Quiet," commanded Poppa, shutting Steve up. "This man will speak for himself."

"Well," said Glynn, "it's as Steve told you. I'm more of a

business man, so I imported the canisters. Steve here had the contacts to distribute them."

"I asked *why* you brought the disease here," said Poppa. "I want you to tell me why you did it."

Glynn hesitated again, but Poppa's eyes were firmly fixed on him, and in the end he caved in under their glare.

"I was paid to," he said at last.

A soft sigh travelled around the room in response.

Poppa sat up straighter. "Who paid you?"

"I was paid to bring the disease in. That's all."

Poppa thumped his walking stick on the floor, making us all jump.

"You think you're being funny, is that it?" he shouted.

Glynn shook his head, and stepped back a pace. I didn't blame him. Poppa was bristling with anger.

"I want a straight answer from you," said Poppa. "Don't keep avoiding it. I want truth. Who paid you?"

"It was a consortium of businessmen."

"What sort of businessmen need a disease imported into New Zealand? They must be in a very strange line of work." There was a titter of laughter from the audience.

"They were speculators." Glynn's voice was so low I could only just make out the words.

"Speak up, man," said Poppa. "What did you say they were?"

I had no doubt he'd heard perfectly well the first time, but wanted to drive home his mastery of the situation.

"They were speculators," said Glynn, more loudly this time.

He shrugged his shoulders, forestalling the next, obvious question. "They wanted to gamble on the share market. If New Zealand lost its dairy industry, then other world markets would benefit, and if my clients bought up shares in those businesses, they'd become very wealthy."

"Shit!" I heard Tamati whisper beside me. I agreed with him. The plan was startling in its ruthless simplicity.

I was reviewing the flights I'd taken with Glynn. Had there ever been an indication of the depth of his villainy? In a sense I found Steve's simple thuggishness easier to understand than this calculated, venal project. I felt sick that I'd been used, however innocently, as a tool in such a venture.

There were quiet conversations taking place throughout the room as we all tried to comprehend what the implications of such a scheme might be.

I glanced across at Poppa. His head was turned, listening to something Maia was telling him.

Glynn and Steve still stood together in front of him, uncertain what to do, both looking more like errant school boys than master criminals and terrorists. It might have been funny if you didn't wonder how much damage the two of them had caused already by their actions.

Poppa nodded at Maia at last and turned back to the rest of us. He banged his stick on the floor again, and the room quietened down.

He turned to Steve.

"So, it seems you are not here to save our people with a crusade, but you're simply a tool for a greedy man," he said scathingly.

"But Poppa," Steve replied, "the two don't have to be separate, don't you see? Glynn may have his reasons, but that doesn't mean we can't use …"

"Quiet!" Poppa commanded. "We've all listened to your ideas, and every person in this room now knows just how stupid and evil they are."

He paused in his speech, and visibly gathered himself together.

"You have no idea what you're saying, do you? Your whole way of thinking is wrong and corrupt. We don't own the land. This land owns us, and we are its guardians. You don't even know that's enshrined in law now, do you? You've had no contact with your whanau for years. You know nothing about what it means to be Tuhoe."

Poppa thumped his stick on the ground.

"How dare you come to me here and talk about poisoning the land! How dare you talk of polluting our water and our animals! This is the land, our mother and we cherish her, as she provides for us. How can you stand here, in sight of our sacred mountain, and speak such filth to us? We are the conservators of our lands, not the destroyers. We have fought and spilt our blood to preserve our land. That is the Maori way. I am ashamed of you. You claim to belong to our whanau, yet you want to destroy us and all that we stand for."

Beside him I saw Maia nodding her head.

There was complete silence in the room as the old man spoke. Those who had listened to Steve, tempted by his rhetoric earlier in the day, now looked at the floor and were careful not to catch each other's eye.

Poppa had laid down the law, and that was that.

Steve looked devastated. The fictional world he'd invented for himself to be a hero in had been destroyed by a few pungent phrases. He paled and staggered as if the shock of rejection had finally cut through his drug-imposed invulnerability. Glynn put out his arm to steady him.

Steve stood, rocking on his feet, looking at the old man.

"I need your help, Poppa," he pleaded. "OK, it wasn't about Maori sovereignty, I admit that. The cops were taking too much of an interest in me and Glynn and I needed to come somewhere safe. I hoped we could stay here for a while until things blew over."

"And why should anyone here give you shelter?" Poppa's anger was scathing. "You bring your filthy disease, and your foul drugs – oh yes! - I know about the methamphetamine - into our pristine land. You dare to bring this into our nation, up here to our people? Have you no care for the destruction and damage you could cause? Shame on you. Shame on both of you!" He was so angry he was panting by the end of the rant.

"But Poppa … " Steve wasn't taking his rejection well. He pulled away from Glynn's support to make another plea.

"You think you're so clever with your city ways, coming into Te Urewera to tell us how to live and fight? You forget, we've had prophets before, and we know the difference between real leaders and shoddy con-men. You leave here today. I don't care whether you go in the rescue helicopter, whether you fly out again in your plane, or whether you walk out." The walking stick pounded the floor, punctuating the speech. "You leave and don't ever come back."

The force of Poppa's rage was so powerful, Steve actually stepped back in alarm.

I understood now what Krystal had meant when she talked about Poppa being the boss. Poppa had spoken, and his decision was final. I couldn't see anyone challenging it, and it seemed that, his judgement given, Poppa had lost interest in Steve and Glynn, although they still stood in front of him looking lost.

"Never argue with a kaumatua," said Krystal softly.

Poppa looked across the room to Melody and me, lifted his arm and beckoned us. Maia gave us both a reassuring smile as we approached, which was kind, as I was nervous. It felt a bit like being summoned to meet royalty.

I didn't like having to stand so close to Steve, even if he had been dealt with and sentenced. I could feel his presence behind me, and it lifted the hair on my neck although I knew there was little damage he could do to anyone now.

Melody shook hands, bent towards Poppa for the hongi and gave him a big grin of delight as she rose from the embrace.

"Thank you for letting us be here," she said like a polite school girl.

Poppa was apparently not immune to a pretty young girl smiling at him, and chuckled. "You are welcome," he said as he patted her hand.

Then it was my turn. I leaned towards him, let my nose touch his, and felt the softness of his breath on my cheek. I'd never realised how intimate a greeting the hongi was, nor how much warmth and emotion it could convey. I too was smiling as I pulled away.

"Why are you with these men?" Poppa asked Melody.

"We were kidnapped," she said. "They needed Claire to fly the plane, and Steve said he wanted me as a hostage. Steve hurt Claire."

Poppa looked at my face, then at Maia.

"She'll be OK," said Maia, answering the unspoken question. "The swelling has come down, and the bruises will be gone in a week. But he's *vicious*," she said, glaring at Steve.

"What would you like to do?" asked Poppa. "If you wish to leave immediately the weather appears settled enough for you to fly out, otherwise you're both welcome to stay."

"I should really get myself and the plane back to home base as soon as I can," I said. "But first I'd be grateful if we could find some way of letting everyone know we're OK. Melody's father must be frantic about her, and my boss will be much the same. We need to let people know what's happened to us, where we are, and that we're safe."

Melody nodded. "Dad will be beside himself. Steve wouldn't let me bring my mobile so we've had no way of communicating."

Poppa nodded. "Hey, Tamati," he called across the room.

Tamati had turned to reply when we heard the unmistakable beat of helicopter blades.

"That'll be the rescue chopper," Maia said placidly. "About time they showed up."

The noise grew louder, sufficiently intense to rattle the panes of glass. Half the room gravitated to the windows to watch the helicopter put down.

"Hey, look at that," said Johnno approvingly. "You're getting door-to-door service, Steve."

With no runway required to land the chopper, it was able to settle onto the track a hundred metres away. From where I stood beside Poppa, we couldn't see it land, but there was plenty of commentary from the people close to the window.

"It's not just one helicopter. There's two others coming in as well," declared Krystal. Then she gave a slight cry. "I think it's the police. They're landing right outside."

I heard one of the men shout, "It's a police raid."

CHAPTER TWENTY

STEVE MOVED WITH LIGHTNING SPEED. DISTRACTED by the approach of the helicopters, everyone had rushed to watch them land and no one had been looking at him. In one stride he'd grabbed me with his good arm, and swung me around against his body, pinning me against his shoulder.

"What the … " He'd caught me completely by surprise, but for the moment I wasn't frightened. I knew his arm was badly damaged, and I'd no qualms about hurting it some more to escape him. I resented bitterly finding myself held, face against his shoulder, as if we were in some obscene embrace.

The contact disgusted me and I twisted violently around in his grip, trying to free my fists to smash down on his wounded wrist.

"Oi!" cried Poppa, suddenly noticing. "Steve, let her go."

There was a babble noise around us as others registered what was happening.

"I don't think so," snarled Steve. "This isn't your business, old man."

I ignored him and continued to struggle. If I could free my arms they would be effective weapons.

Then an object was shoved hard in my left side at waist level.

It was such an unexpected development I stopped writhing.

"Do you feel that?" Steve's voice purred above my head. "Remember the gun? It's in my pocket. If you, or anyone else, try anything, a bullet will fly straight into your kidneys. Understand?"

Holy crap! How could I have forgotten the gun! Bugger. Krystal had talked about finding his P kit, but hadn't confiscated the gun or knife.

I heard a gasp from Glynn. "Hey, wait on, mate," he said urgently. "Steady up, this won't help us."

Steve ignored him.

I didn't dare move, and stood rigid within the circle of his injured arm. His hand might be useless, but he still had enough strength in the rest of the limb. I knew Steve was as dangerous as a cut snake at the best of times, and being banished by his Poppa probably hadn't put him in a good mood. I felt him fumbling around with his left hand, and realised he was trying to pull the weapon out of its concealed pocket. Everyone was now focused on the drama unfolding in the room. Tamati had leapt forward, but when he realised Steve was armed with a gun pointing at me, he'd frozen in position.

"Let her go," demanded Melody. "Let. Her. Go." Her voice rose shrilly into the stunned silence of the room. She tried to pull on his left arm and was shoved away roughly.

"Shut up, you little bitch," said Steve. "Remember, I can kill her any time I want, so don't give me any shit." He'd worked the gun free and held it by my side. I wondered how accurate a shot he would be with his left hand. Not that it mattered. He could shoot me anywhere he chose at this close range.

Poppa looked as shocked as the rest of the room but recovered quickly and banged his stick on the ground for attention.

"Quiet!" he shouted. "Stop acting like a mad man. Steve, let the woman go," he ordered.

I felt Steve move behind me, and realised he was shaking his head.

"No, old man. You didn't want to help me, so you can shut the fuck up now. Do you think I'm going to let the pigs get me? I'm not going back to prison again. Not ever. I'd rather die than be shut up again." His words dripped with scorn and anger.

I saw shock move over Poppa's face.

"You didn't know that, did you, old man. You ask why I haven't been up to visit you? I was in Paremoremo prison for five long years. That's why you didn't get a Christmas card from me, or a phone call on your birthday."

He took a deep, shaking breath. "I thought I could trust you to help, but you've turned your back on me. My fucking whanau! What a joke you all are. But I'll tell you something for free, old man. Half the people in this room wanted to join with me and my plan before you stopped them. They were really keen, and you can't keep control forever."

He was so worked up, a spray of saliva flew out with his words. "You're old, Poppa, and your ways are over. It won't be long before someone else takes your place. Young Maori are taking control now. You don't want to help me, that's fine, but you don't get to tell me what to do now."

"Let the woman go," Poppa repeated. "Don't make a bad situation worse."

Steve gave a snort of amusement. "She's my hostage. They can't hurt me if I've got her in front of me. It's why I brought the women with us."

He tightened his arm, drawing me closer against him. I could feel his body quivering with tension. He turned to Melody.

"You, blondie," he said, "walk in front of us to the door, and open it. I want to see what's out there and what the pigs are up to. And no funny business. The rest of you stay back in here. Remember she gets it if you try and screw me."

Melody's eyes blazed fury when she looked at Steve, but she was helpless. Her eyes met mine and we shared a look of deep frustration.

We'd thought our troubles were over, but instead they'd just escalated.

She shrugged, conceding defeat, turned and walked, very slowly, out of the room towards the front door.

Steve pushed me ahead, his arm still pinning me against him.

"Open the door," Steve commanded Melody.

Steve pushed her through first, then me as a shield in front of him. It meant he had to peer over my left shoulder to see, but it also meant his left arm was free to aim his gun anywhere he chose.

The scene outside was chaotic. Although the helicopters were on the ground, their blades were still spinning, so the noise was intense.

There were a lot of people about, and I realised that while Steve had been forcing Melody and me to the front door, the other occupants of the house had escaped via the back door and were currently scarpering out of harm's way. I recognised some of the bystanders. Nothing like a lunatic armed with a gun to get people moving.

I hoped Poppa and Maia had managed to get out safely. Poppa would be in no position to run anywhere, and given what had been said between them, I wouldn't trust Steve not to hurt him if he got the chance.

I realised Glynn hadn't come outside with us and assumed he'd taken the opportunity to run. I'd felt he was uncomfortable with the direction Steve was taking them since we'd first arrived in the valley. This last scenario must have been one step too many. He had, after all, described himself as a business man. I didn't imagine an armed siege had been part of his plans.

The Eastland Rescue helicopter was shiny white with its bold logo and red and gold stripes. In contrast, the police choppers were dark charcoal grey. Krystal had described them as being right outside. Standing on the porch with a gun shoved into my side, they seemed a million miles away.

Steve stood and watched. For once he wasn't fidgeting. Instead he seemed mesmerised by the activity.

I wondered whether Steve had any idea what he hoped to achieve by using Melody and me in this way. He couldn't have planned it. He'd just responded instinctively, grabbing any advantage he could, when he'd heard police were outside. It felt intolerable that help and safety were only a few hundred metres away in front of us, and yet we were helpless because of the threat of one sawn-off shot gun.

There was a good deal of action going on around the helicopters. I wondered how the air ambulance crew were supposed to work in with the police. Steve's damaged arm still had to be treated. I knew little about the effects of whatever drug he was taking, but at some time the effects must surely wear off and he'd be in a lot of pain.

I was impressed the police had managed to find us at all. After their failure to show up at Wairoa, if I'd given them any thought it was to assume no one would be able to track a transponder up into these hills. Once Melody and I had seemed to be safe, I hadn't considered them at all.

It was a long time before Steve apparently had seen all he wanted to, and pulled me back into the house.

"Blondie," he said, "get back here." For a mutinous moment Melody looked as if she'd refuse, but common sense prevailed and after a brief hesitation, she complied, shutting the door behind us.

Steve pulled me back into the room we'd used for the meeting. It was empty. I was pleased to see that Poppa and Maia had managed to get out. Steve gave a grunt as he looked around.

At last he stepped away and eased his clamping arm away from my body. It was wonderful to be free of his touch, but as I stepped out of his grip I discovered my knees had turned to jelly once again.

"You two sit over there," Steve said, indicating the window seat where Krystal had been sitting earlier.

I was happy enough to obey. Not only were my knees shaky, but my pulse was racing and my breathing was tense and ragged.

The window seat allowed a clear view of the activity outside. Civilians had now been efficiently cleared from the scene. Those people who remained were clearly professional, and I noticed, armed. I suppose I should have been reassured. Guns in the hands of the good guys had to be better than in the hands of the bad guy. Right?

Wrong. From where Melody and I sat, either side had an equally good chance of pinging us.

"I hope they don't open fire." Melody's words echoed my thoughts. We exchanged sober glances.

It was all too easy to recall news reports of hostage stand-offs where things had gone wrong and innocent lives been lost in the crossfire. I deeply respect the New Zealand Police Force – hell, I'd been sleeping with one of its more attractive representatives for the last few months – but accidents can happen.

I smiled at Melody, while my thoughts automatically drifted to Jack.

"What's the time?" I asked.

She checked her watch

"One o'clock," she replied.

Still early afternoon then. So much had happened over the last twenty-four hours that time had become a fluid concept and I was surprised how little time had actually elapsed.

Jack would have been back in New Zealand for a few hours now. I wondered if he'd been told what had been happening. I knew from experience how fast news can travel within the police force. I'd like to think he'd called me when he landed, and wondered why my phone hadn't been answered.

No point in thinking about him now, I told myself, and deliberately erased him from my mind. There'd be time for gentle reflection and soft emotions later, if Melody and I survived the next hours.

For now, I needed to be focused on the present, and ready to take advantage of any opportunity to escape.

Steve paced restlessly around the room. I turned my head to study him and place him in a context I could understand. I'd once watched a tiger at the zoo, that strode up and down the glass window that divided him from the watching public. It, too, had been restless, unsettled and dangerous. I tried to extend the analogy to Steve. His febrile, edgy energy drove him, no doubt of that, and he'd had that air of danger about him from the first time I'd met him.

I ran out of metaphors. A tiger? Probably not. There was something glorious about a tiger. If I had to deal in animal metaphors, Steve was more of hyena or a wild dog.

Bored with his pacing, Steve at last flung himself into the chair Poppa had been sitting in and lit a cigarette. There was nothing relaxed about his posture. Even sitting, he couldn't seem to be still. One of his legs jiggled up and down incessantly, a movement he apparently wasn't even aware of. I studied it for a while, wondering how much energy it must take to keep a leg in motion like that. I knew Steve hadn't slept since we'd arrived at Maia's house; he'd barely dozed off on the flight, and heaven knows whether he'd got any sleep the day before. The man had to be running purely on nerves and drugs now.

The radio crackled into life. "Steve," said a disembodied voice.

I saw Melody jump and grimaced at her reaction. The sudden intrusion of the outside world into our isolation came as a shock. Steve surged to his feet and began to search the room, eventually locating the console on a small table at the back of the room.

The radio was an older model but similar to the one we had at back at base. Steve hesitated a moment before reaching out for the handpiece.

"You pick it up and press the button to talk," I said helpfully.

He picked it up, and stared at the radio for a moment. Eventually he pressed the transmitter button.

"Yeah? It's Steve Freeman."

The reply was instant.

"Hi Steve, we just need to know how you all are. We know you've been wounded. The rescue helicopter is here to get you to hospital. Do you want to come out now and get on board?"

"And let you bastards take me? No."

"Are the women all right, Steve?"

"The women are fine. I'm not letting them go until I get what I want. If you want the Mason girl, then I want cash. If her dad wants her back in one piece, he'll have to pay the price. Until then, she stays with me. The other one I'll keep until I'm safe out of here. I might need her to fly me, and anyway, if you threaten me, she dies."

"We'll need to talk about your request, Steve. I'll call you back shortly."

Melody and I looked at each other. She pulled a face.

"I suppose we should be grateful the whole thing's coming to a head at last," I remarked. "At least the police have made contact."

Steve dropped the transmitter and looked at us. "Shut up, the both of you," he said as he turned and sat down again. His leg resumed its tense juddering.

I stood up. "I'm just putting some more wood in the burner," I said when Steve started to order me back.

"It's getting colder, and if we don't keep the fire going it will be really cold later when the sun goes."

He shrugged, and let me load the pot-belly stove up with wood. As I'd thought, there were only glowing embers left inside. I took my time, feeding the fire with kindling and encouraging the small flame, before adding larger logs.

The work steadied me, and Steve's acquiescence made me bolder.

"I'm hungry," I said. "I guess we all are. Shall I go into the kitchen and see what I can rustle up to eat?"

That was apparently a step too far.

"You get back here and sit down." Steve had risen to his feet, yet again pointing the gun at me. "You're not going anywhere. You think I'm stupid or something?" There was a note of panic in his voice which worried me. A panicked Steve would be a dangerous Steve.

"OK, OK," I said as I returned to the window seat. "Don't get your knickers in a knot. I was just asking because it's been a long time since any of us have had anything to eat. I thought I could make something simple and hot for us, like grilled cheese on toast. A hot drink as well. It might make us all feel better."

"I am hungry," echoed Melody wistfully. "You could watch us and make sure we didn't get up to anything," she offered.

Steve didn't respond. After a moment I gave-up, and settled back to watching what was happening beyond the window. I was too frightened of Steve to challenge him directly. Melody gave me a dismal look, and I reached out to hold her hands. Her fingers curled around mine. I could feel her hand trembling, and tightened my own fingers reassuringly. We exchanged nervous smiles. At least we had each other's support through this ordeal.

In the distance another helicopter was coming in to land. It was small in comparison to the rescue chopper. My eyes narrowed as I watched it. It was too far away for me to read the markings, but I recognised it as a white Hughes 300. Paraparaumu Aviation had an identical aircraft. Roger had taken me up a couple of times and allowed me to handle the controls, so I identified the type with certainty.

I knew it was improbable that Roger had actually flown up here, however concerned he was about his missing C172, but the familiar sight of the chopper had, for a moment, filled me with hope, and now, as I realised my folly, with a surge of what could only be called home sickness.

I leant back, let my cheek rest against the cool glass, and shut my eyes.

CHAPTER
TWENTY ONE

W E SAT IN SILENCE. I WAS WEARY and despondent and Melody looked much the same. Behind us, Steve twitched and jiggled on his seat, alternating with long minutes of restless prowling around the room.

Boredom itself created its own fears and tensions.

I heard my tummy rumble.

Melody, hearing it as well, gave a giggle.

"We need food," she said. "I'm starving."

"Tell me about it," I replied.

Steve heard us talking.

"You two shut up," he said. His eyes narrowed on Melody in an assessing gaze.

"Maybe there's something else we can do to pass the time," he said suggestively. "What do you say, blondie?"

I heard a sharp intake of breath from Melody as she registered the threat.

Steve stood and approached us. Melody shrank back on the seat.

I tried to think rationally. Surely his injury would render him incapable of attacking us. He had a gun, of course, but presumably a rape would involve putting it down? I'd just braced myself to launch an attack when the police called up on the radio again.

The crackly voice calling his name distracted Steve. He looked blankly around the room for a second before registering the source of the noise and moving towards the radio.

As Steve picked up the transmitter, Melody glanced at her watch. "That's an hour," she said in a shaky voice.

"What?" I asked. I was too rattled to be thinking clearly.

Once again, her courage under fire amazed me. I tried to pull my shattered nerves back together.

"It's been an hour since the last contact. I read somewhere that it's standard procedure in armed offender incidents. You know, call up every hour and keep the pressure on. I suppose they hope the gunman will be rattled into making a mistake or something."

"Hm," I muttered, "or else goad him into doing something stupid to the poor hostages." I was watching Steve. He seemed twitchier and more highly strung than ever. I didn't feel this was a positive sign.

At the very least he had to be seriously sleep-deprived which must have been affecting his rational behaviour.

"What do you mean, negotiate?" Steve was asking. "I've fucking told you what I want. The girl doesn't leave here until I've got the cash."

"Surely that's impractical," I whispered critically to Melody. "Even if anyone wanted to help him, there's hardly an ATM here to draw money from. He'd be better to organise a transfer to an offshore account or something." I admit freely that my knowledge of criminal activity was limited to TV programmes. I was vague on details, but I definitely connected offshore accounts with money gained from criminal activity.

"We need to see the women. How do we know they're alive? What guarantee can we give her father that Melody Mason is all right and worth ransoming?"

"Of course she's still alive. Look in the bloody window. She's sitting right there. I haven't laid a finger on her." Steve's voice was rising in volume and pitch.

"Oh, for fuck's sake," he said eventually. "Fine. I'll bring her to the door, but you'd better keep your people right back. Mason can come closer, but only him. I'll have my gun on her the whole time, so no smart moves."

"Does that mean Dad's here?" Melody breathed.

I raised my brows. It sounded like it.

Melody's face lit up.

"He'll be accompanied by the negotiator in this case. He needs to be there." The voice on the radio was adamant.

"Al right then. The two of them. But only them. I want their hands up where I can see them. Keep the rest of your men back. I won't hesitate to shoot if you try anything."

Steve gestured to me. "Get back over here."

I was too slow for his liking, so he strode across the room and hauled me up with his left hand.

"Don't play dumb," he threatened. "Get back in front of me. You too," he said to Melody.

He pulled me close to his body again and held me in the curve of his right arm. Melody walked ahead to the front door.

"Open it," he ordered. "Just remember there's a bullet with her name on it if you do anything stupid."

Melody gave me an apologetic glance before turning and opening the door.

The men walked towards us. Still too far away for us to identify him otherwise, Jim's white hair was easy to pick. I watched him increase his pace as he saw his daughter. Lord knew what the poor man must be feeling. Every jerky stride he took as he accelerated towards us spoke of his tension and anguish.

In front of me Melody stood straight and silent, staring at her father. She never uttered a word, but her shoulders, so close in front of me, shook with the strain of holding herself there. It was a peculiar form of torture, to be so near those you care about and the safety of their presence, and be unable to reach for them.

The men came closer. I couldn't bear to watch Jim's pain and averted my gaze to take in the police officer beside him. My body jolted as my breath caught in my throat. I converted the gasp to a hasty cough to conceal my reaction, and I looked across the metres between us into Jack's dark eyes.

His face was impassive. He gave no flicker of recognition

or any other emotion as his eyes scanned me. I saw his glance linger on my bruised face, then check the rest of me. His steady pace never faltered as he crossed the distance. I might have had no more significance to him than a painting in a museum.

I couldn't imagine how he had got up here to Te Urewera so quickly. I'd imagined him stuck in Wellington in a management meeting, not within feet of me in this remote spot. With all my being I wanted to cross the distance between us and throw myself into his arms. We hadn't been a couple for very long, but in the time I'd known him, I'd always been able to count on his support and affection. I ached to go to him.

I bit my lip, steadied and forced myself to avoid his gaze and stare a few inches over his head. Maybe he was a hallucination I had conjured into being. Jack's presence was so unexpected I'd lost the self-discipline I prided myself on. I made myself take a couple of deep breaths and relax my shoulders. I found it helped settle my breathing which once again had grown ragged.

In this unstable state I watched the men draw nearer. When they were no more than ten metres away, Steve moved.

"Stop," he said. "No closer." He propelled me forward to stand beside Melody at the front of the porch. Melody flinched as Steve pushed beside her, but said nothing.

Jim saw, and reached out involuntarily to her. It was a tiny gesture, instantly controlled and withdrawn, but Steve responded immediately.

"Don't move," he threatened. "If either of you takes another step, she gets it." He indicated Melody with his chin. Jim stood obediently motionless, but it was clear what it cost him. He was as blanched pale as his daughter, his eyes hard. And although he stood unmoving, I saw his hands were clenched in tight fists by his sides.

Roger had, some weeks ago, warned me not to fuck with Jim. I couldn't remember the exact words, but Roger had referred to Jim as being tough, and possibly a bit of a villain.

Villain or no, I suspected if Jim ever managed to meet Steve without Melody as a shield or the protection of a firearm, Steve would be history. I imagined a very large number of people owed him favours he'd be happy to consider redeemed if they gave him Steve's scalp.

My attention switched back as Jack, who was still ignoring me, spoke.

"Your name is Steve?" he asked politely.

Steve nodded.

"My name's Jack. I'm hoping we can negotiate and resolve this situation safely so no one needs to get hurt." Jack's voice was calm, warm, reasonable and as soothing as a cup of hot chocolate.

"There's nothing to negotiate," Steve snapped, apparently impervious to Jack's pleasantness. "Give me the money and safe passage out of here and you can have the girl."

"How much do you want?" Jim asked. There was nothing soothing about Jim's voice. Raw emotion roughened each word.

Steve shifted beside me and took a deep breath.

"A million." The phrase was so explosively uttered, both Melody and I turned to stare at him. The force of his words seemed to have startled him as well. Perhaps he'd never imagined the actuality of saying them.

He cleared his throat.

"I want a million bucks in cash," he said to Jim. "Then she's yours."

"I'll have to organise it." Jim's voice was equally curt. "Are you sure that's what you want? It will take time for me to get that amount of money in cash and then take hours to get it up here. You realise this is a long way from anywhere and the roads are blocked? I can't make it happen quickly."

I felt Steve shrug. "I'll be waiting."

His grip on me tightened as he drew me backwards to the front door.

"Back up, blondie," he ordered Melody. "Turn right around and get back in the house."

"We need to sort things out, Steve." Jack's voice stopped us. "You can get through this without making the situation worse. Let the women go free. If you extort money, it will be another charge against you. Don't do things now that you'll regret later.

Let us work together to end this in the best possible way."

Steve's body jerked in response.

"You're the police," he snarled. "Do you think I'd trust you? I know your tricks. You can keep your courts, and your justice. I'm not going back inside again." He waved the gun somewhere in the vicinity of my head and I flinched involuntarily. My eyes met Jack's but he gave no reaction.

"She's my shield," continued Steve. "As long as she's in front of me, you won't try anything, so piss off, pig. Take your negotiations and shove them where the sun don't shine."

He shuffled back a few more paces with me.

"Get my money," were his last words before Melody and I were in the house and Steve had slammed the door.

CHAPTER
TWENTY TWO

WITH THE DOOR SAFELY CLOSED BEHIND us, Steve released his hold on me. This time he eased away carefully, as if he was starting to register the pain of his arm, and I watched as he leaned back against the wall for a moment.

I took advantage of his stillness to walk briskly down the hall towards the kitchen. I'd just about made it before he spoke.

"Get back in the lounge," he ordered.

I turned and shook my head.

"I'm going to get us something to eat, and a hot drink," I said firmly. "We can't go forever without eating."

"And I need to go to the bathroom," stated Melody.

Steve's shoulders slumped. "Fine." He had to be as hungry as the rest of us.

I didn't wait for him to reconsider his decision but entered the kitchen.

I wanted to be alone for a moment to recover my composure. Jack's unexpected presence had deeply shaken me. I felt both better and worse knowing he was outside the house – better because I loved him and felt safer knowing he was close by, working to set us free; worse because it heightened my fear that the stand-off with Steve might not have a happy ending and I might never have a chance to say goodbye.

I shut my eyes and said a brief prayer to a god I wasn't certain I believed in. I had tears in my eyes when I opened them again which I rubbed away hastily. Showing weakness in front of Steve was unlikely to be a good move.

Like the rest of Maia's home, the kitchen was spotlessly clean, utilitarian and tidy, except for the discarded cups and mugs left behind when the meeting had broken up.

I was aware one of the doors in the kitchen led outside. Freedom was tantalisingly close, but Steve came in and leaned against the door frame, gun in hand, watching every move I made.

There was a two-ring gas hob with a slide-under grilling arrangement. I put the kettle on to boil while I investigated the safe for food. I found bread, cheese and mustard, heated the grill and assembled the makings of grilled cheese on toast. I was generous in the number of rounds I cut. I wasn't sure whether methamphetamine users got the munchies as they came down from a high, but I assumed Steve would have a healthy appetite. Melody and I were ravenous anyway.

Melody helped me carry everything into the living room, then put more wood in the fire.

We sat around the pot-belly stove to eat our impromptu picnic. The warmth of the food and the fire gradually began to penetrate my system, easing out some of the knots and tensions of the last twenty-four hours. Even Steve seemed more relaxed, although he ate surprisingly little before he gave up. He'd shoved the gun back into his pocket and fumbled about with his good hand, lighting another cigarette.

Melody and I didn't care. Our appetites would have put navvies to shame as we each fed our hunger.

I wondered whether Steve really expected to collect his ransom and effect an escape, or whether he just refused to admit to himself that his chances of doing either were negligible. If ever I'd seen a man in denial, it had to be Steve. At least he'd been distracted from whatever sexual impulse had triggered the nasty little episode we'd had earlier.

I glanced at the window. The mist had swept back in again, and the afternoon light was dying. It must be bitterly cold outside for the men standing around waiting. They wouldn't choose to spend the night out in this weather although I supposed it was part of their job.

I stood to tidy up the plates. Steve looked up as I moved and started to say something, but was interrupted by the radio.

I took the opportunity to whisk my way out into the kitchen with the tray of dirty dishes. The back door called me with its siren song of freedom, but Melody had remained in the room with Steve, and I couldn't desert her.

I reheated the kettle and returned to the lounge with cups of hot coffee.

Just in time. Steve had slammed down the transmitter and had started towards me. He was only partly mollified by the hot drink I proffered.

"Don't do that again," he growled. "You stay here where I can see you."

"OK," I agreed. I went back to the window seat and watched the men outside. Melody came to join me.

"What happened with the radio call?" I murmured.

"Don't know," she said. "He had his back to me and was whispering. He's not happy again though."

She was right. The brief period of calm was over. Steve was back to his routine of twitching, pacing and leg jiggling. He lit yet another cigarette and marched around the small room puffing furiously. In between inhalations we could hear him muttering to himself.

He came towards us and looked out of the window. There wasn't much to look at, but it managed to annoy him all the same. He paced back across the room to the far wall, let out a frustrated roar and smashed his good hand into the wall. It must have hurt, because he gave a furious yell, and stepped back, shaking his hand.

Melody and I glanced nervously at each other. He was winding himself up again.

"What's the matter?" I asked, figuring it was better to know what the problem was than for us to sit here and watch him prowl with no idea of what was driving him.

"They're trying to dick me around. That's what the matter is," he said. "They're saying they can't get the cash up here until tomorrow because the weather's turning bad. Fuck it. Where there's a will there's a way, isn't that so?"

I thought about the improbability of any bank holding a million dollars in cash that was readily available. His plan was daft.

He came over to us and glared at Melody. "You'd better hope Daddy comes up with the cash, or I'll be returning you to him one finger at a time." He flung away from us and resumed pacing the room.

"Fuck off, Steve," I muttered under my breath. He heard, and swung towards me.

"You think I'm just threatening? Hell, if I can take the tail off a cat, I can cut fingers off a girl."

The words had the same effect as a punch to my gut. I'd heard him use the phrase "'curiosity killed the cat',' and dismissed the usage as coincidence. Then, I hadn't been able to bridge the huge gap in my mind between a normal paying passenger, and the unknown but barbaric monster trying to frighten me. Now I stared at him in sick fascination, immobilised by the horror his words conjured up. He was utterly evil.

Melody looked terrified, as well she might. At least he'd put the gun back in his pocket so it was out of sight and we'd seen no sign of a knife.

I reached over and covered her hand with mine in a futile gesture of support. Beneath my hand, her fingers curled and clenched, and I gave them a gentle squeeze. She was shaking again, and I put my arm around her briefly for a hug. I felt tears well in my own eyes and blinked them away. Fear was taking its toll on both of us but I was sure any sign of weakness would fuel Steve's bully-boy attitude.

We went back to staring out of the window. My thoughts were gloomy. In theory, Melody and I, working together, should have no trouble subduing Steve. There were two of us, and he had only one useful arm. Even if the drugs rendered him largely immune to pain, the damage he'd sustained would curtail the amount of movement and usefulness of the limb.

It was the gun that was the leveller. We might well be able to overcome Steve, but if one or other of us was seriously hurt or killed in the attempt, it would be a pointless victory. Unless we could find some way of separating him from the gun, we were best to wait until the cavalry came to rescue us.

Beside me Melody stiffened.

"There are vans out there now," she said.

I stared towards the helicopters. A fine mist had settled in. Not enough yet to reduce the range of visibility, but sufficient to flatten the light, effectively reducing clarity.

Melody was right. Without us noticing, two large trucks had arrived and parked near the choppers.

"They're TVNZ vans," said Melody.

Melody's eyes were evidently better than mine. I had trouble picking out the details, but eventually I agreed I could see a faint logo on the sides.

"Hey, Steve," I said. "You're about to get your fifteen minutes of fame. The press has arrived, or at least the TV news has."

"What?" Steve rushed over to the window and stared out. "Well, what do you know?" he said slowly. "The road must be open for traffic again."

All three of us stared at the trucks. Steve was correct. They had to have been driven up, and if news crews could make it here, then so in due course, could the ransom money. I could almost hear the cogs in Steve's brain turning. I wondered what difference this would make to his plans. Certainly our inaccessibility couldn't be used as an excuse any more.

I imagined Jack would be in touch soon to progress negotiations with Steve.

Right on cue the radio spoke again.

While Steve was distracted talking on the radio, I put my head next to Melody's.

"I've been wondering whether we can win our freedom

ourselves," I murmured.

She glanced across at Steve. "How?" He's still the one with the gun. I don't fancy getting shot if we piss him off."

Steve's gun was still in his pocket, and he was using his good hand to hold the transmitter, but I knew what she meant.

"No," I agreed. "But maybe we should concentrate on looking for an opportunity. He only has to slip up once, and we could do it. When I went to make the coffee I realised the kitchen door opens to the outside. If we could get out and behind cover, we'd be free, and the police could use all the force they want to against him. They're only delaying moving in because they know he's got hostages. If we got ourselves out of the way, the siege would be over." And you and I could get back to the people we love, I added silently.

"You're wasting your time," Steve replied to whatever had been said on the radio. "I don't need medical attention."

"Well, there's someone here who thinks you *do* need medical attention, and who really cares about you." Steve was quiet. It was torture being able to hear Jack's voice and not being able to respond or go to him. I skipped the next few exchanges as my thoughts focused on how much I needed Jack. I came back to reality to see that something said had clearly rattled Steve.

"No, shit no," he replied urgently. He was still refusing whatever had been proposed when his voice changed.

"Hi Mum. You shouldn't be up here." His voice veered between resigned, resentful and sheepish. The transformation from hardened criminal to small boy was so abrupt that Melody giggled, which earned her a furious look. He was still glowering at her as he walked towards us across the room and looked out of the window.

We could plainly see a small woman standing in front of the police line.

"Fuck," I heard him mutter as he returned and picked up the hand-set.

"No. Yes, I know Mum, but you can't believe everything they tell you. They don't care about you or me, it's just a game for them. They'll use you to get at me. You shouldn't be here."

"I don't want you to get into worse trouble, dear. And they've said you're badly wounded. You must give yourself up so you can get help."

Steve became more urgent.

"That's a load of crap, Mum. Do you really want them to take me again? You know what happens to Maori in the justice system. I've got brown skin. You think I'll get a fair go? Hell no! They'll shut me away again."

I resisted the temptation to snort and contented myself by rolling my eyes at Melody. Steve getting sent back to prison would have nothing to do with his race, and everything to do with his dodgy dealings.

"Please, Steve. Be sensible, love. You can't win this. Let it go. You know I want the best for you. I don't want you to be in prison so long that I'm too old to recognise you when you get out." Her voice gave a sob.

We watched as she fumbled in her pockets for something to wipe her nose with.

"Hey Mum, no, that's not fair." He tried to step closer to the window. The wire connecting the transmitter to the radio was at full stretch. If he pulled it much harder it would disconnect. To make room for him, I slid sideways from the seat and stood up.

Steve took my place and put a knee up on the seat, leaning towards the glass as if trying to get closer to the woman who stood outside. His distress was evident. The left hand, holding the transmitter was white to the knuckles. His right arm was in its sling.

"Mum, it will all work out, I promise," he urged. "I've got it all planned. It will be OK." His voice broke on the promise. "You've got to trust me, Mum," he pleaded.

I walked over to the wood stove, picked a log out of the wood basket and turned back. Steve was still peering through the glass, ignoring what I was doing. Melody's eyes widened as I approached.

It was surprisingly hard to bring myself to hit him in cold blood, but I steeled my resolve, lifted the wood and swung it at his head. He gave an ugly squawk, his good hand flew up to his ear and he pivoted to face me. For a second he stood silently staring at me. His hand fell from his ear, and I could clearly hear an excited gabble from the radio. I braced myself for the retaliation that never came.

In slow motion his knees bent, his eyes rolled back, and he collapsed limply on the floor.

"That's for Nelson," I said.

Melody had jumped to her feet, and we stood looking down at him.

"Oh my God," she said eventually. "Do you think he's dead?"

I hoped not, but I had no way of knowing the difference between a killing stroke, and one that would render him unconscious. My concern made my voice unnecessarily harsh.

"Get that gun from his pocket, would you?" I asked.

I bent, picked up the transmitter, and held it to my mouth. There was silence at the other end.

"I need to speak to the police," I said.

CHAPTER TWENTY THREE

MELODY SAT ON THE WINDOW SEAT, the gun in her hands.

"Careful what you do with that thing," I cautioned. "I'd hate you to shoot me by mistake."

She gave a cheeky grin. "I have control," she said, using the aviation phrase that prefaced the passing of control from one pilot to another.

I smiled and shook my head at her. Her guts and resilience were amazing for a girl who'd had to listen to Steve's threat to carve her up.

I knelt beside Steve to check whether I'd killed him. To my relief, I detected a faint, irregular, thread of breath. I loosened his collar. I found a string around his neck and tugged at it to loosen its grip around his throat. When that had little effect, I unbuttoned the top two buttons of his shirt hoping to ease the passage of air into his lungs.

I had exposed a pendant.

I glanced at it as I peeled the shirt back, and stiffened. The carved bone manaia was familiar and unique. A memory flashed of a young man with laughing eyes telling me of the gift he'd received. A man, whose broken body had lain lifeless on a cold, wet pavement a few hours later.

I reached out, turned the pendant over and looked at the back. Intertwined, in a lovely cursive script, were the letters A C. I bit down hard on my bottom lip.

A hand on my shoulder broke my concentration and I dropped the pendant.

"Excuse me, love, but could you step back so we can take a look at him?"

I looked up at the man in ambulance crew uniform, nodded, and climbed to my feet. He gave a hand to steady me as I stood and faced him.

A frown crossed his face as he took in my bruises.

"You OK?" he asked.

I nodded.

"Better than he is, anyway," I indicated Steve.

He gave me a thumbs up as I turned away.

Ambulance crew and police crowded the room.

One approached Melody who sat on the window seat watching the action, the shotgun held slackly in her hand.

"I'll take that for you, shall I?" he asked as he reached carefully for the gun. He'd only just gained possession of the weapon before Melody, ignoring him, jumped to her feet, gave a strangled sob, and launched herself across the room.

I turned. Two other men had come into the room. I watched as Melody flung herself into Jim Mason's arms. She burrowed against his shoulder, but I could see Jim's face, his eyes shut fast as he held her to him.

When at last he opened them, his tears were obvious as he hugged his daughter, and spoke softly to her. My own eyes naturally flooded in response, and I looked away. The explosion of such raw emotion in that reunion was too much for an onlooker to easily bear.

I composed myself and turned back to look at the man who stood beside them, saying nothing, gazing steadily at me.

I found it exquisitely hard to meet Jack's eyes and eventually dropped my own to look at the floor. It was impossible to read his expression, but one thing was for certain - there was no wide, welcoming smile on his face. Love, fear, relief, desire, grief, shame and joy; the vast range of my own swirling emotions left me paralysed and shy.

With all my heart I wanted to emulate Melody and fly across the room to his embrace, but inhibition held me rigid. What I'd wanted to be easy and joyful between us had turned to prickly complication. This was not the reunion I'd imagined with such anticipation when I'd primped and pampered myself the night before.

It was a shock to realise that had been less than twenty-four hours ago.

It occurred to me Jack might be angry. Our relationship so far had been punctuated with a series of dramatic events and he'd told me once he'd like a restful girlfriend. I wondered whether this latest adventure compromised his professional reputation. It wasn't hard to imagine the police force took a dim view of its officers confusing their professional and personal lives.

"Claire?"

He'd stepped up beside me. "May I have a word?" His tone was courteous, impersonal.

I nodded numbly. He held my elbow as he guided me through the press of men in the doorway, across the hall and into the room on the opposite side. There was a click as the door closed behind us and we were alone.

He released my arm, folded his own and leaned back against the wall, leaving me standing in front of him.

"Look at me," he said, in that same unnaturally calm voice.

I forced myself to meet his gaze, and the intensity of his attention locked me in. We stood motionless for long moments, just looking at each other. Jack was utterly still, allowing the silence to build and develop as it would. My breath caught, became uneven, and I licked my lips nervously. I couldn't mistake the passion in his eyes. Although I stood steadily enough, I felt my body soften as untold threads of tension dissolved in relief and were replaced with the energy of a new dynamic.

It felt like forever before his hand reached up to run a finger gently down my damaged cheek.

"He hurt you." The statement was flat, the voice unexpectedly harsh.

I nodded. "Only a little. It's not bad," I assured him. "It's over."

"Did he do anything else?" Again, the cold sharpness of his tone startled me, causing me to flinch.

I'd begun to shake my head in reply when, finally, light dawned. Jack was afraid. I was close enough to smell it on him and read it in his eyes. He'd been afraid about what Steve might have done to me. I'd been right about the anger I saw on Jack's face, but it hadn't been directed at me.

I gave a husky laugh of relief, as I understood the problem and smiled up into his face.

"He only smacked me a few times," I told him. Relief made me discount my bruises quite cheerfully. "My face may not be pretty, but that's the only damage. He didn't touch Melody either," I hurried to say. "He was scary, but in the end we hurt him more than he did us."

Abruptly my nervousness fled. This was Jack, whom I loved, who'd spent hours being terrified for me, and even now was treating me with the care due an antique vase. I'd never expected to provoke such intense concern and care from a lover. This was new territory in our relationship for both of us.

I stepped forward, his arms came around and he held on to me, as the Leonard Cohen song has it, like a crucifix. We clung together for a long time, seeking the simple, tactile comfort of each other's body. My senses were in overdrive. I was hyper aware of the texture of his jumper, the ribbing around his wrist where it pressed against my skin. I breathed in the warm Jack scent of his skin and listened to the subtle bass blood rhythm as his heart rate slowed and his breathing, so carefully controlled, settled to a normal pattern. His hair was longer, his skin a deeper tan. I relished the changes being apart had wrought as much as I welcomed his familiarity.

"I was afraid I'd never see you ag …"

"I was desperate. They told me you were …"

"I thought of you. I kept wondering where you were; whether

you were back in New …"

"I couldn't get here fast enough. The bloody helicopter was so slow …"

"How did you," "When did you," "Are you sure you're …?"

It was the most disjointed conversation two people could share, and yet it explained things to our mutual satisfaction.

At last we abandoned words, which at best were dysfunctional for what we needed to express. He eased my head gently away from his sweater and forced me to look at him. His eyes were open, seeking my consent all the way, as, with exquisite slowness, he brought his lips down to mine which had automatically parted in anticipation.

There was neither kindness or gentleness in that kiss. Love, sexuality and relief, of course. But there were deeper strains of anger at the fear our investment in each other had cost us, a roughness as we recognised how immutably bound together we were. While I welcomed this knowledge, I was shocked at my new-found vulnerability and inclined to be resentful.

It was the knocking on the door that forced us apart.

"Sir? Are you in there, sir? We've completed the search and the house is secure."

By the time Jack had the door open I was sitting demurely on the chair by the dressing table, hands folded on my lap, presenting a fine vision of a woman helping police with their enquiries. My hair might be mussed, my lips swollen and my colour a little high, but nothing unexpected, I hoped, for a woman who'd spent the day as a hostage.

We returned to the living room. Maia had been allowed into her house and was busy sorting out the mess.

"I'm sorry we made it untidy," I said, as I watched her clearing up a coffee mug tucked on the floor behind the leg of a chair.

"Don't be silly, girl. I'm just glad it's all had a happy ending," she said. "You go and sit down. The police will want to talk to you."

I joined Melody and Jim, back in position on the window seat. Jim stood as I approached and grinned at me. He looked ten years younger. Melody had obviously filled him in on all the details.

"Quite some excitement," he said to me. He leaned forward to give me a gentle hug and a kiss on the cheek.

"It's had its moments," I said wryly, "but we've come through. Good to see you here. How did you arrive so promptly?"

"Roger flew us up," he said. "He's still waiting outside. The cops haven't let him in yet."

"That'll please him." I said, smiling. "Not. Patience isn't his greatest virtue."

"Well, maybe, but he was desperately worried about you," said Jim. "He'll be glad to see you when the police have decided it's safe enough. Speaking of which ...."

I looked across the room to where Roger had just been admitted. He saw me and gave a big grin as I rushed across to hug him. He hugged me back with equal enthusiasm.

"You're here," I said with real pleasure. "Bless you for flying up."

"I didn't have a choice," said Roger. "I had Jim over there and that policeman of yours badgering me to come up and get you. I was forced into it. Anyway, I was worried about what you might have done to my aircraft."

"Of course," I laughed, and gave him another hug out of sheer exuberance. I was alive, safe and some of my favourite people were here with me.

"Now that's enough of that, Hardcastle," said Roger hastily. He's not a man given to expressing overt emotion. I gave a chuckle.

"Have you actually left Paraparaumu Aviation unattended, without you at the helm?" I teased.

"Greig and Nick can manage just fine," he said offhandedly. "It will do them both good to work together and get over the nonsense they've put us through. Maria's there as well and will keep things running smoothly." By which I understood we were back on an official footing and that no pesky emotion need intrude on our relationship. Roger's as tough and as self-contained as they come, but his hug had been warm and genuine. I smiled happily.

Official process took over. Steve was helicoptered off in the air ambulance. He'd woken up, had his good hand cuffed to a police officer and been escorted off to hospital. I was relieved to find I hadn't killed him. In an unexpected kindness by the police I'd been pleased to hear his mother had been allowed to fly as far as the hospital with him, although I did wonder how strained their conversation might be.

Melody and I were interviewed and our statements taken. We were free to go.

It was late in the afternoon, but the sky had cleared when Roger borrowed Tamati's quad, and the two of us drove down to the paddock where I'd parked the plane.

Roger, Melody and Jim were going to take the opportunity to leave while the weather was good.

"I assume you'll hang around and bring your man back yourself?" asked Roger, as we checked the aircraft over.

"I suppose so, unless he has police business. In which case I'll fly back on my own. You don't mind if I stay here the night, do you? I doubt if I could pilot a bicycle anywhere safely at the moment," I said.

Roger nodded and looked at the country around my impromptu landing strip. "OK. When you fly out, what's your plan for taking off from here?"

I stared blankly at the mountains towering over us. My brain seemed to have disappeared. I couldn't have planned my way to a bath, let alone how to get out of the valley in a plane.

Roger glanced at me, read my exhaustion, and took over.

"You'll need to stay away from downdraught off those hills if you can. If the wind stays as light as this, your best route is to get off the ground and turn left in a climbing turn. Keep the nose of the plane down. For Christ's sake don't just point up at the sky, or you'll stall."

He pointed to the surrounding mountains. "Don't let them intimidate you. You'll feel claustrophobic, but there's probably more space to work with than you imagine. Don't panic and be tempted to fly steep turns. A gentle bank is probably all you need, and you'll be safe. Keep spiralling up until you've got airspeed and height before you try to get out of the valley. And remember the top of the ridge is not your horizon. Keep your wits about you."

I nodded. "That's pretty much how I came in to land."

Roger gave me an approving nod. "You made a decent fist of it, I'll give you that. Do the same on the way out."

He took me back to Maia's and I said goodbye to Jim and Melody. Roger assured me he'd phone Kate for me when he got back and reassure her that I was safe and well.

"You get a good night's sleep then girl, and we'll see you back tomorrow. Try not to get into any more mischief," said Roger.

I grinned and waved as the chopper lifted. Already one of the police helicopters had left, and I could see the TV news vans pulling out. The show was over, the drama ended and real life could resume.

CHAPTER
TWENTY FOUR

I WAS IN THE KITCHEN WITH MAIA, helping to dry dishes when Jack came across with another officer.

"Claire, this is John Letts." I nodded at the man. I saw he was carrying the notes of the statements we'd made.

"Hi, Claire. We want to know what happened to the other guy?" he asked.

"What other guy?"

"Grylls or something?" He peered at his notes. "The guys who held you hostage. Didn't you say there were two of them?"

"Glynn," I corrected. "Yeah, he helped abduct us and hijacked the plane with Steve, but he left when Steve grabbed us as hostages this afternoon."

"You mean he wasn't in the house when you bashed Steve over the head?" asked Jack.

I winced at the bald statement.

"No. He'd bolted ages ago, with the others, when Steve pulled his stunt. I assumed the police had already picked him up," I said.

I stared at them in disbelief. "You mean, he's still out there?"

There was a moment's silence as we processed that fact.

"Shit," said Jack.

Orders were given, the remaining police were dispatched, and the search for Glynn began from door to door. It was soon obvious he'd disappeared. None of the families in the settlement had seen him after they'd scurried out of the meeting with Poppa. He wasn't holed up in any sheds or outhouses.

"How could they not have taken any notice of him?" I asked. "He's a stranger here and must stand out like a sore thumb."

"When Steve grabbed you and Melody, there was a rush to get out of the house and it was everyone for themselves," explained Jack. "Some crowded around us at the helicopters to tell us what was happening, so there was a lot of shouting and excited carry on. There's a robust gun culture among the Tuhoe, and some of the young lads wanted to assist us. Unfortunately, their idea was to storm the house, so we had to discourage them. The rest decamped to their homes and shut the door on the world. It was a bit chaotic, and of course the police were focused on was what was happening to you and Melody back in the house."

"Well, I'd be surprised if anyone in this valley was prepared to help Glynn," I said. "Poppa pretty much shot him down in flames, so he's persona non grata here."

"Could he have stolen your plane?" asked John.

I shook my head. "No, Roger and I just checked it, and it's still there. He wouldn't know how to fly it anyway. I've got the keys in my pocket, and we'd have heard it take off if he had managed to start it by swinging the prop."

I shrugged.

"We'd probably also hear a loud bang as well as he crashed it," I added for good measure.

"Where's it parked?" asked John.

"In the big paddock around the corner, further down the track you guys landed on."

Jack nodded. "I saw it as we flew in. It's only fifteen minutes' or so away. It would pay to get it checked out in case he's holed up near there," said Jack. "Are you up for the walk, Claire?" I nodded agreement.

After the stagnant hours of being stuck inside, it was refreshing to be out in the chill of the evening. It was on the edge of dusk, but it would be a clear night, and I'd borrowed a warm jacket from Maia to fend off the cold. I should have been unnerved that we still had members of the armed offenders squad as an escort, but Jack was beside me, and in spite of the circumstances, I felt a surge of happiness.

We reached the aircraft much quicker than I'd expected. I was pleased to see the little plane again, still sitting safely in the clearing and patted its high wings.

"It's not a horse," said Jack, amused.

"It carried me, and several other people, safely," I retorted. "The least I can do is be nice to it." I double-checked to see there had been no interference with the aircraft, although I was certain that Roger and I would have noticed it earlier.

The men spread out and checked the scrub and bush surrounding the paddock, but there was no sign of Glynn.

"Scarpered," said John in disgust. "So now we've got a fugitive running around out there, and it will soon be night."

I looked at the dark, bush-clad hills surrounding the valley.

"I can't see him heading into the Ureweras on his own. He's a town boy, not Man Alone." John missed the literary allusion, but I saw Jack understood. He grinned appreciatively. It amused him when snippets of my academic past slipped into conversation.

"What's he like?" he asked.

"Small," I replied. "Shorter than me. English. He came out here five years ago or so. He seemed quite nice when I flew him as a passenger. Certainly I thought he was the more reasonable of the two of them. He's Steve's uncle, did you know?"

Jack nodded.

"At first Glynn was the one in control. Even when they kidnapped us, it was Glynn who told Steve what to do and settled him when he got overly aggressive. Right up until this morning I thought he was the brains of the operation. But once we got up into the hills here, Glynn sort of lost the plot."

"Go on." John was listening.

"Well, I'd gathered they were on the run, but I don't think Glynn was very keen on what they were running to. When we got up here, he looked really unhappy and out of his depth, and that was when Steve took over and became more aggressive and unpleasant. Of course, Steve was coming home to whanau and assumed they'd accept him, while Glynn couldn't have looked more alien and uncomfortable."

"So you're saying Glynn hasn't gone bush?"

I shook my head.

"I'd put money on it. I don't know if there was any survival stuff in their packs they took up to Maia's place, but I doubt it. They were carrying the foot and mouth canisters, and I suppose there'd be drugs as well. They weren't planning on living rough. Were the packs still there?"

"We didn't find anything," said John. "Maybe he took them when he vanished."

"Then where the fuck did the man go?" asked Jack.

We trudged back to the village. I could feel the men's frustration. By then they must all have wanted to clock off and go home. Instead they had a rogue criminal to track down.

We passed the chopper, still parked up on the track.

Jack stopped. "Cars," he said. "There were vehicles here, and they've gone. Did Glynn cadge a lift out with someone?"

"They had the big TV vans. Could he have hidden inside one?" I suggested. I remembered I'd watched them pull out.

With this new scenario the police launched into action.

Radio calls were made, outside assistance called in and road blocks set up. We were so far off the beaten track of course, that it was a considerable drive for those who had to set them up.

If a vehicle left this valley and made it back to the main road, (I use the term loosely in this remote area), there was a choice of going east or west. Before then there was only the one road out of the Maungapohatu; a steep, twisty route that needed to be driven slowly.

"Even so, we can't rely on them getting picked up on the Maungapohatu Road," said Jack gloomily. "Let's just hope they get them further down."

"Do you have to leave with the armed offender guys?" I asked as I watched the men packing up.

Jack smiled down at me. "Nah, I've told them I'm on victim

support duties this evening. I'll fly back with you tomorrow if I can?"

"I'm not that much of a victim," I said indignantly.

"OK," he said equably, "then let's call it my witness protection scheme. You admit you'll be a witness at the trial?"

I shuddered. "I won't look forward to that. What will they charge them with?"

"Dunno. They slapped a couple of minor charges on Steve so they could bring him in, but I understand he's wanted for questioning about a murder in the Sounds. Then there's the drug dealing, which I understand he admitted in front of any number of witnesses."

I remembered I hadn't told Jack about the pendant around Steve's neck. That led naturally to me saying he'd been responsible for sending me the parcel with the cat's tail.

"Fucking psycho." He frowned.

"You're certain it's the same pendant? You think you could swear to that?"

I hate being pushed into making absolute statements.

"As far as I can be," I said. "I only saw it the once remember, but it's quite distinctive. Also, when I turned it over, AC was carved on the reverse. Andrew told me that night that they'd had been carved into the back and those were his initials."

John came across to say goodbye.

"Claire's got something to tell you," Jack said. I repeated my story.

"No shit," he said when I'd finished. "That could be a break-through. I'll let Wellington know. I don't know anything about that case, but the officers working on it will want to talk to you when you get back home."

We watched as the helicopter flew off into the evening. The beat of the blades faded into the distance and the valley was quiet.

CHAPTER
TWENTY FIVE

DINNER WAS TO BE A SHARED AFFAIR at Johnno's family home.

In the interim I had a shower. Hot water came courtesy of the wet back on the pot-belly, and I was pleased I'd taken the time to keep the stove going during the afternoon. It felt glorious to have the hot water run over my body and wash the day away.

Maia lent me deodorant and a new toothbrush. I struggled to do anything with my hair. My scalp still hurt like crazy, but I managed to make myself look reasonably presentable, if you ignored the odd bruise or two. It wasn't quite up to my usual level of grooming, but I picked that no one was going to care. Even though I had to change back into my worn clothes, I felt a million times better for freshening up.

I joined Maia in the kitchen where I prepared vegetables as my contribution to the evening meal, while she assembled a large trifle. Tamati brought in a few loads of firewood and restocked the pile by the wood stove, while Krystal got the kids organised.

Jack, fresh from his own shower, joined us. He'd washed his hair which now had a nicely tousled look. I felt a shiver of appreciation pass through me when he caught my eye and smiled.

We walked together to Johnno's place.

The house was packed. I recognised people I'd met that afternoon, but there were many others to be introduced to. A constant stream of women carried bowls and plates into the kitchen or set them out on the bench. I was hugged by nearly everyone and made to feel very welcome.

The men had gathered outside on the back porch where the barbecue was cranked up. The savoury scent of fried onions mixed with the rich smell of cooking meat and hovered as a pungent cloud floating in the chill air above the porch. It was bitterly cold, but I was amazed how many men wore little more than a T-shirt and shorts. Clearly they bred them tough up here in the mountains.

It was a warm, welcoming and very happy evening. The food was superb. I commented on the quality of the meat and Tamati laughed at me.

"That's venison from the bush," he said, "and those chops are wild pork. We don't serve supermarket rubbish here."

I grinned. "Man, the mighty hunter?"

"Too bloody right," he returned. "We get proper food. You wouldn't find any of us settling for the meat you townies eat."

I gestured up at the ice-cold sky, which was lit by a million stars. Even though I lived in the country, and there were frequently beautiful nights to be seen, the ever-present light pollution from Paraparaumu township stripped the night sky of some of its intensity. Up here the night was intensely dark, and the stars shone with added brilliance.

"On a night like this I could be tempted never to be a townie again."

Johnno, who'd joined us said, "You won't feel like that tomorrow morning when the mist is thick on the ground and its so cold you can't wriggle your toes."

"It doesn't look like it's misty." I was surprised - it was such a beautiful evening.

He explained, "The temperature only has to drop another degree or so, and the mist will roll in thick and fast. It'll lift by mid-morning though, so you'll be OK for your flight home."

I was relieved. Much as I was enjoying the evening, I needed to get back home, and soon.

Later I introduced Jack to Poppa and watched the two assess each other. Jack summed up the old man in a second and turned on both his charm and his best manners.

Presumably Poppa approved of Jack, because he greeted him with genuine warmth. Soon, in a uniquely Maori way, they were discussing their respective tribal ancestry.

"You're Tainui?" asked Poppa.

"Waikato Tainui, yeah, mainly. Although I also have whakapapa to Ngati Porou, through my grandmother," replied Jack.

I left them to it. An overseas writer once remarked that conversation with a New Zealander was like reciting the telephone directory. With Maori, the process is even more intense because they remember lineage that can go back centuries and tribal intermarriage is an integral part of their heritage.

Jack and Poppa settled down to an enjoyable discussion of genealogy.

"You don't find many like him," Jack told me later in private. "He's got a pedigree that reaches back to pre-history, and a pride and dignity you don't often see these days in anyone. Do you know what he spent his working life doing? He was a professor at Auckland University, then he became a leading Treaty of Waitangi negotiator and served as an informal advisor to government on Maori policy. His influence on New Zealand policy has been enormous. Now he's come home to spend his retirement here. No wonder he's respected."

"Holy crap," I said. "I didn't realise all that."

"An amazing man," said Jack. "Look at the physical presence he has. He could be a king. You suddenly realise what Maori must have been like when Captain Cook sailed in and met them."

It was a rowdy, cheerful evening. Later Johnno got a guitar out, the room quietened and he played while Krystal sang. She had a lovely voice – true and mellow. I was tired and let my head fall back against Jack's shoulder while the lovely song flowed around me. Later others joined in with their own guitars, and the singing became communal and happily rowdy.

Krystal tapped me on the shoulder. "I'm taking the kids back home," she said, "so I'll say goodnight."

I stirred myself from the warm support of Jack's shoulder.

"Can I come with you? I asked. "I'm starting to drift off here, and I'd best get to bed. I didn't get much sleep last night."

"Sure."

Jack decided to come with me, so we made our farewells.

We found Maia chatting in the kitchen with her friends. "You off? Fair enough. This lot here will carry on for hours. When you get home, drag the mattresses out into the lounge," she instructed. "You'll be warm sleeping there by the fire. Krystal will give you a couple of sleeping bags."

Once outside, Jack drew out his mobile and punched the numbers.

"Dammit, no signal," he muttered.

"I don't think there ever is up here," I said. "You'll have to use the radio back at Maia's."

I felt him give a light shrug.

"Doesn't really matter. I was just calling base to see if they picked Glynn up this evening. It can wait."

Jack and I lagged some way behind Krystal and the kids. It was extremely dark, but Jack must have eyes like a cat as he had no trouble steering us in the right direction. The cold was so intense it made my eyes water. Even with my jacket collar pulled up I could feel my cheeks chilling in the icy air.

"Cold?" Jack's voice was warm as he put his arm around my shoulders.

"Freezing," I replied, "but the pay-off is looking at the stars. I don't think I've ever seen a night so beautiful."

He pulled me closer in a brief hug but didn't break his stride. I needed his arm for guidance because my attention was riveted on the sky. The deep black allowed the stars to display themselves in their infinite variety. Usually the night sky appears as a one-dimensional child's painting – deep blue with yellow stars painted on it. Tonight, uncluttered by any external light source, the depth and dimensions of space were apparent. There were close stars and faint, far-distant ones. The misty Milky Way ran like a river through them.

As I watched, a shooting star flared across the night.

"Look!" I exclaimed.

We stopped and watched its arc through the darkness.

"We have to make a wish," said Jack softly. He was very close, the arm around my shoulder drawing me into his side. I could feel his breath stir a loose wisp of hair across my cheek, smell the fresh warmth of his skin's scent. I felt his lips kiss the top of my head.

"I already have," I replied.

"So have I." His voice had an undercurrent of laughter as we resumed walking.

Corny? Well of course it was. I don't suppose there's been anything original or new in romantic dialogue for centuries. Did it fill an emotional need? The answer was an unequivocal yes. On the surface the interchange was banal, but it served as a conduit for a much more sophisticated emotional dialogue that ran beneath. My soul reaches out to your soul. Our vocabulary limits what we can express in words. Sometimes metaphor is the only tool we can use.

I was smiling as we walked.

When we reached Maia's house, Krystal was already wrangling the children into bed.

I helped Jack drag a couple of mattresses into the living room, stoked up the fire and went in search of sleeping bags.

We lay side by side in front of the fire, the only light coming from the flames that flickered in the cracks around the firebox door. It was warm and cosy, and for the first time today we were completely alone. Not, mind you, sufficiently alone to risk wilder sexual activities. Krystal and her kids were in the next room, and Maia and Tamati could be back at any time. We shared the innocent intimacy of being together in our sleeping bags. It was like being seventeen again. I snuggled close, happy to be safe and beside him. I was sufficiently tired that I'd be asleep in minutes anyway.

"This isn't quite the way I imagined our first-night reunion together would pan out," said Jack, lifting his lips from mine.

I giggled. "It's like being in a tramping hut. Friendship, but no sex."

"Hm," Jack's growl demonstrated his opinion of that as an option.

We lay quietly for a while. In spite of my weariness, it took me some time to relax after all the tensions of the day.

Eventually Jack stirred beside me.

"Today I was afraid I was going to lose you," he said quietly.

I reached up and lightly touched his face. "And I was terrified I wouldn't have a chance to say goodbye."

He kissed my fingers as they floated over his lips. I took the opportunity to snuggle up even closer.

There was a long pause. He cleared his voice.

"I lost someone I loved once before. I don't think I could bear it if something happened to you." Jack's voice had roughened with emotion. I held my breath.

"I've never told you, but I was married once." The words hung in the silence between us. I was afraid to move.

"What happened?" I asked eventually.

"She was killed in a car crash."

Hearing it from Jack, and registering the depth of anguish in his voice as he spoke, was almost unbearable. I reached across, found his hand and squeezed it. His fingers tightened on mine.

"We'd been very much in love. When I lost Samira, I didn't think there was any point in going on." He gave a short, unamused, laugh. "I threw myself into my work to blot out the pain."

"I'm so sorry," I said. It was such a useless, inane thing to say, but what else is there?

"Then I met you, and you taught me to love again," Jack continued. "I didn't even know how deeply I needed you until I saw you today on that step with Steve's gun pointed at you. I was terrified he'd kill you."

I stretched out and gripped as much of him as I could hold.

"I'm here; I'm safe and I'm with you," I said.

Later there would be more details he could tell me to flesh out the story. But for now it was enough we had each other.

We clung together for a long time. I suppose love is made up of moments like these. Moments when anguish cracks our defences open a little, making us more honest and allowing others entry through the barriers we keep around our hearts.

I had a fleeting thought of the time I'd spent moisturising and epilating to please him. It seemed such a silly, girly thing to do when compared to the serious emotions we'd experienced today. Although, in its own way, it had been just as much a statement of Jack's importance to me as anything else I could do.

I smiled into the darkness before closing my eyes and finally abandoning the day.

CHAPTER
TWENTY SIX

I LOOKED OUT OF THE WINDOW AT AN opaque world. The mist, as Johnno had predicted, covered the valley. I could barely see the darker grey silhouettes of trees that edged the garden.

"It'll burn off soon," promised Maia, who was busy feeding the children. "Help yourself to Weet-Bix or toast," she added.

I smiled at the kids, who smiled back shyly before dropping their eyes. I grinned, picking they didn't get to see many strangers up here.

I bit into freshly buttered toast while I waited for the jug to boil for coffee. "What's the jam?" I asked. The intense flavour exploded in my mouth.

"Damson," she said. "We've an old tree in the garden that we use to make jam and Damson gin. It's not a bad taste."

"It's delicious."

By the time Jack and I had tidied our sleeping bags, had breakfast and helped Maia and Tamati with the chores, the mist had lifted, revealing a perfect blue sky. It would be a beautiful day for flying. I had to flag my normal pre-flight tasks of getting weather information for our route, or calling in a flight plan. With no phone or Internet, I would be flying by the seat of my pants. I had a pleasing sense of being an Amelia Earhart or Jean Batten.

There were hugs and kisses as we said our goodbyes. I'd brought nothing but trouble and drama to the valley, but the hospitality and kindness of its inhabitants had been overwhelming. I wouldn't, as I told Maia, forget her help and support in a hurry.

"Don't be silly," she replied. "You've given us more excitement than we've had up here for years. The whanau will remember this as a great adventure."

Tamati took us out to the plane on the quad. The only sign of yesterday's drama was flattened and well trampled grass beside the track. Otherwise the valley had returned to its remote, pristine beauty. We'd been warmly welcomed here, but it was easy to imagine a consciousness in these hills that wanted us gone. The land had stood for millennia, and we were a temporary intrusion. I'd been allowed to land here when I'd needed help, and I hoped would be allowed to leave safely, but I was alien in this place. It wasn't hard to believe the fairy folk, the patupaiarehe, still haunted these mountains. All my Irish ancestry resonated with the atmosphere. I gave a slight shudder.

Jack checked his phone for signal again.

"Bugger," he remarked. "Not only can't I get signal, but the battery's flat as well. I didn't get the chance to charge it last night."

"I think the only reason I've missed my phone is as a clock," I said. "It's been peaceful being off line."

"Hm." Jack gave an irritated sniff and shoved his phone back in his pocket. "The sooner we're back to civilisation, the better."

I looked down the length of the paddock and gritted my teeth. Normally, the night before an important flight I lie in bed and visualise the tasks I need to do. Last night had been taken up with other concerns. This morning, with Roger's briefing buzzing in my head, I looked at the country around us and realised the magnitude of the task ahead of me.

"It's going to be a bumpy take-off run," I warned.

"I have faith in you," Jack smiled at me. I blessed his

comfortable reassurance. He might not be a pilot, but he wasn't stupid and I was certain he understood how little margin for error we had.

We raced across the uneven ground, bouncing and shaking. I tried to keep the plane on the ground long enough to build up speed, but it was a relief to be airborne. I concentrated on keeping the nose of the aircraft down and letting the airspeed build to safe levels. As it was, it felt like only seconds before we'd reached the hills bordering the valley. I banked the plane away, beginning a slow, shallow spiral upwards. The space I had to operate in was tight, but Roger had been correct - as long as I kept in a medium turn I could keep within the circle of the valley walls. I was so focussed on keeping a watch outside the aircraft while simultaneously monitoring the instruments in the cockpit that I had no time to be as terrified as I should have been.

We seemed to have been turning in circles forever before a subtle change in the quality of the light alerted me that at least half the circumference of our orbit was now in clear air. We were above the level of the range. I gave us one more turn to gain a few extra hundred feet of altitude then turned south.

Jack had been admirably quiet and had allowed me to concentrate. I glanced at him to see if he was OK. He saw me looking.

"I had perfect faith in you," he repeated, answering my unspoken question.

I wiped the palms of my hands on my jeans and gave a little laugh.

"Just as well one of us did. That valley's a bit too tight for a fixed wing aircraft."

He reached out and briefly covered one of my hands with his, giving it a reassuring squeeze.

"Good work then."

The rest of the flight home was easy. The weather was kind, the winds were light, and the miles floated past beneath our wings.

"I prefer flying legally," I said to Jack, after I'd cleared Napier's airspace. "I don't think I broke too many rules when we flew up the other night, but it was unnerving not to be able to talk to Christchurch control, or any of the towers. I didn't realise how much security they represent."

Jack chuckled. "Are you saying you're not a rebel?"

"Apparently not. It seems I'm a very law-abiding citizen when it comes to aviation."

"That's a relief," he said. "Do you realise it's the first time I've flown with you?"

He was right, although I hadn't thought about it.

"There's a first time for everything," I said, and gave him a grin. "Of course, if you want to try flying yourself, you're welcome to give it a go." I indicated the yoke in front of him. There are, after all, certain advantages to being an instructor.

He shook his head. "Nah, that's your job. Just get us home."

"Pete's learning to fly," I reminded him.

"Ah yes, Pete. I'm looking forward to catching up with him," he said grimly. "There's a few things we need to discuss."

I grinned. "I think he's planning on putting quite a bit of effort into *not* catching up with you anytime soon," I said.

"He might well do," was the dry reply.

We flew over the ranges, passed south of Palmerston North, and had our first view of Kapiti Island in the distance. Its triangular fin - emerging from the water - dominates the seascape for the length of the coastline from Mana to Whanganui and being in sight of it represents home to me.

"Nearly there," I said. We were in territory as familiar to me as the palm of my hand. Previously I'd taken for granted the familiar way-points, radio procedures and landmarks that comprised 'my patch'. Today I cherished them all. When I'd piloted us north the other night I'd been afraid I might never see any of this again. I reminded myself everything had worked out in the end, and we were on our way to a happy ending. Still, the thought of what could have been lost coloured my thoughts.

Jack must have picked up on the tenor of my thoughts because his hand again covered mine, where it held the yoke, and gave it a squeeze, although he said nothing. I glanced at him.

"Have you plans for the evening?" I asked. I referred to the meetings I knew he'd abandoned to fly up to me yesterday.

"I most certainly have plans," he said and gave a wicked grin. "I'm not sure I should discuss them with you while you're flying a plane, though. They might distract you," he said piously. The effect was marred by the warmth of the look he shot me. I felt a surge of anticipation that jolted me out of my previous introspection.

"Then I'd better get us back safely," I said.

Nick came running over as soon as we pulled up outside the hangar.

"You're back," he said. To my surprise he gave me a warm hug.

"Shit, you had us worried when we got here yesterday morning and found the plane missing. The old man was beside himself. It was only when he got home last night and told us everything was OK with you that we were able to relax."

"It's been a hell of an adventure," I said. "If you shout me a drink, I might even tell you about it."

"You'll have to wait until after we shut up shop," said Roger, who'd made a leisurely approach over from the offices to greet us. "Incidentally Hardcastle, you'd better put the hose over that plane: it's got grass stains and cow-shit spattered all over it."

"What state's the chopper in then?" I asked him. Clearly there'd be no prodigal son type re-enactment from Roger.

"Clean and tidy, and don't be cheeky," he advised. "How you survived a long flight with her, I don't know," he said to Jack. "She'll be impossible now. I suppose she'll want to be treated like a heroine."

Nick and I smiled at each other. God, it felt good to be home again.

Jack left to get back to the office and salvage what he could of the work day.

"I'll see you at your place," he said. "We can go and grab a quick meal, then spend some time catching up."

"Sweet as," I said.

I thought I heard Roger give a soft snort, but when I looked at him his gaze was fixed innocently enough on the Air New Zealand flight coming in to land.

I raised my eyebrows at Nick, who choked on a laugh. I threw him an evil look. Just because I'd been away twenty-four hours, there was no excuse for insubordination.

"Give me a hand to get KIM over to the hose so I can wash her," I asked him as I reached for one of the struts to pull the plane across the apron.

A couple of hours later, when we'd closed the hangar doors for the day, Nick honoured his promise of buying me a drink. Greig had returned from the charter he'd flown that day, and we settled down in the office while I filled them in on my adventures.

"Importing drugs is common place enough. Police and customs arrest smugglers almost every week," Roger remarked. "But foot-and-mouth disease? That's horrific. The implications for New Zealand are almost unimaginable. Is it even possible?"

"That's what Glynn claimed," I said. "There was an item on the news a few nights ago about a foot-and-mouth scare. I was busy so I didn't tune in, but that must have been the start of the crisis."

Roger grunted. "Google it for us," he ordered Greig. "I didn't catch up with the news yesterday, I was too busy flying your fan club around the country to rescue you. By the time I got back last night it was too late to watch TV."

"And he enjoyed every minute of it," interjected Maria. "Mind you, we were very concerned when we got to work yesterday and found a plane missing and eventually realised you were involved."

"Did you find my note saying we were going to Wairoa?" I asked.

Maria bit her lip and shook her head. "Not until quite late in the piece, I'm afraid. I only noticed it when I sat down at the desk to work. Before that we'd been running around trying to find out why the lights were on and the hangar doors open. It took a while for the pieces of the puzzle to fall into place. We found the offices open, then you didn't come in to work or answer your phone, so Nick went around to your place to see if you were there. He found the house open and your car still parked outside. Next thing we found out was that Melody had been taken and a ransom note left. Roger had called the police by then."

"It was a bit of a jigsaw," admitted Roger. "I'd only just arrived at work, and was still wondering why all the lights were on, when I got a phone call from a guy who lives next to the airport, complaining about a plane breaking curfew in the middle of the night. I told him it was nothing to do with us, but then I went outside and found the hangar open, and the Cessna 172 gone."

Roger opened his can of beer.

"Next thing we're fielding phone-calls from police and air traffic control who want to know why an aircraft squawking an emergency code had been tracked north from Paraparaumu in the middle of the night. It was only then Maria noticed your scrawl, and the pieces of the jigsaw started to fit together."

"I'd have spotted it earlier if things hadn't been so topsy-turvy," said Maria. "As it was, we'd started to get the full picture of what had happened and where you'd gone when Jim Mason came in here demanding we fly up to rescue his daughter. He'd just got back from Auckland after his court case to find his housekeeper hysterical, Melody kidnapped, the police called and a ransom note waiting for him."

"Then your boyfriend called to check on you," said Roger. "We filled him in with what we knew. He'd already picked up on a police alert, so he said he'd get an Air New Zealand flight across to Napier, and please could we pick him up from there, as he thought you had been taken into the Ureweras. I tell you, yesterday was a long day."

"Tell me about it," I agreed. "It's great to be back here with you all. I'm shattered. Nick, I owe you a drink, but can we take a rain check on it? I need to get home beforc I go to sleep in this seat. Can someone give me a lift?"

Nick elected to drive me.

"It was bloody creepy when I got here yesterday morning," he said as he negotiated my drive. "When I found there was no one here, and no indication of where you were, it was like finding the Marie Celeste. Spooky and worrying."

"I certainly found it pretty worrying when Steve broke in," I agreed. "I suppose I'm going to have to up my level of security around here again. I still can't work out how he got in."

"Do you want me to come in with you and check everything is OK first?" asked Nick.

"Thanks, but no. It all looks fine, and I had all the bad guys away on the trip with me, so they can't have caused any more chaos," I said.

"See you tomorrow then," Nick said as I climbed out. My car was blocking the turning circle, so I waved as he backed down the drive.

How can the familiar seem so strange? I'd only been gone a day, but there was a distinctly empty feel to my home. It had been left unlocked when Steve had taken me. I walked in and automatically called out for Nelson.

There was no reply.

The kitchen and living room were fine, but, even though I'd expected it, it felt odd to walk into my untidy bedroom and see an unmade bed and my discarded PJs on the floor at this time of day.

First things first. I picked my phone up from behind the bedside table, and checked it out. There were unanswered calls and messages from Roger, Jack, Pete and Kate. I deleted them all. Events had made any earlier conversations obsolete. It was surprisingly comforting to have my phone back. I'd taken it for granted until it was taken away from me and realised how much I depended on it for my safety, social contact and even time keeping. Its battery was low, so I plugged it in to charge.

Then I had to make a decision: showering first, then chores, or getting the jobs done, then relaxing. The chores won.

I stripped the bed and put the sheets in the wash then lit the fire in the living room to warm the house up, before returning to make the bed up with clean sheets. All obvious things to do as Jack had indicated he'd be coming around later, but I knew I was marking my territory and removing all trace and memory of Steve. It was why I hadn't chosen to shower first. I needed to imprint myself on my home again.

I looked around with satisfaction when it was all neat and tidy again. I ignored a transient niggle that asked whether I was getting anally retentive and had lived alone too long. I shrugged the thought away, ran a hot shower, and finally got to strip off my dirty clothes.

It felt good to be clean again even if it was more a purifying ritual banishing the shadow of Steve and Glynn from my life.

I returned to the lounge and stacked up the fire before pouring myself a large glass of wine and stretching out on the sofa to watch the news on TV.

I was home and warm, dry and clean. It felt like heaven.

CHAPTER
TWENTY SEVEN

THE OUTBREAK OF SUSPECTED FOOT-AND-MOUTH disease led the news. Samples had been taken from the infected farm, and a strict quarantine imposed on all other farms in the area. There was to be no movement of stock and no sale of produce. The movements of people were restricted and anti-infection measures set up.

I felt desperately sorry for the farmer who was interviewed. No, he said, he had no idea how his animals could have become infected. He just hoped it was some other minor and insignificant condition that presented similarly and not the dreaded foot-and-mouth. In the meantime, he had to wait for test results from the laboratory.

The man's patent misery tore at me. Bloody Glynn and Steve and the trouble they'd caused. It seemed unkind that the young woman reporter who conducted the interview looked so fresh and chipper, when it was obvious this man's life had imploded on him.

A political commentary followed. The Minister for Primary Industries, well-groomed and looking safely removed from the personal tragedy playing out down on the farm, painted a bleak future for New Zealand's trade.

I glared at the screen and muted it. Enough misery for one day. I wondered whether the police had managed to catch up with Glynn. There was no mention of it on the news. It was unnerving that he might still be out there, working his mischief.

There was something slightly hypnotic about watching the presenters on TV soundlessly mouthing words. My eyes began to droop although it was still early, and I was dozing when Jack arrived.

"I thought I'd buy some Indian takeaways," he said. "I hope you don't mind. Once I've settled down here I don't think I'm going to want to go back out again." He dumped the bags on the kitchen bench.

I pushed myself upright and went to join him. "Good thinking. I was just about asleep as it is."

He pulled me to him and gave me a warm kiss.

"Welcome home," I said when he released me.

He grinned. "Hold that thought," he said.

I smiled as we busied ourselves serving the food. Once, our hands brushed as we both reached for a fork, and the frisson ran right through me. I glanced up. He was gazing straight at me. I gave a slight embarrassed smile, and dropped my eyes as I stepped away from the bench with my plate of food. The intensity of my own reactions made me shy. I prided myself on being independent and I didn't want to swamp Jack in a flood of emotion, but my need for him unnerved me.

We were quiet as we ate. I'd been hungry but hadn't realised it.

Jack sat beside me and indicated the silent TV screen. "Are you practising lip-reading?"

"No, I only put it on to see if there was anything on the news about Steve and Glynn. Did they find Glynn?"

"Not yet." Jack's voice was grim. "The roadblocks weren't set up in time, so they missed the TV vans as they went through. They caught up with them in the end, but not until they'd reached Rotorua."

"Did they have Glynn?"

Jack shook his head. "No, they confirmed they'd picked up a

man matching his description on the road out of Maungapohatu. He'd claimed to be a DOC worker, so they gave him a lift, but he'd asked to be dropped off on the outskirts of Rotorua. The search teams are out there now looking for him."

"Bloody unlikely Department of Conservation worker," I snorted. "He had townie written all over him. I'm surprised they believed his story. What about Steve?"

"I gather he's been patched up and is now behind bars. He wasn't granted bail."

"Let's all hope his arm goes septic and he dies of blood-poisoning."

Jack gave me a glance, but said nothing. I wondered whether I'd sounded too harsh.

The phone rang. As I picked up, Jack stood, gathered up our empty plates and took them to the sink. I watched him rinse the dishes, and wondered what that glance had meant.

"Hi, it's Pete. I just wanted to find out whether you got home and how you were. Are you OK?"

"Yes," I said. "I'm back home safely. Another adventure over. Jack's here. Do you want to talk to him?"

There was a slight hiccup of panic from Pete.

"Shit no," he said. "Send him regards and all that, I'll catch up with him soon enough. I only wanted to check up on you. You two have a nice evening."

"I'll pass the message on," I said, amused. Heaven knew what Pete was expecting Jack to do to him.

I went across to help Jack with the plates.

"Pete sends his regards," I said.

"Hm," was his non-commital reply.

I grinned to myself. No doubt the two men would sort matters out between them. I knew they were old friends.

I tidied up the remains of the meal. I love Indian food, but the pungent spices can permeate a room so I took the empty containers outside to the rubbish bin.

Out of habit I called for Nelson, but there was no reply. In truth, I knew it was futile to persist, but I couldn't relinquish the faint hope he could still come back.

Jack was loading the fire when I returned. He stood as I approached him, and opened his arms.

I walked into them and felt him enfold me in his warmth and care. We stood together for a long moment. I felt the edgy tension running through me gradually relax and my breathing softened. I understood then that being with Jack was my happy place.

"You've had a rough time," he said at last, and kissed my forehead. He drew me down to the sofa. I sat back and he perched on its edge, looking at me.

His hand reached out and traced the yellow bruise on my cheek. "How do the bruises feel?

"Better," I said. "There was no real damage done. The worst part was how shaken it made me feel. I'd make a hopeless boxer. I'd bolt if someone came at me with raised fists."

He smiled slightly. "Is that why you were sending death wishes to Steve?"

"I suppose." I shrugged at the idea. "He was just so vicious and unpredictable it was terrifying. He threatened to cut Melody's face at one point, the vicious bastard."

Jack winced. "Bastard indeed. I imagine he'll get dealt to in jail, if that's any consolation."

I pondered that and gave a little laugh. "Stupid of me, I know, but isn't. There's a part of me that is too high-minded to want him bashed up randomly by some other criminal. I'd rather do it myself. What I really want of course is to turn the tables and make him afraid of me. I didn't like being frightened."

"Well, you dealt with him effectively enough. Both times you hit him had fairly dramatic results. When his system is free of all the drugs, I imagine he'll regret bullying you." There was a thread of humour in his voice.

I hadn't seen things in quite that light. "I did OK, didn't I?" I said pleased. Bless Jack, he was restoring my self-esteem. I reached my hand to his thigh and gave it a gentle squeeze.

"You've made me feel much better."

"That's my job," he said as his hand came down to cover mine.

We were looking at each other now, and there was no mistaking the communication and urgency we shared. I turned my hand to grasp his, and stood up, pulling him with me.

"Then let's go and make each other feel even betterer," I said.

There was little finesse as I tugged at his shirt to remove it, or as he peeled my jeans from my hips. At first we discarded clothes with a fury of impatience, frantic to reach the skin beneath, but as the last garments fell, the tempo changed, and we stood together allowing our hands to move slowly, rediscovering each other's naked flesh.

Jacks hands rose to cup my breasts. He played with them gently, his thumb skimming the peaks. He rolled my nipples, then tugged gently. I swear there's a direct thread between nipples and G spot. I moaned softly, and relaxed into the sweetness of the sensation. I felt my insides melt, and my hips stretched towards his as I caressed the planes of his skin.

I reached for his sex to hold him and urge him on, but Jack was far too experienced a lover to allow me to wantonly drive the pace of this reunion.

"Gently, gently. We want this to last," he chuckled as he drew me down on the bed underneath him. He gathered my wrists in one hand and held them pinned above my head while his other hand and his lips roved at will over my helpless body. I writhed and bucked uncontrollably when he plundered deep between my thighs.

"It's not fair," I gasped at last, as Jack began to tease the sensitive nub at my core's centre. "You're still in control of yourself and I'm unravelling."

"No one ever said life was fair," he murmured, but he released his hold on my wrists and obligingly moved as I climbed on top of him.

"Do your worst then," he challenged. And I did. I shot him a look I intended to be sophisticated irony, but probably just looked lust-crazed, and took my revenge. We'd been together long enough for me to know the intimate keys to his body.

My hands stroked, my mouth suckled, and with both I focused on drawing Jack closer to the edge. He was groaning uncontrollably when the rhythm of my teasing changed and I abandoned tormenting him as I yielded to the driving pace of my own need. He felt the shift and rose to meet my hunger. We weren't even remotely gentle with each other. We had twinned with more primitive, ancient rites and were sufficiently bold to embrace the forces we had summoned.

Together we rode a complex wave - a cord of need, twisted together from physical sensation, reconnection, love - and finally, expiation for the pain we'd suffered over the last twenty-four hours.

We were both sweat-drenched when we'd finished. I gave a wry thought to the crisp, clean sheets I'd wasted on the bed. Truth be told, we'd have been equally content on a bed of sacking.

I lay on Jack's breast with my eyes closed, trying to control both my heartbeat and my emotions – not an easy task when I was aware of Jack's ragged breathing as he attempted the same beneath me. The rawness of our coupling had both healed us and blasted us apart. I wondered how we could recover our relaxed relationship after such a climactic event.

It was several long moments before Jack gave a gentle ripple of his chest muscles and dislodged me from my paralysed grip on his torso. I rolled sideways, easing myself away from him, only to be enclosed by arms which wouldn't let me move further than a position right beside him.

"Where do you think you're going?" he mumbled.

I gathered he was half asleep and was torn between amusement and irritation.

"I need to clean up," I explained, "and so, incidentally, do you."

I was rewarded with a gentle snore.

I gave a small grin, allowed him a couple of minutes, then gently eased myself free and stood looking down at him. He was beautiful. Jack would always be a handsome man. Now, reclining in satiated glory, he was a Greek statue. I couldn't decide whether he was a Zeus or a somewhat debauched Bacchus, but his physique ranked up there with the immortals. I enjoyed studying him now, in all his naked glory, and eventually gave a small sniff of female superiority. Magnificence in a man can be so transitory.

* * *

"So, what happens next?" I asked.

I was buttering toast while Jack poured himself coffee.

He shrugged. "You might hear from the police, but you've already given them a statement, so it would only be if they need supplementary details. Otherwise they'll leave you in peace."

"Ops normal then," I mumbled around my slice of toast. "What about you?"

"I complete the interrupted debrief of my work in the Solomons, and then it's back to the grindstone for me as well. Of course, I've still got leave owing to me if you're interested."

Our previous plans to go on holiday together had been hi-jacked when Jack got his overseas posting.

"God, I need a holiday," I said wistfully. Visions of sun-drenched beaches and warm tropical nights flooded my imagination. I turned my gaze to the window where rain was trickling down the pane. Yesterday's fine weather was over and we were back to winter.

"We'll talk about it this evening," he said as he kissed me goodbye.

I took my time getting ready for work. I felt slow and heavy this morning. Jack and I had enjoyed what he'd described as a 'rematch' in the hour before dawn, and I was feeling the effects of all that pleasant debauchery. My eyes were heavy lidded, my lips still swollen, and I was, not unpleasantly, sore.

"I need a lay-day," I'd complained when the alarm went off. I'd tried to bury myself under the duvet.

Jack had chuckled. "You just had a lay-night. Stop your whinging, woman. Get to work and support me. I'm the one who did all the hard work." He'd laughed as he dodged the pillow I'd thrown at him and taken himself off for a shower.

CHAPTER
TWENTY EIGHT

I'VE SAID BEFORE THAT I LIKE MY JOB, and I don't just mean the fun of flying. Even the routine, boring, chores of day-to-day work have their own pleasure and purpose if you're in a good environment. With the rain pouring down outside, we were all office bound, which for once suited me fine. I was in the mood for a quiet day.

"You should be doing this," I remarked to Greig when he came into the briefing room to see what I was doing.

I was updating the briefing notes we used for teaching students. Of course, every flying instructor develops their own copy during their training as a C Cat Instructor, but somehow mine had ended up living in the briefing room and were used as the default manual by all of us.

"Say what?" asked Greig.

"You need to do your B Cat," I said. "As part of that you could upgrade these. They're looking awfully tatty these days."

Greig snorted. "Are you saying you want to use my notes? After you're always so rude about my handwriting? I don't think so."

I grinned at him. "I'd forgotten that bit," I admitted. "Still, you should get your B Cat. You know I'm right."

"Stop hassling him," ordered Roger. "He's already agreed with me that he's going to start in two weeks' time. Isn't that right?"

"Really? That's great," I said.

Greig looked sheepish.

"I discussed it with Roger the other day," he told me.

I smiled. A smile that turned into a yawn.

"Didn't you get much sleep last night? You're yawning, Hardcastle, and you seem a bit cranky," asked Roger innocently but with amused, knowing eyes.

I glared at him, and saw Greig rapidly conceal a grin.

"Piss off, the pair of you," I said crossly.

Roger laughed, and left me to it. Greig, I noticed, looked slightly embarrassed as he, in turn, left.

"Frigging men," I growled, then let the moment go, and let the gentle minutiae of my work enfold me.

I was updating my battered notes on the theory behind Climbing and Descending when Maria called me to accept a phone-call.

Wouldn't you know it? It was T-bone.

"Claire Hardcastle? It's DS Jenner."

"Hi," I replied without enthusiasm.

"I believe you've given evidence in another police case that places a suspect within proximity of a death on the Kapiti Coast?"

I had some trouble untangling that sentence, then realised what he was referring to.

"Yes, if you're talking about the manaia around Steve's throat," I said.

"Can you tie the same suspect to the murder in the Sounds?" he asked.

"What do you mean?" I asked. "You already know I flew Steve and Glynn down to Nopera. Is that the proximity you're asking about?"

"I know that, but is there anything additional, after reflection, you can add to your statement that could provide a direct link to the Sounds murder?"

"Not that I can think of," I said. "I told you everything I knew when you interviewed me, and nothing else has come up since."

"You were abducted?"

"Yes."

"So you were with the suspects for what, about twenty-four hours, and neither of them said anything relevant to you?"

"About murder? No," I said. "Oddly enough the subject didn't arise. I didn't ask them any questions about murdering people, and they didn't confess anything." I let irritation sound clearly in my voice.

T-bone rang off, and I stomped out to the office to tell Roger and Maria about the call.

"Obviously, I'd have told the police if either Steve or Glynn had said anything," I said. "The man's a moron."

"I suppose it's logical for him to try and make that connection, though," said Maria. "Just think how convenient it would be if Steve's arrest solved two murders."

"Two birds with one stone," Roger said thoughtfully. "Actually, it's not Steve or Glynn that connects the dead men, Hardcastle. It's you."

"Me?" I was indignant. "I haven't gone around killing people."

"No, but you've got an uncanny knack of being in the vicinity of the action," he said. "It's getting to be a habit."

"Well, I didn't ask for it."

Roger made a noise that sounded like 'humph'. "We've also got to work out how we cover the expense of the jaunt you took up country," he said. "Who pays for the plane? There's several hundred dollars' worth of fuel and mileage charges to be covered. Are you putting your hand up for the bill, Hardcastle?"

I was shocked. "Shit, no," I said. "You don't honestly expect me to pay for that, surely?"

Sometimes Roger staggered me. I opened my mouth to tell him, with great emotional depth and feeling, exactly what I thought of the suggestion, when Maria intervened.

"It's OK, Claire. He's teasing," she said firmly.

Roger turned to her. I saw him framing a reply, which withered when Maria nailed him with a glare.

"OK, I'll send it to the police then," he said. He sounded a bit like a sulky boy.

I shot a grateful smile at Maria, who nodded her head serenely. "I think that would be best," she said to Roger.

I was still fuming over Roger's words an hour later when he called me out from the briefing room.

"Detective Senior Sergeant Alistair Taylor wants a word with you," Roger announced from where he stood in the doorway.

"Oh my god, not another policeman," I complained.

"You must be their most popular witness," Roger replied.

I went through to the main office area. The man waiting at the counter was tall. Although he was very thin, every other feature seemed to be outsized. His hands and feet were enormous; his head seemed too long and large for the head supporting it, and I noticed he had large feet. He would, I thought, have made a convincing vampire in a classic early Hollywood movie. Alternatively, he could have been Nick Cave's brother.

I felt my eyes widen as I introduced myself.

"Hi, I'm Alistair Taylor. Would you have the time for a few words? John Letts told me you might have some useful information." His smile was warm and friendly, his tone lightly amused. It was such a complete contrast to his sepulchral appearance.

"Come on through," I invited, showing him into the briefing room. We sat down and he opened his laptop.

"What can I help you with?" I asked.

"I want you to look at this pendant and tell me about it."

He pulled an envelope from his pocket, and tipped its contents onto the table.

Andrew's pendant lay in front of me. I reached forward and turned it over. AC, the initials I'd seen before, was clearly carved on the reverse.

I looked up at Alistair. "I told John I identified this as belonging to Andrew Camborne." I took a breath as I tried to accurately recollect the moment. "I'd met him on the evening of the night he died. When I admired the carving he wore around his neck, he told me it had been a gift to him. I think he said it was an antique, but I particularly remembered him saying his initials had been engraved on the back so he could never lose it."

Alistair nodded. "John told me it was around the neck of the man responsible for the armed offenders call-out in the Ureweras?"

I nodded. "Yes, it was around Steve's neck. I found it when I loosened his collar to try and help him breathe after I'd knocked him unconscious."

Alistair gave me a warm smile. "Would you be prepared to make a statement to that effect."

I shrugged. "OK. Does this mean Steve was responsible for Andrew's death?"

"We think so." I realised Alistair was being cautious.

"Can you prove it?" I asked.

He gave a wry smile. "The million-dollar question! Now we know the pendant represents a proven connection between the two men, we're looking for any evidence that might provide clues about Andrew's death. Steve's vehicle and property is being examined by forensics, and although, you understand, it's too early for me to confirm the particulars of their findings, it's looking positive. And you've just confirmed that the victim – I mean Andrew – wouldn't have willingly handed the pendant over to anyone."

I nodded again. "I'm sure he wouldn't. He was very proud of it. I can't imagine any situation in which he'd have parted with it."

I signed the statement Alastair typed out for me.

"Do we know yet why Steve would have killed Andrew?"

Alistair sighed. "The best we've got out of Steve is that a journalist had been sticking his nose into his business and had to be stopped. Mind you, he hasn't admitted to the murder, nor did he name Andrew."

"What happens now?" I asked.

"I'm sure you'll hear as soon as we find anything," he said. "It will be on the news, and I understand you have a couple of friends in the force. I'm sure they'll let you know."

I nodded warily. I don't know the rules surrounding disclosure of information to the general public, but it had occurred to me that Pete at least, had occasionally been indiscrete.

"One other thing."

I looked at Alistair.

"I believe you filed a complaint with police about a cat's tail that had been sent to you, and your own cat being missing?"

I nodded.

"I'm certain Steve was responsible. He more or less admitted to it."

Alistair nodded. "I think you should know a search of Steve's property turned up a cat's body in the garden."

I felt myself begin to shake. I didn't want to know what he was going to tell me.

His voice was softly reassuring when he continued: "The animal was wrapped in a plastic bag, and the way it was wrapped leads us to think it may have come from a veterinary practice. We believe it was euthanised and only mutilated a long time after death."

"You mean they killed Nelson before they took his tail?"

He shook his head.

"We think this animal had been dead for a while."

I stared at him. "What?"

He gave a slight smile.

"Among the people we've identified from contacts on Steve's cell phone was a veterinary nurse. It's possible she provided the animal for him. In which case that tail may not belong to your own animal."

"So, Nelson could still be alive?"

Alistair shrugged his shoulders.

"That I don't know. But the cat we found in the garden wasn't anyone's recent pet. We think it was an animal euthanised earlier and kept in a freezer for some weeks."

"Ugh." I tried to absorb his information and ended up shaking my head. I hoped Nelson hadn't been tortured, but he was still missing, which was what mattered to me.

"I'm sorry," he said kindly, clearly reading my distress. "I know how important pets can be."

We parted politely. I contrasted Alistair with T-bone Trev and marvelled how one could be so abrasive while the other elicited my cooperation with no more than a quirked eyebrow and a gentle smile.

CHAPTER TWENTY NINE

JIM CALLED ROGER TO FIND OUT HOW I was, and to remind us all that he was shouting a round of drinks at the bar that evening to celebrate Melody's solo circuit.

Roger passed the phone across to me.

"Let's celebrate," Jim said. "We can drink to Melody's solo, to you both being safe, and to me for winning my court case and being back at home."

I smiled as I agreed.

I used my mobile to call Jack, tell him I'd be celebrating at work that evening, and did he want to join us?

"Sounds good," he said. I heard the warmth in his voice.

It's the simple things that add value to our lives, I thought. Not that I considered the addition of Jack into my life was simple. I was referring to the convenience of having a mobile phone in my pocket for immediate contact with the rest of the world. I'd missed it when deprived of it.

The pleasure of having Jack back was incalculable. I acknowledged it put a bit of a dent in the self-reliance and independence I prided myself on, but Jack was rapidly becoming an essential part of my happiness. I shrugged and decided not to over-intellectualise the issue. What happened, happened.

Greig and I had locked up the hangar at the end of the day and repaired to the office when the phone went once more.

"Hi, it's me, Pete."

"Hi, Pete," I answered.

"They've got the bastard," he said. "Picked him up late this morning."

"Who? Do you mean Glynn?" I asked.

"Yes. They caught him in the act of trying to plant the virus in a farm's water supply. Well, the farmer caught him first. Glynn was behaving suspiciously around a water trough, so the farmer went to check what was going on. I guess he wasn't impressed by what he discovered, or by whatever story Glynn told him. By the time the police arrived, Glynn had experienced a few accidental falls while waiting for them and wasn't in too good a condition."

Pete sounded amused.

"You mean the farmer beat him up?" I asked.

"No comment. But Glynn's now in custody, so that's a good result."

"They've got Glynn," I said to the others in the room. "A farmer caught him trying to poison the water."

I returned to my phone call.

"At least I don't have to worry anymore about him turning up here," I said. "That's great news."

"All good between you and Jack?" Pete's voice was tinged with nervousness.

"Yes, all good," I replied. "I take it you haven't caught up with him yet?"

"No. That's all I needed to tell you. See you later." He hung up abruptly.

I was mildly amused by Pete's fear. I assumed Jack wouldn't actually beat him up, however angry he was, but I worked in a masculine environment myself, and nothing would surprise me when it came to men. I decided it wasn't my business how they sorted out their differences.

Most students buy a round or two of drinks for their instructor when they go solo. Jim's idea of celebrating went well beyond that. Not only did he open a tab at the bar offering free drinks for everyone who turned up, but he'd organised catering as well. Nick and Greig munched happily on canapés and sausage rolls.

"This is a bit of all right," said Greig, helping himself to another hot savoury.

"So's she," said Nick. I turned to see he was looking at Melody.

She'd recovered well from her ordeal. Her hair was back to bouncy perfection, her clothes discreetly expensive and tidy, and she looked for all the world as if nothing had ever troubled her privileged young life.

I watched her laughing at something Roger was saying, her sulky teenager pose well and truly abandoned. Instead, her animated little face was alive with enthusiasm and excitement. I felt a twinge of envy. I'd worked all day, was still in my uniform, and my face bore a psychedelic array of bruises which weren't nearly as concealed beneath my make-up as I would have liked.

We watched Nick make his way across to her and congratulate her.

Greig raised his eyebrows. "Looks like Nick's got a new interest," he said.

"Not a bad choice," I agreed. "She's a champ. He could do worse." And, I added mentally, she could do a lot worse as well. Nick would be ideal boyfriend material, being a thoroughly nice young man and a vast improvement on Steve.

I looked towards the door, searching for Jack. He was late.

Jim peeled away from the group surrounding Melody and walked over to us.

"Thank you, Jim," I said. "You've done us proud."

"My pleasure. There was a lot to celebrate."

"Here's to Melody," I said, taking a sip of my drink.

"And to you and Roger," said Jim. "You helped Melody through a difficult time. She's been a different girl since she started flying."

No kidding, I thought, remembering her composure as she bandaged Steve and organised everyone. I suppose we'd provided a form of extra-curricular training that few aviation schools could match.

"She was pretty impressive yesterday," I said. "Considering how awful our ordeal was, she remained calm and competent through it all. She's quite a girl."

Jim smiled in reply.

"Did you say your court case went well?" I asked.

"It went extremely well," he replied. "It was a silly case for them to take against me in the first place, as I knew I hadn't done anything wrong, so I was cleared on all charges."

"Congratulations," I said.

"Well, yes and no," said Jim sombrely. "While I knew I wasn't personally responsible for any wrongdoing, there were rumours floating around that my company was involved in something dodgy, and I wasn't having my reputation threatened. A couple of weeks back I launched an internal investigation. It didn't take the IT forensic people long to uncover some disquieting stuff on Glynn's computer. It took me rather longer to fathom out just what he was doing."

"He'd worked with you for some time?" Roger had joined us.

"The best part of five years," said Jim. "I guess that was part of the problem. After that length of time, I trusted him implicitly and probably wasn't keeping my eye on him as much as I should."

"What was he doing?" asked Roger.

"Fudging the invoicing. Creating invoices for expenses that didn't exist and lodging payments that didn't relate to our operation. Effectually he was using my company's legitimate accounts for money laundering. I didn't know where he was getting the funds from, so once I'd discovered the discrepancies, I put it in the hands of the police."

"Holy crap," I said. "How long had it been going on for?"

"As far as we can tell, only during this last financial year," said Jim. "Which of course is why it hadn't been discovered. The accounts don't get audited until next April."

"By which time he'd have launched his foot-and mouth-virus throughout the country, been paid, and would probably have done a runner," I said.

Jim shrugged. "I guess. The police, in their wisdom, decided to raid his place, and that was what triggered Glynn and his nephew to abduct you and Melody. I can't tell you how angry I was when I figured out what had happened. The police owe you and Melody a colossal apology for stuffing things up."

"The police owe who an apology?" Jack had arrived and walked over to join us.

"For the stuff up that allowed Glynn and Steve to evade their raid and kidnap our two girls," said Jim.

"Ah, that stuff up," said Jack thoughtfully. "I imagine a few harsh words will be exchanged during the debrief for that operation."

"All's well that ends well," I said. "Yesterday's behind us, tomorrow lies ahead." I didn't want to waste time dwelling on what had gone before. I wanted to concentrate on the future and on spending time with Jack.

"With that in mind," said Roger, "you need to prepare a briefing for our next meeting, Hardcastle, explaining the route you flew into that valley, how it worked and why."

"OK," I said, surprised and gratified.

"Then you can continue the briefing with an explanation of why, under no circumstances, you or anyone else will attempt such a suicidal landing again." That was typical Roger, I thought. A compliment with a sting in its tail.

"I thought she did very well," said Jim defensively. "Melody was full of praise for her skill. She said she was awesome."

Roger sniffed. I recognised his conflict. He was as proud as punch that I'd carried out that landing successfully, but utterly determined to make sure neither I nor any other instructor risked our necks attempting such a feat again.

I decided discretion was called for. "I'd be happy to prepare a briefing," I said.

I congratulated Melody again as we left and was rewarded with an enormous grin and a bone-crushing hug. She was still shy of Jack but smiled prettily at him when he congratulated her.

"I'll see you in a couple of days. Then the real work of training to be a pilot begins. We haven't even begun to discuss the theory exams you need to study for."

Melody stuck her tongue out at me. "Spoil-sport," she said.

Jack and I had decided to go to the *Thai Lagoon* for our meal. It was one of my favourites, serving exceptionally good food at very reasonable prices.

We went back to my place first so I could change and freshen up.

While he waited for me, Jack switched on the TV news.

"Hey, Claire, come here," he called a few minutes later. "Listen to this."

"… the samples taken from cattle on the south Waikato farm suspected of being infected with foot-and-mouth disease, have been identified as belonging to an attenuated form of the virus. The Pirbright Institute, a research facility in England, confirmed today that their tests have established the strain present in tissue specimens from the affected animals came originally from their secure unit which specialises in research into, and the development of, attenuated viruses. The term 'attenuated' describes viruses which are already dead, having been deliberately killed in the laboratory. The protein remaining from the deceased matter is used in the development of vaccinations to protect against or prevent the spread of virulently contagious diseases. The laboratory stresses that, although a few animals who presumably came into direct contact with the source of the infection have shown mild symptoms of foot-and-mouth disease, they are not infectious, nor is there any possibility of the virus being spread to other animals or farms.

"Policy in New Zealand requires animals displaying such symptoms be destroyed immediately, whether subsequently found to be infectious or not.

"Police in the United Kingdom are investigating how a theft of such potentially deadly material could have occurred from the Pirbright laboratories. Pirbright opened new, state-of-the-art facilities in 2014 and extended them in 2015. They were believed to be totally secure. The director says he is astounded that such a failure could have occurred as the institute prides itself on its rigorous safety systems and controls, and has promised complete cooperation with the police to determine how samples of the virus could have ended up in New Zealand.

"Further in today's news: Police have today apprehended a man in the Bay of Plenty whom they believe can help them in their investigation into what they are now calling 'a deliberate attempt to sabotage New Zealand's economic future'."

Jack and I stared at each other. In the end I gave a nervous giggle. "Are they saying that after all we've been through, the virus they were using was useless?"

"Well, hardly useless," said Jack. "New Zealand's foot-and-mouth scare was reported around the world so I suppose there will be repercussions for us internationally. Glynn and Steve have also caused a good deal of distress, and the infected cattle will be destroyed, which is going to be devastating for the farmers involved. Even if they get compensation," he added. "Most farmers I know really care about their stock and almost know them personally, so it will be horrible for them."

"In which case, I'm pleased Glynn got beaten up," I said. "You should have heard him when he told Poppa about what he was doing. It was just a business deal for him. He didn't care about what happened to the people who suffered or lost their livelihood because of him."

"Which makes him not so different from any other criminal," said Jack wryly. "If there's one common thread running through most crime, its lack of empathy for the victim."

"Steve was certainly like that," I acknowledged. I'd already told Jack about my interview with Alistair Taylor.

"He's a good guy," Jack had said. "If he's on the case, Steve's probably history."

It was a relief to sit down at the restaurant and order our meal. Even so, we weren't alone in our fascination with the foot-and-mouth story. I could hear snippets of conversations from other tables where the news was being discussed, and the implications of the dead, harmless virus were examined.

"That's why I don't believe in vaccinations," one young woman declared. "Look what they're made from, and we're putting dead bugs into our children."

"Don't be silly, Sarah," an older woman sitting beside her chimed in.

Their debate continued. I raised my eyebrows as the argument became heated.

Jack and I looked at each other. He reached his arm across the table to me, and I put my hand into his. His fingers curled around mine.

"It's good to be back," he said.

I nodded. "It's bloody good to have you back. I hate to sound a wuss, but I missed you."

"Me too," he said. As I assumed the mangled grammar meant he'd missed me as well, I felt a glow of happiness.

We said nothing for a while, just sat quietly and in harmony until our food arrived and we were forced to move.

As it happened, I was ravenous, and had no problem redirecting my attention to the food. I was well into my Thai savoury pancake when Jack, who'd been eating at a slower pace, put down his fork and said, "I was late getting to Paraparaumu Aviation this evening because I saw Pete when I left work."

"Oh?" I raised my eyes from the rather yummy prawns I was eating, and focused back on Jack. I wasn't sure I wanted to hear the details of the conversation with Pete.

"Do I need to call an ambulance?" I asked politely.

He shook his head and smiled. "No. I ranted and raved a bit, but Pete was already suitably penitent and apologetic. I couldn't really do anything else but accept his apologies. And, no thanks to him, the story has had a satisfactory outcome. Mind you, I told him I'd kill him if he ever again tried to involve you in a police operation."

I refrained from telling him just how terrified Pete had been about meeting with him, which led to an interesting insight. I'd never lie to Jack, but equally, I wouldn't betray Pete to him either. I justified my conflict by telling myself that they needed to sort the matter out themselves, but a part of me knew I regarded Pete as a slightly delinquent younger brother who I disapproved of but would protect in equal measure.

"I'm glad you're both talking to each other again."

He shrugged. "It's done."

He picked his wine glass up. "Here's to us," he said.

I followed him in the toast. "To us."

"Excellent," said Jack putting his glass down and turning to his food.

"We still need to organise the shared leave we were supposed to have two months ago. Are you still on?" he asked.

I nodded.

"Maybe we should work out a plan, stick to it, and this time really get away," I said. "I'll talk to Roger tomorrow and see what we can work out."

It was still early when we got home, although the night was pitch black. Winter is a very depressing time. I loathe the dark mornings and early evenings. The foul weather we'd had all day meant it was darker than ever as we climbed out of the car and made our way to my front door.

Jack had just opened the door for me when I heard it, a thin wisp of a sound, almost blown away in the wind.

"Quiet," I said urgently as I stretched every sense I had to focus on the call.

In spite of my efforts I heard nothing more. My shoulders sagged as I realised wishful thinking had once again misled me.

I sighed. "No. It was nothing."

I moved to cross the threshold and reminded myself I was ready to face the truth. Nelson was dead and I'd never see him again.

That time we both heard it. Jack stiffened beside me and I gave a small cry.

"Nelson, Nelson!"

Slowly, barely visible, a pale shadow in the darkness, a small creature made its way out from underneath the bushes that lined the drive.

"Nelson," I breathed as I went to scoop him up and carry him into the house.

I put him on the kitchen bench and examined him. He was

appallingly thin - his ribs obvious beneath his dull, dirty coat - but he had a tail! I was absurdly grateful that he appeared to be in one piece even though his voice was a mere croak, nothing like the rich, noisy calls Nelson was known for.

I lifted him, turned him over and examined his pads. They were rubbed raw, the wounds oozing and painful looking.

"Oh, Nelson." I buried my face against his neck. "What happened to you?" Even his purr was cracked and muted as he rubbed his cheek against mine.

I hugged him like a child hugs a teddy bear. When at last I could bear to pass him to Jack I busied myself filling bowls with water and food.

I was absurdly happy when he finally began to eat. I was careful to limit his food. Much better to feed him one teaspoon an hour for the next few hours than to let him bolt his food and be sick. If I was any judge, Nelson had spent several days without food, and I'd need to be careful not to overload his system. I'd make an appointment at the vet for him to be checked over.

Later I lifted him onto my lap and settled on the sofa within the warm comfort of Jack's arm.

I beamed at Jack. "There is a god after all."

He kissed the top of my head. "Do you know what I'm thinking?"

I shook my head. He looked vaguely embarrassed, hesitated, and then launched into the first line of the Sister Sledge song.

"'We are family'."

I blinked to contain the emotional rush of moisture that rose in my eyes.

Nelson gave his cracked, death-rattle purr as I reached my hand out to Jack.

"I love you," I said quietly.

Please continue reading for a bonus excerpt from Penelope Haines's third instalment in the *Claire Hardcastle* series –

STALL TURNS

CHAPTER

ONE

WE WERE LOST, OF COURSE. I'D BEEN certain of it for some minutes, but as a tactful woman, I'd refrained from pointing it out. Now Jack had stopped the car and was peering at the battered signpost that marked the crossroads.

"I don't remember Pat mentioning anything about a Retakure," Jack said reading the place names in puzzlement. "We must have gone wrong somewhere."

He parked at the side of the road, and studied the directions he'd written down.

"He didn't mention a war memorial?" I asked. On the opposite side of the road stood a white stele. Bronze plaques screwed to the base listed the names of local men fallen in the world wars. There were probably hundreds of these memorials dotted around rural settlements in New Zealand, paying tribute to the price we'd paid as a nation honouring our international alliances. Pat would almost certainly have mentioned such a local landmark.

I'd listened to his directions myself as Jack had written them down. The route Pat had described had followed vague and strictly locally sourced criteria which had foiled the skill of the GPS navigation system installed in Jack's car.

"Turn left at the forestry block and follow the road for about 10 km. You'll be tracking alongside the river, so you can't go wrong. When you get to the fork in the road, turn right. You'll see the Fitchett's place on your left. About 5 km on you'll reach the crossroads. Turn right again and then take the second road on the right. The old woolshed will be on your left. The farmhouse is 2 km further on. You'll probably recognise the old place once you get there. You can't miss it."

Famous last words!

Of course, Pat hadn't mentioned the roads would turn to gravel soon after we'd left the highway, making it hard to distinguish between farm tracks and promulgated roads. We'd already wasted time driving up one such track, only to come up against a shut gate marking the place as a private farm. Nor had Pat thought to tell us there were several more turnings and crossroads than those he'd specified.

Consequently, on that fine spring morning, Jack and I were well and truly lost in the hilly countryside that lies south west of Te Kuiti.

"You don't remember this place from when you last visited?" I asked hopefully.

Jack shook his head. "I've only been out here once before, and I was about ten then," he said ruefully. "I suppose I'll remember the farmhouse when we get there, but nothing else seems familiar. We'll have to turn back, and see if we can pick the route up further back."

"Why don't we find the nearest farm and ask for directions?" I said. "They're bound to know where Pat's run is if it's anywhere near here. Farmers tend to know their neighbours."

Yes, I know real men don't ask for directions, but I was relying on Jack's common sense to get us past male stereotyping clichés.

Jack's "Hmm" didn't sound convinced, but he obligingly

turned the car towards Retakure.

A short distance further on, just past where the road curved around the bend, we came to a wide gateway framed by a high square archway that spanned the entrance. On each side of the gates the bordering fence line was neatly planted with low shrubs. The track that passed beneath the arch and led away up the valley was wide, well gravelled and tidy. Clearly this was a substantial and prosperous property and a marked contrast to other farms we'd passed that morning which had displayed utilitarian values rather than aspiring to being aesthetically pleasing.

"There must be someone about," I said as Jack turned into the long drive. Sure enough, in a few hundred metres we'd reached a sizeable woolshed, with a red ute parked in front of it.

"Stay there," said Jack. "I'll go and see if I can find someone."

I watched as he tried the woolshed door which must have been locked. He gave me a wave as he made his way through the sheep yards around the side of the building towards the rear.

It was too nice a day to remain sitting in the car, so I climbed out and looked around. Well-fenced and maintained paddocks ran into the distance. Beyond them, cleared land gave way to the bush covered hills which framed the valley. It was a beautiful spot. I leaned back against the car's bonnet and listened the silence. The only sound was the gentle sound of bees buzzing in the clover filled paddocks.

Jack had parked our car near a small stream, its banks fringed, not with the usual flax, but with bulrushes. I've always admired the austere architectural design of these oddly shaped plants, so I made my way through the long spring glass to have a closer look at them.

Getting to the plants was more of a mission than I'd anticipated. Not only was the long grass unpleasantly damp, drenching the bottom of my jeans, but I hadn't appreciated that the long stems of the bulrushes were well protected at their base by a mixture of pig-fern and blackberry tangled among the plants. I picked my way over the uneven ground until I'd reached the nearest plant, only to discover I'd been misled by an illusion. The kebab shaped heads of the bulrushes were clearly well past their use by date and must have been hanging there since last summer. Those that remained were shabby, their rich velvet coating rubbed away in uneven patches. What I had assumed were entire flowers were ghostly shapes held together by the spiders' webs which covered them.

"Well, that's depressing," I muttered to myself.

I had to bend to untangle the mess of fern, bidibids and blackberry clinging to the leg of my jeans. I glanced back at the woolshed. Jack hadn't reappeared. I didn't want to return on the track I'd used to come out here – it was too tangled and messy to tempt me again. I thought I could see a clearer route to my right that would take me between a couple of clumps of reeds, and looked free of any entangling creepers.

I wasn't savvy enough to see the area in front of those clumps, cunningly disguised by the long grass, was swamp. I hadn't taken two steps before I had sunk ankle deep into the morass. I floundered across to the reeds, and by balancing on their roots, hauled myself out of the smelly wet mud.

By now I was beside myself with fury. Yes, it was entirely my own fault and stupidity, but that didn't make me feel any better. My shoes were soaked, my jeans foul and I stank: a rich mix of rotting vegetation, sour mud and stagnant water. Worse, I could imagine Jack's hilarity when I made it back into the car. At least, I thought viciously, his laughter would die once the stench I now carried with me like a toxic plague infested his vehicle.

I took a deep breath before launching myself from my safe-haven, and across more swamp to the next clump of bulrush reeds. I stumbled on snags concealed in the quagmire and grabbed gratefully onto the rough blades of the reeds to pull me to safety.

My right foot had been gripped so firmly by the mud that I had to bend and pull it out by hand so as not to lose my shoe. There was a nasty sucking noise as it emerged. My shoes of course were ruined. I couldn't imagine any wash cycle that could clean them up adequately and render them fit for purpose again.

I looked around to plan the next stage of my trip back to the car. The ground ahead looked solid, but then, I'd been proved wrong before. I checked behind at the route I'd taken already, to see whether I could improve on my plan. Probably due to extricating my shoe from its grip, my passage through the morass had caused other matter to rise to the surface. I squinted at the thin white branches that emerged from the mud.

They were probably what I'd trodden on. I was lucky they hadn't caused me to trip and fall face first into the swamp. I'd half turned away to concentrate on the next half of my escape from the quagmire before my brain focussed on what I'd just seen and screamed for my attention.

I turned to face the branch. Shit. It wasn't a collection of thin twigs I'd seen, but the very identifiable, if skeletal, shape of a human forearm and phalanges. If I'd just seen the ribcage, I suppose I'd have assumed it to be the remains of a long dead sheep or cattle beast. As it was, the structure and shape of the arm and fingers was unmistakeable. And I'd just trodden and tripped over it. I felt a surge of nausea. Too late I realised the debris hanging off those twigs wasn't vegetable matter from the swamp, but probably rags of skin.

"What are you doing?" called Jack. He was back at the car, watching me. "You look a little worse for wear."

"Come over here," I shouted.

"Are you stuck? Do you need a hand?" Jack's amusement was palpable. "I'm not going to get myself all dirty for you. If you were silly enough to go in there, you can get yourself out."

"Just come here." I gritted my teeth against the sickness in my stomach. I couldn't face forming the words that would explain I thought I'd found a body. Let Jack work it out for himself.

Jack must have registered my distress, because he stopped teasing and came across to help.

"Are you OK?" he asked when he reached me.

I nodded. "Look at that." I pointed towards bones although I didn't look at them again. I wanted Jack to tell me I was silly; that there was nothing there to worry about.

"What?" He looked where I was indicating. "What's the probl . . . . ? Oh, holy crap. What have you found?"

"They came up when I stirred the mud up by wading through

it. I tripped over them. I thought they were some sort of snag. It's a person, isn't it?"

He put his arms round me and hugged me too him. I was shaking with reaction.

"You OK?" he asked at last once I'd settled a little. I nodded. It wouldn't help matters if I went to pieces.

"You go and sit in the car," he ordered. "I'll just have a closer look. Then we need to phone the police."

Jack, in fact, was a member of the police force, serving as Detective Senior Sergeant Body.

I plodded back to the car. I didn't want to watch whatever examination he carried out.

There was still no one about so I took the opportunity to change into a spare pair of jeans and take my shoes off. I bundled the soiled clothing into the boot. I couldn't do much at present about cleaning myself or my clothes, but at least I'd improved my smell quotient.

Jack was still investigating the swamp and its contents. I looked away, swept by a purely selfish wave of frustration. Jack and I were supposed to be on a much overdue holiday, the first we'd shared since we became a couple. We'd met when I was a suspect in a murder case he was investigating, and so far, either his work or mine had intervened each time we planned to take a break together.

The only reason we'd managed to organise this holiday was because I'd recently been a victim in a kidnapping case. As I'd be needed as a witness at the trial of the perpetrators and there was some gang involvement, the police had suggested it would be better if I were out of the reach of persuasion or retaliation until after the court case.

If I was forced to go into hiding, then as far as I was concerned, Jack was going with me. It took some negotiating, or as Jack put it, his people spoke to my people, but eventually both his boss and mine had agreed, and we'd been granted four weeks leave.

My boss, Roger, had looked a little sick when he made the concession, and I'd been hit with a wave of guilt at abandoning him. I knew perfectly well that in a small business like

Paraparaumu Aviation, each staff member and their contribution was important, and in my absence, Greig and Nick, my colleagues, were going to have to pick up the slack.

Less high-mindedly I knew they'd also be picking up all my flying hours and wondered whether I'd have any students left to call my own when I came back from leave.

Maria, our office manager had sensed my conflict. "Work/Life balance," she'd reminded me. "Don't worry about us Claire, we'll be fine, and you need to get somewhere where you can be safe for the next few weeks. Enjoy the break. It's high time you got away."

I'd agreed, but even so, every time an aircraft passed overhead, my head snapped up, automatically to follow its path across the sky. Some addictions are hard to break.

To date our holiday had consisted of driving to Kihikihi to meet Jack's family. They were lovely, warm, welcoming people who had made me feel at home, but even so, it wasn't quite the romantic idyll I'd been hoping for.

We were only up this god-forsaken valley because Jack's uncle Pat had invited us both to join the spring muster, held every Labour Day weekend, on the hills at the back of his farm. It had sounded like an opportunity to see a real slice of kiwiana, so I'd agreed enthusiastically enough when the plan was proposed. It was to be the last family related activity before Jack and I headed north to Turangi for two weeks of privacy and intimacy.

Now, with the discovery of a corpse, we were likely to be detained and delayed, and if I knew Jack at all, he wouldn't be able to resist the challenge of investigating exactly why a skeleton was residing in the swamp. I hoped with all my heart that the bones were centuries old and didn't relate to recent criminal activity that would involve us in a crime scene.

DEAR READER,

Thank you for reading *Straight and Level*. I hope you enjoyed it.

I was fortunate to spend several years working as a light aircraft pilot and instructor, flying out of Paraparaumu Airport. It was inevitable that I would one day use that beautiful and dynamic environment as a background in my novels.

The character of Claire first appeared in *Death on D'Urville*. She is an amalgam of women pilots I met during my flying years. As a breed they are sassy, courageous and confident women. I hope this series pays tribute to them. Although gender equality has meant an increasing number of women choosing aviation as a career, they make up only a small proportion of the overall number of pilots, a fact I still find surprising.

I realised early on that there were simply too many stories and adventures centred round aviation for me to contain them all in one novel, so a series was born.

As an author and teller of stories, I love feedback from my readers. You are the reason I write, so tell me what you liked, what you loved and what you hated. I'd love to hear from you.

You can write to me at penelope@penelopehaines.com.

Finally, I need to ask a favour of you. If you're so inclined, I'd appreciate a review of *Straight and Level*. Loved it, hated it – I'd just enjoy your feedback. As you may know, reviews can be tough to come by. If you have the time, please leave a review on Amazon.com or Goodreads.com. You, the reader, now have the power to make or break the book.

Thank you so much for reading *Straight and Level* and for spending time with me.

Penelope

ACKNOWLEDGEMENTS

It takes help from a large number of people to put a book together. To each of you who helped me create *Straight and Level*, some in small ways, others hugely, my heartfelt thanks.

First in line are the wonderful team in my office – Kelly Pettitt, Ruth Holman and Belinda Hughes, – who were pressed into service as beta readers. I owe an inestimable debt to Kelly in particular for her frank but constructive criticism during the various revisions of the original draft and for her meticulously detailed notes. Kelly is also responsible for the cover artwork, the photograph of me inside the back cover, the design of the layout and was a godsend as my personal IT division every time I ran into problems with the computer or with formatting.

Sergeant Graham Gubb at Police National Headquarters kindly answered my many questions about police procedure, and Jeffrey Paparoa Holman gave me excellent advice about the Tuhoe. If, in spite of their assistance there are any errors, they are entirely my own.

Sue Reidy and Tina Shaw provided invaluable criticism, guidance and encouragement during the revision process, patient and helpful in the advice they offered. I also owe thanks to Debbie Watson for early proofreading. Finally, my deepest thanks to Adrienne Morris who edited and proofread the final manuscript.

My gratitude to my husband Cavan who sustained me, helped in a thousand ways and never fails to encourage me.

My thanks to Reilly for spending the long hours with me and wagging encouragement; Pascal who lay on my lap as I typed away at the keyboard; and Cash, on whose broad back I cantered away from the frustrations inherent in the creative process.

ABOUT THE AUTHOR

Penelope came to New Zealand as an eleven-year-old after a childhood spent in India and Pakistan. As an only child, reading was her hobby – she read everything that came her way, a habit which has continued throughout her life.

On leaving school she trained as a nurse, without fully considering that a brisk default attitude of 'pull yourself together and stop whining' might not be an ideal prerequisite for the industry. Conceding, at last, that nurturing was not her dominant characteristic, she changed career path and after graduating with a BA (Hons) in English Literature, moved into management consultancy, which better suited her personality type.

After some years of family life she worked as a commercial pilot and flight instructor, spending her days ferrying clients into strips in the Marlborough Sounds and discouraging students from killing her as she taught them to fly.

Penelope lives with her husband, dog, cat and horse in Otaki, New Zealand.

Death on D'Urville was the first novel in her *Claire Hardcastle* series.

Straight and Level takes place some three months after *Death on D'Urville*.

Stall Turns, the third in the series, continues to follow Claire's adventures.

Her previous novels are *The Lost One* and *Helen Had a Sister*.

All novels are available in various formats from Amazon. com.

Paperback editions can be purchased within New Zealand from Paper Plus, Unity Books and other reputable bookstores and suppliers. Alternatively, they can be ordered from Penelope's website - www.penelopehaines.com, and you can visit Penelope on Facebook @penelopehainesbooks.

www.ingramcontent.com/pod-product-compliance
Lightning Source LLC
Chambersburg PA
CBHW021002260626
47169CB00006B/1908